Bride & Groom

Also by Susan Conant
in Large Print:

Ruffly Speaking
Black Ribbon
The Dogfather

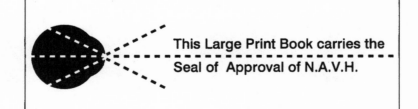

This Large Print Book carries the
Seal of Approval of N.A.V.H.

Bride & Groom

A DOG LOVER'S MYSTERY

Susan Conant

WHEELER
PUBLISHING

Published in 2004 by arrangement with The Berkley Publishing Group, a member of Penguin Group (USA) Inc.

Wheeler Large Print Compass.

The text of this Large Print edition is unabridged.
Other aspects of the book may vary from the original edition.

Set in 16 pt. Plantin by Liana M. Walker.

Printed in the United States on permanent paper.

Library of Congress Cataloging-in-Publication Data

Conant, Susan, 1946–
    Bride & groom : a dog lover's mystery /
    Susan Conant.
      p. cm.
    ISBN 1-58724-619-8 (lg. print : hc : alk. paper)
    1. Winter, Holly (Fictitious character) — Fiction.
2. Cambridge (Mass.) — Fiction. 3. Women journalists — Fiction. 4. Women dog owners — Fiction. 5. Serial murders — Fiction. 6. Dog trainers — Fiction. 7. Weddings — Fiction. 8. Dogs — Fiction. 9. Large type books. I. Title: Bride and groom. II. Title.
PS3553.O4857B75 2004b
  813'.54—dc22   2004041779

To my dear friend Meredith Kantor,
in loving memory of Abbey, the perfect mix.

As the Founder/CEO of NAVH, the only national health agency solely devoted to those who, although not totally blind, have an eye disease which could lead to serious visual impairment, I am pleased to recognize Thorndike Press★ as one of the leading publishers in the large print field.

Founded in 1954 in San Francisco to prepare large print textbooks for partially seeing children, NAVH became the pioneer and standard setting agency in the preparation of large type.

Today, those publishers who meet our standards carry the prestigious "Seal of Approval" indicating high quality large print. We are delighted that Thorndike Press is one of the publishers whose titles meet these standards. We are also pleased to recognize the significant contribution Thorndike Press is making in this important and growing field.

Lorraine H. Marchi, L.H.D.
Founder/CEO
NAVH

★ Thorndike Press encompasses the following imprints: Thorndike, Wheeler, Walker and Large Print Press.

Acknowledgments

For the appearance of Alaskan malamute BISS American International Ch. Quinault's Northern Exposure, CGC, WLDX, WTD, WPD, the amazing North, I am grateful to Twila Baker, who accompanies North herein. Bruce Southworth, B.S.I., responded with expertise and enthusiasm to my plea for help with a Sherlockian wedding ceremony. Thank you! I also owe profuse thanks to the American International Champion of editors, Natalee Rosenstein, to her assistant, Esther Strauss, and to Deborah Schneider, all of whom deserve special awards for patience and support. For generous help with the manuscript and proofs, many thanks to Jean Berman, Roo Grubis, Cindy Klettke, Roseann Mandell, Dru Milligan, Phyllis Stein, Geoff Stern, Jolie Stratton, Anya Wittenborg, and Corrine Zipps.

My boundless gratitude goes also to my own Alaskan malamutes, Frostfield Perfect Crime, CD, CGC, ThD, WPD, my very own

Rowdy, and her young companion, Django, formally, Jazzland's Got That Swing. Like the malamute puppy in this book, Django is a son of Ch. Jazzland's Embraceable You, the beautiful Emma, and was bred by Cindy Neely. Cindy, thank you for my new muse.

To have and to hold from this day forward, for better for worse, for richer for poorer, in sickness and in health, to love and to cherish, till death us do part.

Solemnization of Matrimony,
THE BOOK OF COMMON PRAYER

Chapter 1

Between August 22 and September 27, as I was planning my wedding and promoting my new book, five women were bludgeoned to death in Greater Boston. The murders were premeditated. So, in a happy sense, was my forthcoming marriage to Steve Delaney, D.V.M. As for my book, its title invited the accusation of malevolent culinary premeditation. It was called *101 Ways to Cook Liver.* I am, however, entirely innocent of evil intent toward my fellow human beings. I'm a dog writer. Indeed, I may never recover from the fumes I breathed while testing what are, in fact, more than 101 recipes for dog treats.

My column runs in *Dog's Life* magazine. Holly Winter? I do freelance articles as well, and I contributed the text for a book of photographs of the lavish Morris and Essex Kennel Club dogs shows of the 1930s. *Contributed:* gave in return for royalty payments insufficient to buy one of those coffee mugs you get for donating to public radio. Honest to doG Almighty, I've tried writing about people, but I lack the knack. Anyway, as dog books go, *101 Ways to Cook Liver* had gotten me a decent advance, and as Mac McCloud kept reminding me, my book would sell and keep selling if — and only if — I promoted it even half as energetically as I trained, exercised, groomed, and showed my dogs. Mac's first book, *Dogs with Dr. Mac*, had been holding a solid sit-stay on the canine bestseller lists since its publication two years earlier. Bruce McCloud, D.V.M., who'd just published his second book, *Ask Dr. Mac*, did more for me than merely hand out advice: He suggested that we cooperate in making our work known to the dog-loving public and generously arranged to have me included at signings, readings, and interviews to which he alone had initially been invited. Readings. Well, *101 Ways to Cook Liver* didn't exactly lend itself to public performance, but I was already getting pretty good at following a principle that Mac had drilled into me, which was always to refer to my book as *101 Ways to Cook Liver* and never as "my book."

The first event that Mac and I did together was a launch party and signing on Saturday, August 17, at The Wordsmythe, a big, important bookstore in Brookline, Massachusetts, that probably wouldn't even have stocked my book (pardon the lapse) without Mac's influence. From an author's viewpoint, August isn't the ideal publication date, but then neither is any other month that falls outside the Christmas-shopping Advent, when even poverty-stricken or skinflint library addicts — me, for example — actually spend money on what they purport to love, thus enabling those of us who labor in the fields of canine literary endeavor to feed our dogs and, if the harvest is bounteous, ourselves. But, as Mac emphasized, August wasn't outright bad. Our books would still be on the shelves when doting nieces and nephews browsed for the perfect holiday gift for Auntie So-and-So who was so-and-so crazy about dogs. On the other hand — paw? — my second-floor tenant and first-best friend, Rita, had to miss the launch party because she was away on vacation, as were millions of other potentially book-buying and indubitably fortunate residents of Greater Boston, where the temperature was now, at quarter of five in the afternoon of August 17, a stinking ninety-five degrees.

Steve and I had parked my new air-conditioned car in the shade cast by the back wall of a funky movie theater and were walking my sweltering dogs along the sidewalk toward The Wordsmythe. I had Rowdy's leash, and Steve had Kimi's. Of the four of us, the only one who looked cool in any sense of the term was Steve. He was tall and lean, with wavy brown hair and changeable blue-green eyes, and he wasn't even sweating. I was cursing the weather, as were Rowdy and Kimi, who, being Alaskan malamutes, are congenitally predisposed to define climatological perfection as ten below zero Fahrenheit with a killer wind. World's most incredible question about the Alaskan malamute: *Where did the breed originate?* It was a question I got asked all the time, as did Steve, the relatively new owner of his first malamute, Sammy — properly, Jazzland's As Time Goes By, and just as properly, my Rowdy's young son. Kimi and Rowdy weren't swearing aloud, but didn't need to. They are big, beautiful wolf-gray show dogs who typically stride boldly along with their glorious white tails soaring above their backs. Now, their heads drooped, and their tails sagged. Although I'd spent hours grooming them in preparation for their first appearance as my PR team, they were "blowing coat," as it's called, and my efforts had left me with dogs who seemed mysteriously to be shedding more hair than they'd had to begin with. Furthermore, instead of radiating the breed's characteristic sunniness of temperament, Rowdy kept glaring at me as if summer were my fault, and Kimi was too wilted to mark utility poles and fire hydrants in the male-like fashion of self-confident female malamutes.

"Ma femme n'aime pas la chaleur," said Steve. Translation: *My wife does not like the heat.* He had supposedly been studying con-

14

versational French by listening to tapes. We were getting married on September 29 and honeymooning in Paris — and no, we did not choose our wedding day *only* because it was the date when we expected our dogs to have quit shedding. Anyway, instead of mastering common phrases and expressions that would be useful in ordering food and asking directions, Steve had learned to say exactly one thing in French, namely, the sentence he'd just uttered.

"I'm not your *femme* yet," I said sourly. "I'm your fiancée."

"When we get to France, you'll be *ma femme*."

I'd be Steve's second *femme*. More than a year earlier, after we'd been together for ages, I'd split us up. On the rebound, Steve had married the grossly misnamed Anita Fairley, fair being the last thing she was, unless you count her appearance. In fact, she was an embezzler-lawyer who hated dogs. But Anita really was beautiful, whereas I bear what always strikes me as an unwelcome resemblance to a golden retriever, the breed that raised me. Anita was as nasty to Steve's dogs as she was to him. The marriage was brief. Sammy, Steve's malamute puppy, had brought us back together.

Steve's divorce had become final on August 2. We'd celebrated by taking all five of our dogs to Acadia National Park. The loca-

15

tion was admittedly somewhat weird, since Bar Harbor, Maine, was where Steve and Anita had gone immediately after their city-hall wedding and where I'd learned of their marriage and first met Anita. But damned if that bitch — a term I ordinarily use in its dog-technical sense — was going to ruin Acadia for me. Besides, my stepmother, Gabrielle, owned a big house on Mount Desert Island, and I was always welcome to use Gabrielle's guest cottage. It wouldn't have been easy to find a motel that would've accepted all those dogs, nor would it have been easy to share one room with the five of them, especially because my Kimi resented the perfection of Steve's German shepherd bitch, India, and displayed her own imperfection by frightening Steve's timid pointer bitch, Lady, the term *bitch* being used in its proper and inoffensive canine sense to mean nothing more than *female*. Also, we drove to Maine on July 31, and I might've shared a room, but wouldn't share a bed, with Steve until August 2. I'm not all that moral, but I *am* proud: I couldn't see myself as an adulteress.

So, on the Great Divorce Day, we celebrated by hiking up Sargent Mountain. The four adult dogs, Rowdy, Kimi, India, and Lady, wore dogpacks filled with bottled water, liver treats (what else?), first-aid kits, and two fat lobster rolls crammed between cold packs. When we reached the top of

16

Sargent, Steve amazed me by producing four items he'd snuck into India's pack. Steve was not a sneaky person. Anything but. Furthermore, although he was rigidly law-abiding and knew that alcohol was illegal in the park, his secret stash included a split of champagne and two wineglasses. Crystal. Not plastic. The fourth item was an engagement ring. In defiance of his undramatic, even self-effacing, character, he tried to drop to his knees to propose, but Sammy assumed that he was initiating play, as, in a sense, he was, and Steve ended up asking me to marry him while I was extricating him from beneath the large and joyful puppy. It was not the first time Steve had asked me to marry him. But it was the first time I'd said yes.

As to the words Steve spoke, what he said was, "As husband material, I'm nothing special, but I'm a damned good veterinarian. And I love you. I love your dogs. I even love your ugly cat. Marry me. You'll never pay vet bills again."

Chapter 2

A big double-sided chalkboard on the side-walk in front of The Wordsmythe invited passersby to a launch party with Dr. Mac McCloud and Holly Winter. I am not petty enough to report that Mac's name was printed in far larger letters than mine. Prominently displayed in the shop window were five copies of *101 Ways to Cook Liver,* at least fifty copies of *Ask Dr. Mac,* and a poster-size glossy color photograph of a smiling Mac hugging a Bernese mountain dog. My book was what's called a "trade paperback," meaning that it was oversized and overpriced. *Ask Dr. Mac* was a hardcover.

"That's not even Mac's dog," I muttered to Steve. "The real dog person in the family is his wife, Judith. Uli is very definitely Judith's dog."

Steve just laughed.

"I know ten thousand times more about dog training than Mac does," I said. "And that's a conservative estimate."

"It's an underestimate," Steve said loyally.

"But if *I'm* jealous, think how his wife feels. Judith has a new book out, too, and it isn't even *in* the window."

Judith Esterhazy, Mac's wife, was what I'm tempted to call a "real writer"; her characters stood on two feet — and not because the other two had been amputated. Judith Esterhazy wrote serious literary fiction. She'd originally been known, albeit not very widely, for her perfectly crafted short stories. Her first novel, published about three years earlier, had received a starred review in *Publishers Weekly*. *Kirkus* had called it "mesmerizing" and "sparkling." It was now out of print. I'm reluctant to talk about the novel she'd just published because I'm not sure that I know how to pronounce its title correctly. It was called *Boudicca*, pronounced, I think, *Boo-dick-uh,* possibly with the stress on the second syllable, and was about Boadicea, the first syllable of which is *bow* as in "bow and arrow," not as in "bow wow wow," and the remainder of which is *uh-diss-ee-uh,* with the stress on the *ee.* Anyway, I'd looked up Boudicca or Boadicea on the web and discovered that she was a Celtic queen who led a rebellion against the Romans in 60 A.D. The information failed to convince me that an unpronounceable title had been a wise choice. But I went on to buy and read the book, which was, indeed, about the Celtic queen, a fearsome creature, strikingly, if bipedally, reminiscent of my own Kimi. I did not tell Judith that I thought that her book was really about one of my dogs. On the contrary, having read the *Kirkus* quotation about her previous novel on the back of this one, I said that I'd found *Boudicca* hypnotizing. In truth, Judith Esterhazy wrote beautiful prose.

When Steve and the dogs and I entered the frigid bliss of the bookstore, Judith Esterhazy was the first person I saw. She stood next to a table with a sign that read NEW AND NOTEWORTHY HARDCOVERS, and was signing a copy of *Boudicca* for a studious-looking young woman who worked in the bookstore. Judith was so thin that it would've been easy to imagine that, like Zola, she subsisted on sparrows. In no other respect did she match my image of the literary novelist, a phrase that connotes, at least to me, rapt concentration on vivid turns of phrase and a concomitant obliviousness to personal appearance. Judith showed no sign of bohemian dishevelment. She must've been in her early fifties, but there wasn't a white strand in her short, straight, glossy brown hair, which could only have been done at one of the fancy salons on Boston's famous Newbury Street. The style was geometrically blunt cut at the back. Her part began at the crown of her head and ended radically to the left, just above the outer corner of her left eyebrow. Her eyes were large and blue. She had prominent cheekbones, full lips, and white teeth. Her makeup was almost invisible. She was dressed, but not overdressed, in a pale gray linen jacket, shell, and pants. As Judith handed the autographed book to the young woman, her face was angular and forbidding, but when she caught sight of the dogs and me, her expression softened, and suddenly she looked warm and lovely. It struck me as demeaning to observe that Judith was pretty when she smiled, as if I somehow thought that she should mask her severity and, with it, her sadness and intelligence, by habitually putting on a happy face and gushing, "Have a nice day!" Still, my observation was accurate.

There was nothing phony about Judith's greeting. "Congratulations! Somehow, after all the work that goes into a book, it's still a surprise to see it as a physical object for sale in a store."

"Your books and mine are hardly comparable," I said. "But thank you. And you're right about the surprise." Then I introduced Steve to Judith and said, "We're getting married at the end of September. And you know Rowdy and Kimi."

As if demonstrating that acclaimed literary novelists can be platitudinously conventional, Judith said, "Married! I hope you'll be very happy. And of course I know your beautiful dogs." As she reached into the pocket of her pale gray jacket, I noticed that despite her leanness, she had the muscular arms and hands of someone who lives with big dogs. Producing two dog cookies, she said, "May I? The recipe is from your book."

I smiled. "In that case, yes. I'm flattered."

"You write clearly. And it's more about training with food than about cooking."

"My publisher hoped that no one would notice."

"You can't fool another writer." Glancing toward the back of the store, she said, "The manager's setting things up. Mac's around somewhere. We have Uli with us."

"Mac told me never to show up at a signing without a dog."

"I wish I had your excuse. Signings can be lonely events. Not that this one will be."

As if to prove Judith right, what felt like a delegation from the Cambridge Dog Training Club entered the store: Ron Coughlin, Diane D'Amato, Ray and Lynne Metcalf, and a few other members. Steve and I trained with the club. We'd served on the board and helped out at the club's obedience trials. As I was thanking people for coming, my cousin Leah arrived with Lieutenant Kevin Dennehy of the Cambridge Police. With her masses of red-gold curls and her voluptuousness, Leah was wildly eye-catching, but not to the point of requiring a police escort. Kevin was here in his personal capacity as my next-door neighbor and friend. His hair was even redder than Leah's. Especially because of his monumental build, they looked spectacular together, but certainly weren't a couple. Leah was an undergraduate at that ivy-choked institution down the street from my house, whereas Kevin was in his mid-thirties and was attracted to women in his own age group. His girlfriend, Jennifer Pasquarelli, was his junior, but not by enough years to make it biologically possible for him to have fathered her.

"Jennifer's sorry she couldn't make it," Kevin said over the *woo-woo*ing of my dogs. "And my mother —"

Mrs. Dennehy was a Seventh-Day Adventist. This was her sabbath. "Of course," I said. "Please don't —"

Leah interrupted me. "Aren't you supposed to be signing books? What are you doing hanging around here like a regular customer?"

I handed her Rowdy's leash. "Make yourself useful. If there's food anywhere, don't let him steal it." Before she could grumble that she already knew that, I lowered my voice and said, "And don't let Kevin buy my book. I have a copy for him at home, and it feels wrong to ask my friends to spend money to be here. But you *do* need to buy Mac's book.

Have him sign it for you. I'll reimburse you."

"I don't want it. All it says is to buy a crate and lock your dog in it forever. If he were writing about children, he'd tell you to forget school and lock them all in jail."

"Leah, what I'm telling you," I whispered, "is, buy the book! We'll discuss this later. And if you have any comments to make about Mac's book or, for that matter, anyone else's, do not make them here."

Leah's voice carries. Fortunately, all she said was, "*Pride and Prejudice*. I loved it."

"Anyone *living*."

Steve extricated me from the discussion with Leah by saying, "Holly, you're wanted at the back of the store." With Kimi on leash, he headed there, and the rest of us followed.

"Have you ever noticed that you're a natural leader?" I asked Steve. "People trail after you. Animals love you. It's revolting. I'm jealous."

Ignoring my remarks, Steve said, "They've done you proud."

One of two banquet-sized, cloth-covered tables held bottles of mineral water and white wine, disposable wineglasses, platters of cheese and crackers, a bowl of strawberries, paper plates and napkins, plastic forks, and a sheet cake with white icing that read, in bright pink, CONGRATULATIONS HOLLY AND MAC. The words floated above the head of a perky-looking pink dog. Attractively arrayed on the second long table were a respectable number of copies of *101 Ways to Cook Liver*, a great many copies of Mac's previous book, and so many copies of *Ask Dr. Mac* that The Wordsmythe's order alone had probably required Mac's publisher to do a second printing. Mac himself sat on a folding chair behind the table. He looked exactly the way he did in the poster in the store's window and on the covers of both his books — tan and robust, with an expression that remained warm even when he was discussing unhappy veterinary subjects, such as cancer and euthanasia. I knew Mac's exact age because I'd looked him up on a web site called AnyBirthday.com. Although he could have passed for forty-eight or fifty, he was fifty-eight. His appearance of youth stemmed, in part, from his obvious health and fitness, but also from a genetic quirk that had kept his hair almost completely free of gray. In fact, if it hadn't been for a little white at his temples and a few strands of white amidst the brown, I'd have suspected him of touching up the color with some product that gave remarkably natural results. His eyes were a clear, almost flat, blue.

Mac had a gift for making close contact with people. His books were popular not only because he promoted them, but because his readers felt that he was talking directly to them about their dogs. In person, too, he felt like an ally. He made good eye contact and had a habit of reaching out, sometimes with a hand, always with his voice. At the moment, he was engaged in what seemed to be a serious conversation with a wiry blond woman who was standing next to him with her head lowered. She seemed intent on catching every word he said. Considered individually, her features were unattractive. She had small, narrow eyes and a weak chin. Even so, the woman was pretty in an exceptionally lively, wired way. Her short curls seemed to spring energetically from her scalp.

It was Mac who broke off the tête-à-tête. Rising to his feet, he greeted me with a smile and said, "Holly! Take a seat! You have fans waiting. You know Claire Langceil, don't you?" He pronounced it *Lang-seal*. "I've just had some terrible news about someone I used to know. I was telling Claire. But take a seat and get to work!"

My memory of the next half hour is somewhat blurred. I remember signing books while people told me about their dogs and said flattering things about my *Dog's Life* column. It took all the concentration I had to pay attention to the people while trying to write legibly and to make sure that I spelled all the human and canine names correctly. Dog writers do not, of course, merely autograph books in the barren fashion of what I should perhaps call mainstream writers: "To Harvey" or "Best wishes." Rather, a typical dog-book inscription goes something like, "To Linda, Nikki, Tipsy, Bounder, Lulu, and Zippo," or "To the beautiful Golden Retrievers of Halomyst Kennels," or "To American/Canadian Ch. Perfectly's Wediditagain, CD," or, in the case of my inscriptions, "To Peter, Sasha, Chinook, and Katy — Woo-woo-woo from Rowdy and Kimi." As an afterthought, I scrawl my own name. Anyway, I spent about thirty minutes in a daze of listening and signing and introducing people to Rowdy and Kimi, who were capably handled, respectively, by Leah and Steve, *capability* being defined as effectiveness in preventing the dogs from leaping onto the food table, gobbling up every single thing on it, including the paper plates, and then getting into a tussle about the crumbs.

Once the crowd of strangers thinned, I had time to chat with friends who'd come to congratulate me about the book and, to my embarrassment, to buy it. Kevin Dennehy, who doesn't own a dog, made me sign five books that he insisted were for fellow cops. Mac and Judith's daughter, Olivia, had me sign a book. I knew from Mac that Olivia was in her late twenties, but she looked younger — about eighteen. Her light brown hair fell to her shoulders, and her loose chambray dress

27

reminded me of a pinafore. Olivia had Judith's cheekbones and her air of elegance as well, despite what was unmistakably Mac's athletic vigor. When she heard that Steve and I were getting married in late September, she asked where, and I had to confess that we had no idea. Olivia had been married for only two months and had apparently had a big wedding. Although I insisted that Steve and I wanted a small wedding, she was horrified to learn that we'd not only failed to select a place to get married and hold a reception, but hadn't lined up a caterer, a florist, or, worse yet, someone to perform the service.

As I was explaining that we'd been engaged for only a few weeks and as Olivia was offering to share everything she'd learned about planning a wedding, Judith joined us and went on to second the offer. I was still sitting behind the table of books, as was Mac, who now had Uli with him. The Bernese mountain dog has an average life span of seven or eight years. Uli was twelve. He showed his age. He was bigger than my Rowdy, who weighed eighty-five pounds, but both dogs had the sturdy build and heavy bone typical of working breeds. Bernese mountain dogs have long, silky coats and are tricolored: black with rust and bright white. Uli's markings were symmetrical. He had the desirable "Swiss cross" white mark on his chest and a white tip on his tail. The expression in his dark, clouded eyes was soft and loving. Although Uli was with Mac, those gentle eyes kept seeking out Judith.

As Olivia was suggesting that Steve and I inquire about a wildlife refuge in Lexington that was a wedding site especially suitable for a veterinarian groom and a dog-writer bride, a familiar voice spoke a name I'd never heard before. "Nina Kerkel!" said Ceci Love. Then she said it again. "Nina Kerkel!"

The younger sister of my elderly and revered friend Althea Battlefield, Ceci never settled for just two words; it was inevitable that she'd immediately babble hundreds more, as she rapidly did. "Nina Kerkel! I haven't thought of her for years. To think she's dead! I wonder if Greta knows. That's Greta Kerkel, whose son Hal married that Nina it must have been thirty years ago, although I must say that Greta — well, no, on the contrary, I mustn't say it, must I? Not with the poor girl dead. What did she die of? Holly, did you like the cake? I see that the dog is still left, the picture on the cake, not Rowdy and Kimi, naturally they're still left. Althea is so terribly sorry that she couldn't be here even though it would have been impossible given her age and condition, but you are our favorite honorary niece, now that I think of it, our only one, and we decided to send the cake, do you like it? Althea wants you to know that I am fully authorized to represent her here and to convey her congratulations on your delightful book, which it is — delightful — it's obviously a book, isn't it? And there was something from Sherlock Holmes that Althea made me promise to quote to you, but I've forgotten what it is."

Ceci was, as usual, a vision in champagne. Her hair was tinted that shade, and she wore a pale linen suit with matching pumps. Her actual age was not public knowledge, as I know for certain because I'm the person who had it removed from AnyBirthday.com. I'll tactfully report that Ceci not only could have passed for sixty-five, but frequently did, especially when she had a say in the matter. According to Althea, Ceci's daintiness and lifelong prettiness were, in part, responsible for her apparent frivolity. Also, Althea claimed that Ceci had been indulged first by their father and subsequently by the doting man she'd married, Ellis Love, who was already dead by the time I met the sisters. For whatever reason, Ceci continued to indulge herself in the matter of her appearance and also in the matter of her chronic babbling, which grated on her sister's scholarly nerves. Althea was a devoted student of the entire Canon of Sherlock Holmes. Ceci, in contrast, was a successful student of Messieurs Dow and Jones; her late husband, a stockbroker, had trained her in investment strategies. No one, however, had ever succeeded in training Ceci to apply her intelligence to speaking simply and coherently.

After excusing myself to Judith and Olivia, I hugged Ceci and thanked her for the cake. After repeating her congratulations about my book and offering an unnecessary explanation of why Althea wasn't there, Ceci returned to the topic of the newly deceased Nina Kerkel and the horror felt thirty years before by her friend Greta Kerkel when Greta's son had married a person Ceci consistently called "that Nina." Ceci, I might mention, could pack more damnation into the word *that* than most other people expressed with dozens of explicitly denunciatory terms; I hoped that she never had reason to refer to me as "that Holly." She and I were now standing by the refreshment table, where I was sampling the cake. As she continued talking in her usual jumbled fashion about Nina Kerkel, the cake, her elderly Newfoundland, her sister, Althea, Althea's wheelchair, and my wedding, we were joined by Mac, Judith, Olivia, and some people I didn't know. A few were evidently friends of Mac's. Some were customers of The Wordsmythe. With typical warmth and friendliness, Mac approached Ceci and introduced himself. He'd obviously heard her speak Nina Kerkel's name, but missed what she'd said about *that* Nina. He said, "You knew Nina? I'm still reeling. We worked together at Meadowbrook. Meadowbrook Veterinary Hospital. This must've been twenty-five years ago. Nina was the receptionist."

I heard a whisper near my ear. "Thirty. Thirty years ago. And Nina certainly was *receptive*. It's always interesting to note correspondences between vocation and character, isn't it." Turning my head, I saw that the speaker was Judith. I had no idea why she'd chosen me as her confidante. Maybe I was just the nearest person who'd read her new book.

Although he couldn't possibly have overheard his wife, Mac echoed a word she'd used. His tone was nostalgic. "Nina was an interesting person. Always there, always smiling."

"Nina Kerkel," Judith muttered, "was a little slut."

"What did she die of?" asked Ceci. "I wonder if Greta knows she's dead. That's Greta Kerkel," she informed Mac. "Her son Hal was married to this Nina at the time." In Ceci's lexicon, *this* was slightly less damning than *that*, but only slightly.

"I remember Hal," Mac said. "He was married to Nina when I knew her. They rode dirt bikes together."

"Dirt," Judith commented sotto voce. "How reliably these little messages await the discerning eye and ear."

Oblivious to his wife's commentary, Mac

32

went on, but his voice became somber and low. "What I just heard was that Nina died of an overdose. It's a shame. A loss. Her life must've gone badly downhill."

"Well," said Ceci, "I'll have to tell Greta. She and Nina did not get along. Even so, Greta may want to do something appropriate."

"Such as what?" whispered Judith. "Dance on her grave?"

Chapter 3

Steve and I hung around The Wordsmythe for a while talking to people, browsing the shelves, and letting Rowdy and Kimi ingratiate themselves with everyone. The events manager had me sign some copies of my book. When I'd finished, he affixed labels that read, rather grandly, AUTOGRAPHED. In reality, it's celebrities who give autographs; people like me just write our names. Still, it was the first time I'd ever signed stock for a bookstore. I knew that I was no literary star, but I began to feel like a real author.

The glow was lingering when we got back to what was about to become *our* place and not just mine, the three-story barn-red house at 256 Concord Avenue in Cambridge. The back entrance, the one I usually used, was on Appleton Street, around the corner from Concord Avenue. Together with Rowdy and Kimi, and Tracker, my cat, I occupied the first floor, and Rita, my therapist friend, rented my second-floor apartment. My third-floor tenants had bought a condo and moved out. At the moment, Steve and his dogs had the third floor. When he'd first bought his veterinary practice from my old vet, Dr. Draper, he'd moved into the apartment above the clinic. Later, he'd rented a house for a while, but ended up back in his over-the-clinic quarters. Neither his place nor mine was big enough for two people, five dogs, and a cat. Like most other residents of Cambridge, Steve and I felt convinced that moving to any non-Cantabrigian community within commuting distance of his work would instantly age us twenty years and render us stupid and uncool. Against our will, we'd find ourselves watching television instead of reading. Our Birkenstock sandals would start to grow uppers, and before long, they'd transform themselves into grown-up shoes. Looking in the mirror, I'd discover that I was wearing blue eye shadow. Steve would come to care deeply about eradicating crabgrass from our lawn. Even our animals would be hideously changed. With no Cambridge turf to mark, Kimi would abandon her radical malamute feminism and quit lifting her leg.

To avert such grotesque transformations in ourselves and our companions, we were determined to remain in the identity-defining vicinity of Harvard Square. Also, we liked my house, which was in an interesting, diverse neighborhood and had a fenced yard, although a small one. Our long-range plan was to turn the first and second floors into one big apartment for ourselves. Rita could move to the third floor. Or, if she married the man in her life, Artie Spicer, she'd presumably move to his house or elsewhere. I hated the idea. I'd had lots of canine siblings, but Rita and my cousin Leah were as close as I'd ever had to human sisters. I didn't want to lose Rita.

Because we'd lingered at The Wordsmythe, it was seven by the time we got home, but we'd been nibbling cheese, fruit, and cake, and weren't very hungry. We'd fed the dogs before my signing, so we just gave them brief turns in the yard, first Rowdy and Kimi, then India, Lady, and Sammy the puppy, Rowdy's son, who was now a big teenage malamute but was doomed to be known for life as "the puppy." In my view, the beautiful, sweet, funny, and charming Sammy was actually *the* puppy. Succumbing to my addiction, I checked my E-mail. After that, Steve sat at the kitchen table drinking cold beer while I made a salad. Even for the author of *101 Ways to Cook Liver*, it was too hot to cook.

"Claire is really something," Steve said. "Comical."

I was at the sink washing lettuce, but turned my head to look at Steve. "Is she? I didn't get to spend any time with her."

"You have to feel kind of sorry for her husband. I've met him. Daniel. He seems like a nice enough guy."

"So why do you have to feel sorry for him?"

"A lot of her joking's at his expense. About how rigid he is. Or selfish. Or how Daniel doesn't appreciate her. Claire *is* funny. But she practically says that the only reason she married Daniel was that she wanted a baby."

"Did she get one?"

"Yes. He's five or six now. Gus. She talks about him a lot. Devoted mother. People say one reason she married Daniel was that she thought he'd be a good father."

"Is he?"

"I guess so. That's why he wasn't there today. He took Gus on one of those Duck Boat tours that leave from the Prudential. Amphibious vehicles. Claire tried to get him to forget it, but he wouldn't. She always says, 'You know what Daniel's like.' I hope you never say that about me."

"I say it all the time. Besides, everyone knows what you're like, Steve. You're wonderful. Everyone always says so. And since you're so wonderful, why don't you open that bottle of Reisling that's in the refrigerator. And pour me a glass."

I was slicing tomatoes, chopping fresh basil, and performing other such tasks without having to guard the food from Rowdy and Kimi. The only dog loose in the kitchen was Steve's shepherd, India, who was not a food thief. In fact, India was that rarest of creatures, a truly obedient dog. Rowdy and Kimi were obedient dogs in the sense that they'd indulged the senseless human wish to put advanced obedience titles on them; when they'd felt in the mood and simultaneously found themselves in the obedience ring, they'd cooperated. India, in contrast, reliably obeyed Steve. In marrying him, I was marrying into his family of dogs. India would fully accept me as Steve's wife. Astute judge of character that she was, India had rejected Anita. In her own way, India already loved me, but she worshiped Steve and was truly a one-man dog.

Sipping the wine Steve had supplied, I said, "It would be nice if someone would give us a big wooden salad bowl as a wedding present. Rita is making me register at Bloomingdale's. Maybe I'll pick one out."

Steve was silent for a moment. "You're not really doing that. Are you?"

"*We* are. You and I are. Rita is making us do it. She's taking me to some mall next Friday. You're welcome to come along."

For once, he replied instantly. "No."

"Rita says that left to our own devices, we'd register with some kennel supply place. Cherrybrook. I said that we wouldn't, because we already have all the dog stuff we need."

"We don't need dishes. For us. Do we?"

"Not really. But we do need a salad bowl, and if we take attrition into account, we could use a hundred sets of those wooden salad forks. Rowdy and Kimi eat them."

"Buy a salad bowl. And forks."

"Argue with Rita, not me. And with Gabrielle. She's as determined as Rita." Gabrielle was my stepmother.

"I'm going to have a mother-in-law." Steve sounded as if the idea had just occurred to him, "Me. With a mother-in-law." Anita's mother had died long before she'd married Steve.

"You love Gabrielle. So do I. And we can both be grateful to her for exerting some control over my father. She's the first person who's been able to do that since my mother died." I was immediately sorry that I'd mentioned Buck, who was a good father in his own eccentric and sometimes infuriating way. I said, "The salad's ready."

Steve was setting the table with the precision of the surgeon he was. He aligned the knives and forks exactly where he wanted them. His vet techs and assistants always remarked on what a neat surgeon he was; similarly, he never left dirty dishes for me to clean up, but rinsed them and stowed them in the dishwasher.

When we sat down, he said, "Beautiful. Shrimp. Avocados. Cheese. Maybe if you'd

39

written a cookbook for people, you'd've turned into a great cook for dogs."

"I *am* a great cook for dogs." Then, to avoid returning to the subject of my father, I said, "You know that woman who died? The one Ceci kept going on about? Nina Kerkel. Did you have the feeling that Mac'd had something going with her? Because while Mac was talking about her, Judith kept whispering remarks in my ear. That when Nina was a receptionist, she was all too receptive. That kind of thing. And what Ceci implied was, as Ceci'd say, that Nina was no better than she should've been. Meanwhile, Mac looked pretty nostalgic. And he had nothing but good things to say about Nina."

Steve shrugged. "Maybe. But Judith was in an awfully good mood."

"She was? Not while Mac was talking about Nina. Then, she wasn't exactly in a good mood. Or a bad mood. In a strange mood, maybe. Or a vindictive mood."

"When we were all eating, after you were done signing, Judith was smiling a lot. I noticed because when we first got to the store, she looked real serious. And then later, she was all lighthearted. She was hitting the wine. I wondered if that was why."

"Maybe Mac had an affair with Nina, and Judith was glad that Nina was dead."

"Hey, I meant to tell you. This guy Mac."
"Yes?"

"He has this habit of putting his hands on people."

"I know. Mac reaches out to people. He likes to make contact."

"Keep your eye on Rowdy when he does that."

"Steve, Rowdy doesn't bite! How could you say such a thing about Rowdy?"

"I didn't. What I meant is that Rowdy doesn't like it."

"Who is it who doesn't like it? Rowdy? Or you?"

He took a second helping of salad, heavy on the shrimp. "Rowdy."

"People've told me this before," I conceded. "And I've noticed, too. Rowdy doesn't like strangers to touch me. Especially men. That's true. Not that Mac is a stranger. Rowdy has been to his house with me. But Rowdy won't do anything. I don't need to keep my eye on him. And in case you wondered, I have no interest in Mac, and he's never been anything but friendly with me. He's never come on to me. Never. Nothing even remotely like that. Besides, Mac may be young for his age, but he's old enough to be my father."

"There are women who like that," Steve said.

"I'm not one of them," I said.

Chapter 4

Five days after the launch party at The Wordsmythe, on the evening of Thursday, August 22, a woman was bludgeoned to death in the underground parking garage of a fancy Cambridge hotel. Steve and I learned of the murder early on Friday morning. I'd just spooned scrambled eggs onto our plates, and in compliance with Cambridge law, we were listening to National Public Radio. As proof that I'm neither lying nor exaggerating about Cambridge lunacy, I'll present the relevant city ordinance in its entirety:

Section 9.08.021
Consumption of certain breakfast foods in private places

No person shall consume any breakfast foods as defined in Chapter 138, Section 1045 of the General Laws while on, in or upon any private place between the hours of 5:00 a.m. and 10:00 a.m. without simultaneously listening to National Public Radio as defined in Chapter 1046 of the General Laws. Whoever violates this section may be arrested without a warrant by an officer authorized to serve criminal process. All breakfast foods being used in violation of the section shall be seized and safely held until final adjudication of the charge against the person or persons arrested or summoned into court, at which time they shall be returned to the person or persons entitled to lawful possession. Anyone found guilty of the violation of this chapter shall be punished by a fine of not over one thousand dollars and immediate deportation and permanent exile from the City of Cambridge.

So, as I was saying, to avoid getting booted out of the highbrow community that we insanely chose to inhabit, we were listening to *Morning Edition* on WBUR and thus heard about the murder of Dr. Laura Skipcliff, who'd been killed the previous evening in the garage beneath The Charles Hotel. In fact, it was the mention of the hotel that caught our attention and created a moment of awkwardness between us. There was nothing wrong with The Charles. On the contrary, although it lacked the exclusivity of the Harvard Faculty Club, it was nonetheless the most luxurious and expensive lodging place in Harvard

Square. The cause of our discomfort was that Steve had met the evil Anita, now his ex-wife, in the bar of Rialto, a sumptuous restaurant located in the hotel. Despite that horrid association, which was certainly not Rialto's fault, Steve and I had eaten there several times this summer and had enjoyed the wonderful food and the romantic ambiance. What's more, on each occasion, I'd savored the pleasure of revenging myself on Anita by refusing to let her ruin Rialto for me. Good restaurants, I might add, were Steve's only extravagance. When he'd first bought his practice from old Dr. Draper, he'd been paying off the loan he'd taken out for the purchase as well as his veterinary school loans, but his finances were now in great shape. His clinic was thriving. His staff included three other vets, and he'd wisely poured money into high-tech equipment. Even so, he was earning far more than he spent. He still drove an old van. Furthermore, because he'd had the sense to hire a sharp divorce lawyer, Anita the Fiend had gotten almost no money from him. Anyway, although she hadn't managed to spoil Rialto for Steve or me, the mention of The Charles Hotel caused a moment of discomfort.

"What was she doing in the garage?" I asked. "How did she get murdered there? It's —"

Steve hushed me. "Could we hear the rest of it?"

There wasn't much more. Public Radio isn't usually big on crime. What we heard was that Dr. Laura Skipcliff, an anesthesiologist from New York, had come to Boston for a meeting and had been staying at The Charles.

"The paper won't be here for another half hour," I said. "It'll have the details. But this'll be Kevin's case. Or he'll be the main person from the Cambridge police. The D.A.'s office and the state police'll probably take over."

"Good luck to them shoving Kevin out of the way in Cambridge," Steve said.

Lieutenant Kevin Dennehy still lived with his mother in the house where he grew up, the one on the Appleton Street side of mine. The crimson tidal wave of Harvard's expansion having rolled our way, Mrs. Dennehy could have sold the house for an incredible amount of money and moved elsewhere, but Cambridge was her city. Like his mother, Kevin belonged here. Furthermore, in Kevin's view, Cambridge remained moderately safe only because of his personal and professional presence. Consequently, he didn't dare to leave. Or so he claimed. What was undoubtedly true, as Steve had just suggested, was that Kevin had a deep loyalty to Cambridge, an unrivaled knowledge of his hometown, and the secret conviction that he was smarter than the D.A.'s office and the state police combined.

"One thing you can bet on," I said, "is that Kevin knows at least half the people who work at The Charles, including the people who work in the garage. Either he went to school with them, or they have relatives who are cops, or they work out at the Y with him, or he just knows them. More coffee?"

"To go." Steve had a morning of surgery ahead of him. Instead of sitting around drinking a second cup, he left carrying a red insulated Purina mug. It occurred to me that the two of us combined probably owned at least a hundred canine-embellished cups, mugs, and glasses, some of which had been won by our dogs at shows, trials, and matches. Others had come as promotional gifts from dog-food companies that wanted to endear themselves with pet professionals. If you also counted the trophies won by my late mother's golden retrievers and bequeathed to me, we had enough drinking vessels, bowls, candleholders, plates, and knickknacks to stock a gift shop. And Rita was nonetheless making us, of all couples in the world, register for wedding presents! Hah! In fact, Rita had returned home from visiting relatives who had a beach house in Rye, New York, and was dragging me to Bloomingdale's this very evening. Well, damned if I was going to pick out coffee mugs.

As I fed Rowdy and Kimi, checked my E-mail, made the bed, tidied up, and contemplated the trip to the mall, an unhappy image came to me. Rita and I had gone to the same mall before. Its stores were too pricey for me, but Rita had hauled me along to advise her about selecting a present for my cousin Leah. What I now saw in my mind's eye wasn't the shop-lined interior with its glittering escalators and lush tropical vegetation, but the adjoining three-story concrete parking garage. In contrast to the one at The Charles Hotel, the mall's garage was above ground. Still, it was undeniably a parking garage and almost certainly darker and emptier than the bright, popular, well-patrolled garage beneath the hotel. If only the stupid mall allowed dogs, we could park anywhere we pleased. As it was, we'd have to avoid the garage and use the parking lot instead.

By the time I was ready for my second cup of coffee, the paper had arrived. The murder of Dr. Laura Skipcliff was reported in a section called New England News Briefs and consisted of only a couple of paragraphs. According to the paper, Dr. Laura Skipcliff, fifty-seven, a nationally renowned anesthesiologist from New York City, had been staying at The Charles Hotel while she attended a medical conference at which she'd been scheduled to speak. She had apparently driven her rental car into the hotel's garage at 10:42 p.m. The body had been found by another hotel guest at midnight. Authorities were questioning hotel employees and conference participants, including Dr. Skipcliff's ex-husband, Dr. Dominic DiTomasso. There followed the usual statement that the police were investigating all possible leads, as if they'd consider doing otherwise. Knowing Kevin Dennehy as I did, I felt certain that one of the leads he'd vigorously pursue would be the presence in Boston of the victim's ex-husband. Kevin's experience in law enforcement had taught him to see marriage principally as an institution designed to create motives and opportunities for violence. It seemed to me that the first frustration Kevin would encounter in investigating the murder of Laura Skipcliff would be the aggravating fact of her divorce: Kevin would be irked that Dr. Dominic DiTomasso was Dr. Laura Skipcliff's *ex*-husband.

Chapter 5

The dossier on Laura Skipcliff, M.D., like the other four dossiers that eventually came into my possession, consisted of a neatly labeled letter-size manila folder that contained pages printed from the World Wide Web. Laura Skipcliff's name had appeared on many web sites; hers was a thick folder.

The first page of her dossier showed the results of a search using InfoSpace, a popular "people finder," as such sites are called, a superduper internet phone and address directory. According to InfoSpace, "Skipcliff, Laura" lived on East Eighty-third Street in New York, NY 10021. Her phone number began with the familiar Manhattan area code: 212. Beneath the directory listing, InfoSpace offered the options of getting a map of the area, finding nearby businesses, and adding Laura Skipcliff to an address book. Three lines followed:

Find out more about Laura Skipcliff.
Find Laura Skipcliff on Classmates.com!

Send flowers to Laura Skipcliff.

The next page was similar to the first, but came from another people finder, AnyWho. Its listing was for "Skipcliff, Laura, MD," and specified the street number. The line below the directory information offered the opportunity to get a map and directions to her address, and asked, *Did you go to school with Laura MD Skipcliff?*

The next three pages showed pictures of Laura Skipcliff, photos printed in black and white. The first, which had come from her hospital's web site, was a small close-up of her face, together with a paragraph about her. Her skin was deeply lined, and she had prominent pouches under her eyes. I wondered whether cosmetic efforts had backfired; perhaps makeup had sunk into the creases of her skin, thus highlighting the signs of age. Her hair suggested a woman who'd cared about her appearance. It was dark and cut in an attractive, youthful style, shoulder length and smoothly straight. The second photo was an enlargement of the first. The quality of the original graphics file must have been poor. The blowup blurred Laura Skipcliff's features and grotesquely exaggerated her haggardness. On the following page, however, printed from the web site of a modern dance company, was a group shot of three donors attending a fund-raising dinner. Laura Skipcliff was on the right. She'd dressed up for the occasion. She wore a short-sleeved dress in what I guessed was black. Her hair was a bit bouncier than in the previous picture, and she wore earrings, bracelets, and an ornate necklace. It was now easy to see that she'd once been pretty.

Next in the dossier came information that naive people are shocked to discover is readily available online. A page printed from AnyBirthday.com revealed that Laura Skipcliff's birthday was October 27. She had been fifty-seven at the time of her death. The site offered the unintentionally gruesome opportunity to receive an E-mail reminder when her next birthday approached. The USSearch site confirmed that Laura Skipcliff had lived in Manhattan and that her age had been fifty-seven. For a fee, the site would've gone on to look for judgments, liens, bankruptcies, and a great deal more. Indeed, the people finders and the other free sites all abounded in low-cost opportunities to find out almost anything about anyone: to search Social Security records, court records, and property records. Searchers were also exhorted to click on hyperlinks that would presumably benefit themselves: *Get a home loan, Rent a truck, Refinance now, Save on lodging, Find contractors, Enjoy hassle-free shopping,* and *Meet Mr. Right.*

As it was, the results of free searches left no doubt that Dr. Skipcliff had been a wealthy woman. The web sites of four or five arts organizations listed her as a donor; she'd been especially supportive of dance. She'd served on the board of a well-known dance center in the Berkshires. InfoSpace and AnyWho had provided an address and phone number for her in that lovely region of Western Massachusetts. The town where she'd had what was presumably a summer house was one that posted its property assessments on the web. Laura Skipcliff had owned a house that sat on 2.4 acres. The assessed value of the land was high. The building was assessed at three times the value of the land.

The remainder of the dossier documented Laura Skipcliff's professional affiliations, achievements, and publications. The hospital web site that displayed the close-up of her face also gave her E-mail address: LFSkipcliff@aol.com. She'd attended medical school at Cornell. The papers she'd published had titles that were both impressive and, to me, incomprehensible.

At the end of the dossier were pages about a meeting sponsored by Harvard Medical School to be held in Boston from August 21 through August 25. According to the announcement, Laura Skipcliff was scheduled to present a paper on the morning of August 24 and to serve on a panel that afternoon. The dossier contained nothing about Laura Skipcliff's murder.

Chapter 6

The central tenet of canine fundamentalism is the misleadingly simple-sounding principle that dogs are everywhere. Having embraced this delightful reality, we believers are never surprised to find that interspecies enlightenment lurks in seemingly improbable places. Had I been an agnostic, a skeptic, an outright atheist, a blasphemist, a heretic, or merely the sort of nonpracticing hypocrite who claims to worship dogs but doesn't own one, I'd have been astonished to attain spiritual transcendence in so bourgeois and materialistic a spot as the Bloomingdale's department store at the Chestnut Hill Mall. As it was, the epiphany felt perfectly natural. All this is to say that in entering my name and Steve's in Bloomie's bridal registry, I abruptly and joyously reached a mystical and highly desirable state that had previous eluded me: All of a sudden, I knew exactly what it feels like to be a dog.

Not one to keep divine revelation to myself, I embarrassed Rita in front of the

Bloomingdale's salesperson by blurting out, "Rita, I finally get this wedding stuff! Everything just fell in place. Rita, the wedding is a dog show! I'm the bride. I'm going Best in Show!"

It was Friday afternoon. I'd fought the commuter traffic to the Chestnut Hill Mall strictly out of loyalty to Rita, who was apparently convinced that if I failed to register at Bloomingdale's, my marriage to Steve would be an unlawful sham; in Rita's view, bigamy was vastly preferable to any marriage unblessed by Bloomie's. To please Rita, I'd changed out of kennel clothes — old jeans and a stained T-shirt — and into a respectable pair of khakis and a white blouse. Rita wore a white linen suit. Her short, bouncy hair was streaked by the sun as well as by artifice, and she not only wore heels but knew how to walk in them. Until a few moments earlier, when the true nature of weddings had revealed itself to me, I'd shuffled reluctantly after her while muttering bitter complaints about china patterns and white gowns. Now that I grasped the project, I was thoroughly behind it.

"You know, Holly," Rita said, "I sometimes wonder whether you should be committed." Rita was a clinical psychologist. By *committed*, she meant "locked up," as opposed to "wholeheartedly pledged," as in, *I am committed to the well-being of my animals.*

"I'm committed to getting married," I said. "I'm committed to Steve. And now that I understand weddings, I'm committed to doing this one right. You see, it all came to me while I was registering. I had a distinct sense of déjà vu. And then it came to me that every time I'd ever entered a dog in a show, I'd done exactly what I was doing now, and I knew that I was filling out an entry blank just the way I do for Rowdy and Kimi, only this time I was doing it for myself. Anyway, I'm done grumbling about wedding plans. Registering for presents is fine! What they are, you see, is *trophies*. And what we're doing here today is putting together the *premium list*."

Rita sighed. "Just as long as you don't register for cheap stoneware and cheesy highball glasses, that's just grand."

"In the old days," I said with my newfound enthusiasm, "trophies used to be sterling silver. But it's awfully expensive. Besides, my mother left me the sterling that her dogs won. And I have some crystal, too. You still see crystal at shows, and it's really beautiful. Of course, the trophies I own are mainly bowls and stuff. But we don't need anything to drink out of. Steve and I discussed that. We own a million mugs and glasses."

"That don't match," said Rita, "and have dogs on them."

"Not exclusively. The obedience ones have

high jumps. And some of them have names of kennel clubs. But I do get the point. If we're giving a show, we want to give it with style."

Although Rita was professionally alarmed by the reason for my change in attitude, she seized on my new eagerness and led me through the areas of Bloomingdale's that displayed china, crystal, and silver. Just as some fortunate people are said to possess "an eye for dogs," Rita evidently possessed an eye for expensive household objects. The prices horrified me. The cost of one place setting in the china pattern Rita favored was what I'd have expected to pay for an entire set of dishes.

"It's china," she corrected me. "Not just dishes. And when people buy wedding gifts, they don't want to buy junk."

"My friends can't afford this stuff. And what if I drop it?"

"You won't use it very often," she said.

"Then why am I asking for it?"

"Every culture has its rites and rituals for marking important life transitions. Marriage is a major life event. In our culture, doing what we're doing now is one of the rites of passage that mark it. Besides which, Steve's first marriage was a disaster. He deserves to have everything right this time."

"When you get married," I said, "you can register for the same pattern. At these prices, we'll be lucky to own two place settings each, so we'll share. When we get together for dinner, we'll pool resources, and maybe there'll be enough plates for all four of us."

"Who said anything about me?" Rita asked.

"No one needed to. You and Artie —"

"Well, we're admittedly heading in that direction, I guess," she conceded.

Rita led me through the selection of a china pattern, white with a blue rim. Steve, who'd refused to accompany us, had said that I was welcome to pick out anything that wasn't covered with flowers.

"If you ask whether the pattern is available in dog bowls," Rita warned, "I will kill you here and now."

"I hadn't thought of it until you mentioned it," I said.

We then selected a silver pattern and, over my mild protest, crystal wineglasses. A Bloomie's salesperson then helped us to choose a variety of affordable objects, including salad forks. Well, she intended to be helpful. Some of her suggestions struck me as ridiculous. Steve wasn't the kind of person who'd don the chef's hat and apron that were supposedly popular, and he and I both thought of pizza as something to order at a pizzeria, not as something to whip up at home using a pizza set. An object known as a "tart pan" hit me as a wildly inappropriate wedding present. Brides weren't necessarily virginal these days, but *tart* was going a bit far. A Wüsthof cutlery set — knives stuck into a wooden storage block — seemed like a practical choice for couples who looked forward to years of marital discord and wanted to be sure to have sharp weapons handy when they moved beyond harsh words.

When we'd finished completing my nuptial entry blank at the Bloomingdale's Kennel Club, I thought we were done. Rita thought otherwise. Rowdy and Kimi, I realized, must have the same sensation when forced to return to the show ring for further judging: *We just did that!* Rita did not, however, lead me into another store with a registry for wedding presents. Rather, she caught sight of a display of black undies and exclaimed, "Victoria's Secret!"

"Don't be foolish," I said.

"Do you intend to get married in the old underwear you have on when you wash the dogs? There's nothing foolish about a trousseau."

"A trousseau. Isn't that something men wear for hernias?"

"This is going to be my treat," Rita said. "A romantic negligee."

"Everything in the window is black," I said.

So was most of the lingerie in the shop itself. Furthermore, most items were more suggestive of a brothel than of an altar, which is to say, very suggestive. As if to confirm my opinion that this wasn't exactly a bridal shop, Rita informed me that an especially provocative style of undergarment was known as a "merry widow."

"If I tried to breathe in that thing," I said, "Steve would be a widower. I'm not wearing something that squishes my rib cage. And one thing's settled about my wedding gown, and that's that it won't require a strapless bra. I'm not getting married with some damned choke collar around my midriff."

"Your dress." Rita sighed. "Mine. Leah's. There's so much to do!"

Rita had agreed to be my maid of honor. My cousin Leah would be the only bridesmaid, unless you counted Kimi, India, and Lady, as I certainly did.

I said, "Not to mention a place to get married and someone to marry us and —"

I was interrupted by a woman who came up to Rita, hugged her, and kissed her cheek. Although in certain ways the newcomer was quite attractive, with fine, delicate, pale skin and silky shoulder-length dark hair, something about the combination of that dark hair and her full cheeks reminded me of a character called Little Lulu who had starred in a series of old comic books that my mother had once bought for me at a used book store. Little Lulu, however, had had a round face. This woman's was elongated. Furthermore, it seemed to me that Little Lulu's hair had been parted in the middle, while the woman's was parted on the left. What the woman shared with Little Lulu, I suppose, was frumpiness. In any case, both she and Little Lulu seemed equally unlikely candidates for black lace merry widows, one of which the woman clutched in her hand.

"Holly," Rita said, "this is Francie Julong. Holly Winter. Francie is a birder."

Rita's participation in birding had destroyed my stereotype of birdwatchers as weird creatures who skulked in shrubbery and emerged only to aim binoculars at feathered creatures with stupid names. Artie Spicer, Rita's birding mentor, was a good-looking and normal-acting guy. When the four of us got together, Artie and Steve talked about birds, among other things, but there was nothing in the least bit laughable or freakish about Artie. If there had been, he'd never have gotten so much as a first date with Rita. Although I no longer clung to the stereotype of birders, I was nonetheless surprised to hear that Francie Julong and Rita knew each other from the avian world; from the gushy way she'd greeted Rita, I'd assumed that she, too, was a Cambridge psychotherapist.

"Rita is a much better birder than I am," Francie said. "I just plod along misidentifying everything."

"Not so. We're both out of our league with

60

some of those people at Mount Auburn."

The birding group where Rita had met Artie Spicer flocked together in Cambridge at Mount Auburn Cemetery, a spot as famous for attracting dedicated and knowledgeable observers of birds as for attracting the birds themselves.

Francie said, "Oh, well, we have fun. But I haven't seen you at Mount Auburn lately. I've missed you."

As Rita was explaining that she'd been away, I couldn't help eyeing the drab Francie and wondering whether her conservative, even dowdy, printed dress concealed lascivious undies like the black merry widow she held in her hand. For all I knew, she was wearing a lacy thong instead of ordinary panties. Maybe she even wore real stockings suspended by garters.

"I'm so glad you're back," Francie told Rita. "I'm really excited about the fall migration, and I'd hate to have to face all those confusing fall warblers without you. Holly, it was nice to meet you."

I told Francie that it had been nice to meet her, too. As she headed toward the cash register, I happened to glance toward the rear of the shop. Emerging from the entrance to the dressing rooms was Steve's fiendish ex-wife, Anita, who was tall and stylish. Her hair was long and blond, her expression sour. Dangling from her hand was a garter belt.

She held it with disdain, as if it were a dead rat she intended to whirl around and fling out of sight.

I turned my back to her and whispered to Rita, "Anita Fairley is just coming out of the dressing rooms, and we are leaving this second."

"Coward," Rita said. Still, she followed me out of the shop.

Once we'd escaped, I said, "I am not afraid of Anita."

"I know, I know," Rita said. "You live with two Alaskan malamutes, and —"

"Anita is a very nasty person. And she hates me. Besides, she was brandishing a lethal weapon."

"If one of you ever decides to strangle the other," Rita said, "my money's on you."

The thought that crossed my mind was so vicious that I didn't speak it aloud even to Rita, to whom I can say almost anything. The thought was this: Anita Fairley, recently Anita Fairley-Delaney, had met Steve at Rialto. She probably still went there. When she did, she probably parked in the garage under The Charles Hotel. If a woman had to have been bludgeoned to death in the garage, why on earth had it been the innocent Dr. Laura Skipcliff? Why couldn't it have been that damned Anita Fairley?

Chapter 7

"I'll have the Caesar salad," Rita told our waiter at the mall restaurant. "And a glass of Chardonnay with that. And since I'm not driving, I'll have another margarita while we wait."

I ordered the Caesar salad, too, but also the broiled salmon and a baked potato. Rita was not, by the way, the kind of gustatory hypocrite who eats nothing but salad in public and then goes home to binge on tortilla chips and ice cream at midnight; salad was what she ate, and she stayed slim. In contrast, my leanness was attributable strictly to metabolic luck.

"We did very well," Rita said with satisfaction. "You've registered for gifts, and we got a good start on clothes for you. I know you paid more than you're used to, but you can't go to Paris dressed for a dog show, and the nightie and robe don't count because they're my present."

"I dress very carefully for shows," I said.

"Appearance does count in the ring."

"Where doesn't it?"

"In the eyes of your dogs," I said. "That's one of the ten trillion ways in which dogs are morally superior to human beings. The Parisian dogs would've loved me in ratty jeans."

"And Steve?"

"That's a touchy subject, Rita. When it comes to looks, I'm in no position to compete with Anita. You saw her. She wins. That's it."

"Anita made Steve miserable. She cheated on him. She kicked his dog. She whined and criticized, and she tried to make him into someone he didn't want to be."

"And she is undeniably beautiful."

Rita's second margarita arrived. I could've used a drink, but since I was driving, I took a sip of water and returned to the topic of Anita, who was, as Rita knew, a criminal who'd gotten away with her crime. "The story on Anita is that the wicked flourish like the green bay tree. Could we please discuss another subject?" I introduced one. "Francie seems like a nice person."

"She really is very sweet."

"The way she hugged you, I thought she must be a mental-health type."

"She is, more or less. But she's a researcher, not a clinician. Talk about depressing subjects, though. Her field is the psychology of grief. Mourning. Loss. Parents who've had children die. I can't imagine a more depressing subject. But important, obviously. Still, I don't know how she does it. My work is stressful enough."

"Have you got patients next week? Or are you taking the whole month off?"

"No, I'm seeing people next week. Actually, I have an interesting case. Difficult. I really like this woman, but I'm having a hard time sorting out what's going on with her. She's dropped out. I'm hoping she'll come back."

After the waiter had delivered our Caesar salads, my hearty meal, and Rita's wine, she resumed. "This is a woman sent by her husband because he says she's paranoid. Or so she tells me. I haven't spoken to him. She says he's been repeatedly unfaithful to her. He denies it. He says she's imagining things. It's possible that she's never confronted him as strongly as she needed to. But that's beside the point. What's interesting is that the whole situation highlights what's usually a more muted issue in therapy, which is the question of, um, truth versus accuracy, let's say. There is absolutely no question in my mind — well, very little question — that my patient is telling me the truth in the sense that she really believes that he's had these affairs. She'd pass a polygraph test. In that sense, what she's telling me is *her* truth. But what's the correspondence between her truth and external reality? If there is such a thing?"

"Of course there's such a thing."

"In the literal sense, there is, except that how am I supposed to know what it is?"

"Ask the husband?"

"He refuses to see me."

"That doesn't bode well, does it?"

"Well, I may yet lure him in. And no matter what, there is some kind of personal truth for her in her perception that he's unfaithful. That's what I was offered. It's what I had to work with."

"If fidelity is her primary concern," I said, "she should get —"

"She already has one. In fact, I suspect that that's an issue for the husband, that his wife loves the dog more than she loves him."

"Too bad she didn't marry a veterinarian," I said. "In that way, Steve and I are a perfect match. And when it comes to absolute devotion to him, no one could compete with India and Lady. If you set out to get a one-man dog, you couldn't pick a better breed than the German shepherd dog to begin with, plus India as an individual is very loving and ultra self-confident. India is really a dog with a single mission in life. Her mission is Steve and, to a lesser extent, everyone connected with him. Including Lady. And Lady is completely devoted to Steve because the entire rest of the world scares the daylights out of her. Pointers aren't supposed to be like that, but Lady has her reasons, and she does remarkably well. The miracle is that India never actually bit Anita when Anita went after Lady. But India did growl at Anita. I heard her. Fortunately, India is intelligent enough not to generalize from one wife to another. She and I get along very well. The only serious conflict is between India and Kimi, and that's mainly because of Kimi. Well, and then there's Tracker and my dogs."

"That awful cat," Rita said. "You deserve a medal for keeping that thing."

"Tracker is not a thing," I said. "And I've stopped feeling guilty about not bonding more with her."

"Guilty? Holly, that is an ugly, nasty cat. No one else would keep her for two minutes."

"Steve would."

"You tried to foist her off on Steve, and he refused."

"Only because he knew she'd be safe with me."

As we finished dinner, Rita nagged me about the need to get going on wedding plans. Now that I saw the event in its proper context, as we Cambridge types say, I shared her concern about my formerly casual attitude. Indeed, I'd been to dog shows chaired by people who'd taken their responsibilities lightly. The shows had been disasters. It's one thing to turn your wedding into a dog show, but quite another to turn it into a crummy, disorganized dog show. I wasn't going to let that happen: I felt determined that Steve and I would have the Westminster of weddings.

In fact, when I got home that evening, practically the first thing I said to Steve was just that: "the Westminster of weddings."

"Have you been drinking?" he asked.

"Of course not. We took my car. I drove."

Steve was lying on the bed sipping a beer and watching a DVD of *The Sopranos*. Also on the bed were four of our five dogs: my Rowdy and his India, Lady, and the beautiful-to-die-for malamute puppy, Sammy. Kimi, normally the biggest bed hog in the pack, was holding a sphinxlike pose on the floor.

"If Kimi breaks that down-stay and goes for India, it won't be my fault," I said.

After getting myself a glass of red wine, I rejoined what I was learning to think of as my family. After dislodging a couple of dogs, I managed to squeeze in next to Steve. The *Sopranos* episode was one we'd both seen before, one of the ones about Tony's Russian mistress, so I felt free to tell Steve about my wedding epiphany.

He took the revelation calmly. When Paul told people about what happened on the road to Damascus, they probably stayed pretty cool, too: *Gee, that's nice. And how was the rest of your day?*

"We never intended to leave the dogs out," Steve said. "They were always part of our plans."

"It's the remainder of the plans that I've been neglecting."

"We agreed to keep it small," he said. "Have you changed your mind about that?"

"No. Not at all. Not in the least. But we do need a guest list."

Looking from Tony Soprano to me, he said, "You're not inviting what's his name, are you?"

Enzio Guarini. Steve knew the name as well as I did. So did everyone else in Greater Boston.

"We really have to," I said. "And we'd better ask Carla to do the flowers, too. If we don't, she'll be hurt."

Guarini's wife, Carla, ran a flower shop. Guarini ran . . . well, Guarini ran a lot of enterprises, some legitimate, some otherwise. The principal "otherwise" was the Mob. I'd worked for Guarini off and on, but only in the blameless role of dog trainer. Guarini's own behavior was open to criticism, but thanks to me, his Norwegian elkhounds were model citizens.

"He's your client, too," I pointed out. "And he's very fond of me. We can't leave him out."

"We can't invite every client I have," Steve said. "Just my staff."

"And their husbands. Wives. Significant others. We can't invite half of a couple and leave out the other. Anyway, we need to make a list for Gabrielle. With addresses. She's doing the invitations. Thank God my father married her. But she can't do invitations until we know where we're getting married."

"Anywhere's fine with me," Steve said. "Did you and Rita have a good time?"

"Yes," I said, without mentioning the one bad part of the shopping trip, namely, my having seen his evil ex-wife.

"Did you have a chance to mention the third floor?"

The third floor of my house was sunny, airy, and, if anything, more attractive than the second floor, where Rita now lived.

"No. I couldn't find a tactful way to work it in, except that we did talk a little about Artie. I think they should get married. Rita loves him. I think he loves her. They have a monogamous relationship. They're very companionable and compatible. At a minimum, they could live together. I don't know why they don't."

"Willie."

Willie was Rita's Scottish terrier, a feisty character who had a passion for human ankles, including mine. To the best of my knowledge, Willie had never broken skin, but he did voice his desires. I didn't mind — on the contrary, I liked Willie, whose ankle fetish struck me as a kink that he had the self-control never to act on and the honesty never to lie about. Artie felt otherwise.

Steve continued. "We'd better give it some time. Rita's not dumb. She'll work it out for herself. She's been a real good friend to both of us. The last thing we want to do is make her feel pushed out."

The *Sopranos* episode had ended. Steve switched to the local news on TV. The murder of Dr. Laura Skipcliff got a brief mention. The victim had not been sexually assaulted. Her purse, found at the scene, had contained credit cards and two hundred thirty-two dollars in cash. The report ended with a platitude: Authorities were pursuing the investigation.

"You didn't use the garage at the mall, did you?" asked Steve.

I hadn't. Still, after dinner, Rita and I had hurried across the parking lot as fast as her high heels had allowed. I'd pretended that Rowdy was on one side of me and Kimi on the other. Ahead of us paraded Sammy. For all I knew, Dr. Laura Skipcliff, too, had owned big, beautiful dogs. For all I knew, she'd drawn strength from their imaginary presence until the moment of her violent death.

Chapter 8

From: Gabrielle@beamonres.org
To: HollyWinter@amrone.org
Subj: Worries!!

Dearest Holly,
Your father insists that I convey to you his extreme apprehension about your safety in Cambridge. I have assured him that you are unlikely to frequent the parking garage beneath The Charles Hotel, or any other hotel for that matter, especially now, of course. It is my impression that your common sense passed to you through the maternal line. I trust you to use that heritage.

On the subject of maternal lineage, I want to pose a delicate question concerning the wording of your wedding invitation. As you know, while I never had the privilege of meeting your late mother, I hear marvelous things about her from everyone and, especially now, am acutely aware that you cherish her memory. As your wedding day approaches, how fervently you must long for her presence! And more to the point, for her name, together with your father's, on the invitation. Well, enough beating about the bush! Please answer me in all honesty! Who is to request the pleasure of the company of your guests? Your father? Or Mr. and Mrs.? The Mrs. being, of course, yours truly, as I truly am, and am truly determined not to force my way into a position that a kinder Fate would have permitted your mother to occupy. I must also mention that she, Marissa, would perhaps have had greater success than I have been able to achieve in convincing your father that a wedding invitation is a formal announcement and, as such, requires the utmost in formality and therefore should not be worded "Mr. Buck Winter" or "Mr. and Mrs. Buck Winter," "Buck" being inherently informal, don't you think? I regret to report that in that matter, Mr. Buck Winter has prevailed. Luckily, however, Buck has agreed to wear a suit — the one he bought for our own wedding, so we may rest assured that he will look proper and handsome.

Now, on to yet one more delicate matter. In surfing the web, your father has discovered that the Commonwealth of Massachusetts issues one-day licenses whereby laypersons such as himself are authorized to solemnize marriages. Knowing your father as you do, you will immediately guess the particular layperson he has in mind. As I hope you understand, I fell deeply and permanently in love with Buck within seconds of meeting him at the previously ghastly show when I was an ignoramus about dogs and in need of the rescue he effected. That being said, I think him an unsuitable person to solemnize marriages — for the simple reason, dear Holly, that he would inevitably turn any wedding at all, including yours, into an event indistinguishable from a dog show. It would be a miracle if he even mentioned you and Steve! Plus, you can't possibly want your father running the show, can you? Oh, dear, maybe I am barging in after all. Maybe you love the idea? If not, I urge you to make an alternative plan with the greatest possible speed. What about that nice Episcopal priest with the hearing dog? We ran into her in the Square. That you and Steve are not Episcopalians can't matter in the least, can it? I am and would be more than willing to put in a word for you. If necessary, you might want to convert. ASAP.

Your loving stepmother,
Gabrielle

From: HollyWinter@amrone.org
To: Gabrielle@beamonres.org
Subj: Re: Worries!!

Dearest Gabrielle,
Steve and I want your name on the invitation! As to the solemnization of our marriage, it seems dishonest suddenly to become Episcopalians for the sole purpose of snagging a dog-friendly priest. Anyway, our priest friend will be away at a retreat.

We need to discuss this whole matter. I will call you soon.

Love,
Holly

Gabrielle's E-mail arrived on Saturday morning. I replied immediately and then phoned her the minute Steve left for work. The first thing I asked was whether my father was there. Happily, he wasn't.

"Wonderful," I said. "Look, this whole idea of having him marry us is a nightmare. I don't care what we have to do, but we're going to put a stop to it. I haven't told Steve about it, and I'm not going to tell him, and I need you to do everything you can to make sure that Steve never even begins to hear the slightest hint about it. Buck already has a role in the wedding. He's the father of the bride. That's his role. It's his only role. And not just because he'd talk about dogs. The worst would be that he'd manage to say something mortifying about Steve's previous marriage or . . . the worst would be that he'd say something I can't begin to guess and definitely do not want to hear. Wait! Yes, I can guess. He'd preach for hours about the fidelity of dogs and the infidelity of human beings. I can hear it now. At *my* wedding. Probably with examples. Bill Clinton and Buddy. Gabrielle, over my dead —"

"Your dead body is your father's other worry, of course." Gabrielle had a warm, rich, throaty voice. Her typical tone, which she used now, was confiding. "It's always difficult for parents to realize that their children are grown up." She added, and not as a question, "Isn't it."

"Gabrielle, that murder had nothing to do with me. Nothing. Crime happens in Cambridge just the way it does in every other city. And in the country! The woman who was murdered, Laura Skipcliff, was an anesthesiologist. For all we know, a patient of hers died, and some lunatic relative blamed Dr. Skipcliff. I don't know, and the police don't know. I saw Kevin Dennehy for a second this morning. He doesn't even know what the murder weapon was. Probably a sledge hammer or something like that, but it hasn't been found. No one at the garage or the hotel saw anything useful. Dr. Skipcliff lived in New York. She was here for a conference. It's over. If her murderer was here for the conference, he's gone home by now."

"Why would an anesthesiologist use a sledge hammer? Wouldn't you think . . . ?"

"I don't know. What I know is that I live right next door to a cop, the house has good locks, Steve and I have five dogs, and one of them is India. Would you remind Buck about her? And remind him that for most people, presumably including most murderers, one look at Rowdy and Kimi and even Sammy is a big deterrent. Most people don't realize that malamutes are the world's worst guard dogs. Remind Buck that if anyone actually attacked me, Rowdy and Kimi wouldn't just stand there doing nothing."

Gabrielle responded by saying how much my father loved me. After that, we discussed wedding plans, of which Steve and I had, of course, made all too few. Then I refused her invitation to spend the next weekend in Maine. I offered excuses about Labor Day traffic and the need to work on the wedding. In reality, I didn't want to subject Steve to more time with Buck than was absolutely necessary. Also, Steve and I both had heavy work weeks ahead and wanted the three-day weekend to ourselves.

At the end of the conversation, Gabrielle

said that since she wasn't my biological mother, she had no difficulty in seeing me as an adult, but she still couldn't help sharing a little of my father's worry that I was living in a city where a woman had just been mysteriously murdered. I thanked her for her concern, told her how much I loved her, and said that I felt perfectly safe. I really did appreciate her concern and really did love her. It was also true that at the time, I still felt perfectly safe.

Chapter 9

Six days later, on the evening of Friday, August 30, a woman named Victoria Trotter was murdered as she lay in a hammock on the front porch of her house on Egremont Street in Cambridge. I knew Victoria Trotter, whom I'd interviewed for two articles I'd written, one about her famous mother, the late Mary Kidwell Trotter, a dog portrait artist, and the other about Victoria's own canine version of the tarot. I owned a Victoria Trotter deck of the cards and consulted them every once in a while, strictly to get a reading on themes I might be overlooking in my life and the lives of my dogs, not to foresee what I trusted was the unforeseeable future. Still, because of Victoria's tarot, it's worth noting that I had no premonition of her violent death.

In fact, between the Saturday when I talked with Gabrielle and the Friday when Victoria was bludgeoned to death I paid only routine attention to the security precautions that city dwellers take automatically. As always, I kept the doors to my car and house locked. As I'd always done everywhere and fully intend to do for the rest of my life on earth and for eternity in the beyond, I spent nearly every waking and sleeping moment, indoors and outside, surrounded by big dogs. But I did so solely for the pleasure of their company. Dr. Laura Skipcliff's murder had had nothing to do with me; nothing about it had suggested a threat to my safety.

Even if I'd been worried, I'd have had little time to dwell on my fear during the week before Victoria's slaying. As I'd told Gabrielle, Steve and I both had full schedules. In addition to his practice and my column for *Dog's Life*, we were working on our first cooperative venture, a diet book called *No More Fat Dogs*. On Monday, I had a long phone conversation with Judith Esterhazy, Mac's wife, about wedding sites that she'd investigated when searching for a place for their daughter, Olivia, to get married. Equipped with a list of the names and phone numbers of historic houses, estates open to the public, and large country inns near Boston, I spent a lot of time on the phone learning that most spots were already booked or didn't allow dogs. The only promising site was the Wayside Wildlife Refuge. It had the advantage of being conveniently nearby, in Lexington, and its main building was large enough for us to hold the ceremony and reception indoors in case of rain. Steve and I agreed to visit it over the Labor Day weekend. We drafted the guest list, which was alarmingly long. To our supposedly small wedding, we initially planned to invite more than a hundred people, and Steve and I kept adding names of others who simply couldn't be excluded. To my horror, I found the web site about the Commonwealth's willingness to grant one-day solemnization powers to people, presumably including my father, who wanted to officiate at weddings. More times than I care to report, I checked the big online bookstores to see how *101 Ways to Cook Liver* was faring. It consistently ranked lower than *Ask Dr. Mac*, but only a little lower, so I felt satisfied. Out of curiosity, I also checked on Judith Esterhazy's new book, *Boudicca*. The combination of painfully low sales and splendid reviews was depressing. It's a sad day for literature when a dog-treat cookbook does a zillion times better than a highly acclaimed novel. It's a sad day even for the author of the dog-treat cookbook. On the other paw, of course, it's a perfectly delightful day for big, hungry dogs.

I said just that to Steve on Friday evening as we sat outside after dinner, with country music playing softly from a boom box on the stairs to the house. The fenced yard was one reason I'd bought the place. By suburban standards, the yard would've been small, but for Cambridge, it was decent-sized. Running parallel to the house on the long side of the yard was the brick wall of the peculiar little building that occupied the corner of Appleton Street and Concord Avenue, the "spite building," as it was called, presumably because it was the legacy of some forgotten dispute. Wooden fences at the front and back made the area secure for the dogs. Ivy grew all over the brick wall, and shrubs and perennials testified to my vision of horticultural possibility if not to my acceptance of the reality of Alaskan malamutes. I'd no sooner cured Rowdy of digging when Kimi the Excavator arrived in our lives. Now, just as I was starting to feel hopeful about persuading Kimi that by "horticultural possibility" I meant the hidden gardens of Beacon Hill rather than the battlefield of Verdun, here was Sammy, who had been sired by Rowdy out of Ch. Jazzland's Embraceable You, but by miracle rather than biology had inherited Kimi's self-destructive zeal for tunneling directly to China, where "dog love" refers strictly to an unholy food preference that I'm unable to see as culturally relative. It's not for me to judge harshly if cultural relativism dictates that it's dandy for brothers and sisters to marry each other or that nonagenarians should be set adrift on icebergs to meet life's end, but wrong is wrong, damn it!

Torture is wrong. Child abuse is wrong. So is dining on dogs.

Where was I? Oh, so Sammy the Bulldozer, otherwise known as Jazzland's As Time Goes By, was at this moment using his big front paws to fling dirt in Lady the pointer's bewildered face and was thus distracting me from telling Steve that my book was selling better than the renowned Judith Esterhazy's. I broke off. "Steve, please make Sammy stop. I'm going to build a digging box for all three malamutes, but in the meantime, I really don't want him killing that peony."

Steve refilled his wineglass, took a sip, and said with maddening deliberation, "It's unrealistic to expect a dog yard to look like a flower garden."

We were sitting on the wooden park bench that I'd bought with precisely that expectation. It was about ten o'clock and still stinking hot, but neither of us had wanted to endure another breath of inside air. Hank Williams was singing "Your Cheatin' Heart." The light mounted on the side of the house and the ambient city light let us keep our eyes on our dogs. All five were loose in the yard. When I was alone with them, I let them loose only in carefully selected combinations because I didn't want to risk a dogfight. Steve trusted his ability to stop trouble before it led to bloodshed. Also, if the dogs tore one another to pieces, he'd be able to

83

stitch them back together, whereas my profession left me with nothing more helpful to do than write about what had happened.

"Couples who merge two sets of children have it easy," I said.

"Kids are just as likely to wreck yards and go for one another's throats," Steve pointed out.

I got up and was heading toward the house when Steve read my intention of startling Sammy with a blast of cold water. "Sammy, leave it," he said quietly.

Sammy quit digging. If you live with golden retrievers, you may fail to grasp the astonishment I felt. If you live with malamutes, you will be stunned.

"You should teach at Hogwart's," I said.

"What?"

"The school for wizards in Harry Potter. A teenage malamute just obeyed you. You're magic with animals."

"You're just magic." Steve clinked his wineglass against mine.

Before the potentially romantic interlude could develop, the heavily Boston-accented voice of Kevin Dennehy sounded at the gate. "Anyone want a beer?" That's a translation. The original was *Anyone wanna bee-uh?*

The one who did was Kevin, whose mother banned alcohol and meat from the house they shared. Beer and hamburger were the foundations of my friendship with Kevin.

Soon after I'd moved in, he'd arranged for space in my refrigerator. Now, I unlocked the gate and welcomed Kevin, as did all five dogs, especially Rowdy and Kimi, who bumped against each other in their zeal to get close to him and sing their weirdly human-sounding *woo-woo-woo*s. Coached by the elders of his tribe, Sammy picked up the song. Lady, eternally fearful, hung back. India, who'd been sensibly resting on the ground to avoid elevating her body temperature in the evening heat, remained exactly where she'd been.

Kevin was carrying two cold six-packs. To make room for him, Steve and I moved from the bench to the steps, and Kevin joined us there. Steve and I stayed with the red wine we'd been drinking. When Kevin popped the top off his beer, however, Rowdy and Kimi dashed to him, their eyes gleaming, their tails practically beating out the rhythm of a beer commercial. "Tattle tales," he told them.

For fifteen or twenty minutes, the three of us and the five dogs hung out together. The youngest dog, the inexhaustible Sammy, roused the others to short bursts of running, but the four grown-up dogs succumbed to summer-night lethargy. Lady overcame her timidity enough to station herself next to Kevin, who was chronically guilty of violating my ban on wrestling with malamutes, but stroked the nervous little pointer as delicately as if she'd been a Chihuahua. Steve and I drank wine, Kevin drank beer, and the dogs drank a lot of water from their communal bucket. I updated Kevin on our wedding plans. Steve told him about the book we were writing together and asked about his progress in recovering from the gunshot wound in the chest he'd received the previous spring. Kevin said that his girlfriend, Jennifer, was teaching him Tai Chi and that he was hoping to be able to start running again in October. We discussed the murder of Dr. Laura Skipcliff. The three of us agreed that anyone could've entered the parking garage by taking the elevator in the hotel lobby; patrons of the hotel's bars and restaurants used it all the time, as did people who didn't want to bother searching for on-street parking in Harvard Square. No one, certainly not Kevin, said that the murder would go unsolved, but I somehow felt the presence of a comfortable boundary that relegated the murder to the past and kept it safely separate from the lazy, companionable present I was now enjoying. I slipped into a hypnotic haze induced by the combination of the semidarkness, the wine I'd drunk, the humid warmth of the evening, my love for Steve and our five dogs, my affection for Kevin, and the heartbreaking voice of Patsy Cline singing "Sweet Dreams."

All of a sudden, I was jarred into vigilant consciousness. Kevin's beeper sounded, the cell phone on his belt rang, and the blare of a siren sounded as a police cruiser tore down Appleton Street. Car doors opened. Kevin was on his feet. Simultaneously, it seemed to me, he shouted into the phone, bolted to the gate, wrenched it open, hollered an order to kill the siren, and yelled at me to watch the dogs. Steve was already keeping them away from the open gate. In response to Kevin's bellowing, a uniformed cop, a kid who looked like a Boy Scout, appeared and said, "Lieutenant, there's another one."

"Who trained you? I didn't. I don't want to hear 'another one.' I want to hear what and where, I want to hear it fast, and I don't want to have to ask."

"A woman. Egremont Street. Massive head trauma. No weapon, no witnesses, no perp. The sergeant said to get you."

"Name?" Kevin demanded.

"O'Flaherty."

"Not the sergeant's name! The woman's name."

"Victoria Trotter."

Suddenly, I was cool and sober. "Dear God," I said to Steve, who was closing the gate behind the departing Kevin. "Steve, I know Victoria Trotter. I wrote two articles about her. One, really. One about her, one about her mother. Mary Kidwell Trotter. The artist. She painted dog portraits. Victoria did that dog version of the tarot I own. I wrote

87

about it. Victoria has dogs. Two whippets."

"Where's Egremont Street?" he asked.

"North Cambridge. Off Mass. Ave. on the Somerville side. In the direction of Davis Square. Not all that far from here."

Steve wrapped his arms around me. "I'm sorry," he said. "Sounds like you lost a friend."

"No," I blurted out. Feeling ashamed, I added, "The truth is, I didn't like Victoria Trotter. I didn't like her at all."

Chapter 10

The dossier on Victoria Trotter opened with five pages from web directories. All gave the same information. Victoria's phone number had the same area code and prefix as mine. Her address was 37 Egremont Street, Cambridge, MA 02140. A page printed from MapQuest showed that Egremont was a little L-shaped street and that number 37 occupied the inner corner of the L.

Next were two pages from the City of Cambridge Assessor's Database. The first of those two pages was a plot plan with the property lines of 37 Egremont Street shown in solid black. The house appeared as a shaded area. Dotted lines showed the location of the driveway. On the next page was a table of information about who owned 37 Egremont Street — Trotter, Victoria — together with the block and lot numbers, the square footage of the lot, the assessed value, and so forth. The assessed value was high. The sale date of the property was four years earlier. The assessed value was now a hundred thousand dollars more than Victoria Trotter had paid. In Cambridge, a termite-ridden doghouse that would cramp a Chihuahua has a high assessed value, and correctly so because it also has a high market value that reliably ascends. Ridiculous! I mean, we mere human beings are of frail character, but any dog should have the moral fortitude to resist the lure of that institution with the crimson logo emblazoned with the famous motto and slogan. The motto: the word *Veritas*. The slogan: If you don't have a *Harvard* education, you don't have an education at all.

According to AnyBirthday.com, Victoria Trotter would have turned fifty-six on October 27. The online version of the Social Security Death Index had provided the Social Security number of Victoria's late mother, the famous Mary Kidwell Trotter, who had died twenty-two years ago.

The next few web pages came from the alumni newsletter of a school of veterinary medicine. The lead story was about alumni participation in the dedication of a new administration building. Victoria Trotter had donated one of her mother's paintings, which hung in the lobby. In one of the photographs that accompanied the story, a young Victoria Trotter stood on one side of a large oil painting of three golden retrievers. On the other side, beaming gratefully at Victoria, was the president of the alumni association, Dr. Mac McCloud. Victoria looked much better than she had when I'd interviewed her. She had a thin face with a prominent, aristocratic nose that should have seemed disproportionately large but somehow did not. Her hair was straight and dark. Her skin was light, her eyes almost black. In the photo, her smile looked proud. In person, she'd been arrogant and disdainful, or so I'd thought. She'd had a brittle laugh that she'd produced with grating frequency.

Copies of my articles and pages about Victoria's tarot formed the bulk of the dossier. Some were from the big online booksellers, others from comparatively obscure web sites about dog-oriented spiritualism, mysticism, and extrasensory communication. The Trotter Tarot, as it was called, differed from the traditional Rider-Waite deck mainly in substituting dogs for the usual people on the cards. The suits were identical to the orthodox ones of the Rider-Waite: wands, cups, swords, and pentacles. The drawings were appealing, and they'd certainly appealed to many people. The artwork was expertly executed; the artist was an accomplished technician. What's more, the dogs were rendered realistically, and the impact of the cards was entirely unsentimental. Realism devoid of sentimentality was a hallmark of the work of Victoria's

91

mother, Mary Kidwell Trotter. So was technical mastery. So were the bright but subtle colors that made the Trotter Tarot so attractive. Neither before nor after producing the Trotter Tarot and the companion book had Victoria Trotter ever published any other illustrations of any kind. In my article about her tarot, I'd kept my suspicion to myself because I'd had no evidence and hadn't wanted to risk a lawsuit. But I can't have been the only person to wonder whether the gifted Mary Kidwell Trotter had redone the Rider-Waite deck for her own pleasure and refrained from publishing it because it was close to the original. At a guess, her daughter, Victoria, had had no such scruples and no hesitation about putting her own name on her mother's work. I remembered the dedication of the book: "Most special thanks and love to my late mother, Mary Kidwell Trotter."

The final pages of the dossier consisted of announcements of Victoria's Trotter Tarot workshops, lectures, and courses. She'd served on panels and participated in "interactive plenaries," whatever they were. The freshness, skill, and subtlety of the Trotter Tarot illustrations were nowhere evident in the titles and descriptions of Victoria's presentations. In October of the previous year, at a spiritual retreat center in the Berkshires, Victoria had offered a course called "Useful

Helping Skills in Readings of the Trotter Tarot." In May, at a tarot conference in New York City, she'd given a lecture titled "The Case Example of Emma the Shih Tzu as a Guide to Smoothing Out Kinks in Interpreting the Cards." At an event billed as an Intensive Tarot Studies Program scheduled to take place in December in Bern, Switzerland, she'd been due to offer the following course:

Turning the Tide:
Lessons Learned in Hearing the Soul
Voices of Dogs
Instructor: Victoria Trotter

This innovative course examines the dynamic relevance of utilizing tarot-theory-based models of principles of trans-species intervention with behavior-affected dogs and their human guardians. Topics to be developed include:

• Effect of Trotter Tarot education about canine psycho-emotional concerns on human attitudes and spiritual beliefs.

• Effect of tarot-enhanced communication in elevating canine self-esteem and human resilience in behavior-conflicted relationships.

• Use of Trotter Tarot readings to promote interspecies communication and trans-species unity and global peace.

A short biography followed: "Victoria Trotter has worked with human-canine dyads throughout the Americas and Europe. Illustrator of the beloved Trotter Tarot and author of *Interpreting the Trotter Tarot*, Victoria Trotter is Senior Training Advisor to the International Tarot Foundation."

There ended this dossier.

Chapter 11

"Victoria Trotter was a nasty woman," I told Kevin Dennehy.

So much for saying nothing but good about the dead.

It was nine o'clock on the morning of Saturday, August 31, and Kevin was sitting at my kitchen table drinking coffee, eating his third English muffin, and sneaking bits of it to Kimi and Sammy. I didn't take Kevin to task for breaking the house rule. He'd been up all night. Steve, too, was laboring on Labor Day weekend, although for only a short time, or so I hoped. His clinic had called a half hour earlier about a Belgian Tervuren suffering from an apparent intestinal obstruction. The X ray showed what the young vet at the clinic thought might be a corn cob. But could Steve take a quick look? Oh, my. Never in his life had Steve taken a less-than-thorough look at an animal. Even so, a corn cob was a likely bet, and if Steve saw one on the radiograph, he'd call Angell Memorial

Hospital and have the owner rush the dog there for surgery. By the way, should you care to promote veterinary prosperity at great monetary cost to yourself and possibly fatal risk to your dog, let your dog eat corn cobs, or give him a chance to filch them. Those rough suckers are never happier than when they're lodging in a canine gut.

"I interviewed Victoria two times," I continued. "Her mother was a famous dog artist, Mary Kidwell Trotter. I wrote an article about her. And I also interviewed Victoria about herself, about a dog tarot deck she published. I can show it to you if you want."

"Didn't do her much good," Kevin said. "If she'd seen the future, she'd've stayed indoors last night."

"We didn't stay indoors," I pointed out. Kevin had already told me that Victoria Trotter had been bludgeoned to death as she lay in a hammock on the front porch of her house. She'd apparently spent the hot summer evening lazing around outside, more or less as we'd done. Steve and I had sipped wine. Kevin had had beer. Victoria, however, had, in Kevin's words, been slugging down Bombay gin on the rocks. Steve and I had taken our dogs outside with us. Victoria had left her two whippets in their crates indoors.

The murder scene was easy to envision. I remembered the porch and the hammock from the visits I'd made to interview Victoria.

96

Her house had interested me because it had reminded me a little of my own. Both were red, mine a barn red, hers a darker shade that had struck me as unwholesome, perhaps because it was the color of dried blood or perhaps because my dislike of Victoria had tainted my vision. Her house was somewhat older than mine and obviously Victorian, with yellow-cream trim in a pattern that suggested flowers without actually depicting them. I remember wondering whether my house, too, might once have had pretty trim and a front porch and whether I might someday install a third-floor skylight like the one on Victoria's roof. I'd also been struck by the contrast between the front and the rear of her house, its public and private faces, so to speak. Her house sat on a small corner lot. The front of the house and the side facing the street were neat and well kept. The hammock was attractive, and potted plants decorated the steps to the porch. An evergreen tree near the porch was overgrown, but the foundation shrubs had been trimmed, and tidy hostas formed a thick border along the sidewalk. When I'd parked in the driveway at the rear, I'd been startled. An old radiator had been leaning against the back steps, and other pieces of junk had been strewn here and there.

"Besides, her tarot is mainly for readings about dogs," I said, "not people. And it's not meant for fortune telling. It's supposed to help you understand your dog's past and present. She didn't claim that it was some magical way to predict the future."

"I got no use for all that mumbo jumbo," Kevin said. "So, what was it you didn't like about her? She say something bad about malamutes?"

"She said that they conned law-abiding people into feeding them at the table," I said. "Actually, I said that, and please stop it, all of you. Anyway, one thing I know about Victoria goes back . . . it must be twenty years, long before I had malamutes. I was a teenager. This happened at a show. I was with my mother and some of our goldens. My father wasn't there, which was probably a good thing, because Buck would've been so furious that he'd've done God knows what and gotten himself in trouble. Anyway, Victoria Trotter had a greyhound she was showing in obedience. And she must've known that that isn't the world's easiest obedience breed. Everyone knows that."

Kevin guffawed.

"Everyone who trains dogs. But anyone who shows greyhounds in obedience, or malamutes in obedience, for that matter, needs a good attitude. So, what happened was just that her dog quit on her. I saw this part. I was right outside the ring. It was no big deal. Not that it ever happened with my goldens or my mother's, but on the off-leash heeling, Victoria's dog just stopped and stood still and left her heeling along all by herself. She gave a second command — she told him to heel — which you can do and still qualify. You lose points, but you don't wash out. But in this case, the dog ignored her. He just stood there." I shrugged. "So what! It wasn't as if he'd lifted his leg on the judge or attacked another dog. But Victoria's response — and I didn't see this part — was to take the dog out to the parking lot and beat the daylights out of him. And someone saw her. An incident like that is very serious. The American Kennel Club has strict rules of all kinds about conduct at shows, but in terms of how people react to violations of AKC rules, mistreating a dog is the worst possible thing an exhibitor can do. It enrages people. And this was the daughter of Mary Kidwell Trotter! So, Victoria lost her AKC privileges for I don't know how long, and it was a major scandal. As far as I know, Victoria never showed a dog again. I'd pretty much forgotten about her until I got the assignment from *Dog's Life* to do an article about her mother, and my editor, Bonnie, told me that Victoria lived right here in Cambridge and that I should interview her. That was only a few years ago, just about the time Victoria published her tarot deck and the book that goes with it. And then I got

99

the assignment for the article about her tarot."

"So you stroll into her house and say, 'Hey there, Vicky, how you doing? When did you quit beating your dogs?' "

"Kevin, I did no such thing! I knocked myself out to have an open mind. I told myself that I'd seen her in the ring at that show, but I'd heard about everything else fourth- or fifth-hand. Maybe someone lied. And if not, it happened ages ago. People change. I tried as hard as I could to be fair to her. Not that I believed that anyone had lied. The person who saw her happened to be a guy named Harry Howland, who was and is very reputable and ethical. If Harry Howland said that Victoria was beating her dog, then she was."

"And you tried to forget all that, but you hated her on sight." Kevin leaned down to rub his big chin on the top of Sammy's head. Kimi shoved her way in. Kevin wrapped his gorilla arms around both dogs.

"Not exactly. But it didn't take her long to start condescending to me. She obviously wanted to be a celebrity, even in *Dog's Life*, but she made fun of the name, which was stupid, because it's supposed to be funny. Both times I was there, her whole manner was disdainful. Arrogant. And she was very restless, very edgy. For all that she was the queen bee of animal mind reading, her New Age studies obviously hadn't brought her any

100

peace of mind. Also, her dogs were hand shy. And they were nice dogs. Whippets. That's a sensitive, affectionate breed. They were very sweet. There's no excuse for hitting any dog, but what kind of vicious person hits gentle little dogs like that? And they had been hit. No one could've missed it. So, I kept the interviews short. Professional. I asked my questions, got answers, and left. With a very low opinion of Victoria Trotter." I refilled Kevin's cup and mine.

"Thanks," he said. "Fact is, her dogs weren't in good condition."

"In what way?"

"Locked in their crates in their own filth. No water. Like you said, whippets. Two of them."

"Kevin, you lied to me! When you walked in here, I asked you whether she still had dogs and whether they were okay. And you said they were all right!"

"They are now. And I wanted to hear what you had to say without you knowing about the dogs. She'd only been dead maybe an hour when we got there, and the dogs'd been locked up a lot longer than that." He beamed at Kimi and Sammy. "None of that around here, is there, boys?"

"Kimi is not a boy. But there's certainly no animal neglect around here. That is disgusting."

"Party girl," Kevin said.

"Kimi? She's never been bred."

"You got dogs on the brain. Anyone ever tell you that? Victoria. That's what the neighbors say. Lot of men, lot of booze."

"Lots of suspects," I said. "So maybe Victoria's murder has nothing to do with Laura Skipcliff's."

"Woman alone at night in Cambridge. Bludgeoned. No weapon found."

"A copycat crime?"

Kevin wasn't beaming now. He was looking straight into my eyes. "I don't want you out alone after dark."

"Steve and I own five dogs. Besides, I'm not about to loll around at night in a hammock on an open porch drinking gin."

"Don't walk the dogs. Don't take out the trash. Don't go to your car alone. If you drive somewhere and get home after dark, don't go to your back door alone. And by *alone* I mean without another human. Dogs don't count."

"Kevin, I'm more alone with most people than I am with my dogs."

Kevin repeated his warning. "Stay indoors after dark, Holly. I'm a cop and I'm telling you that in Cambridge these days, don't go out alone at night. Not for two seconds. Don't get cocky. I'm telling you one more time: With what we're dealing with here, dogs don't count. And for all you know, one of your dogs could get killed, too."

"I will murder anyone who even thinks about hurting one of my dogs."

Kevin can be so corny. "Not if you're dead first," he said.

Chapter 12

From: TwilaBaker@QuinaultMals.net
To: HollyWinter@amrone.org
Subj: Mushing Boot Camp

Hi Holly,
I'll be traveling all the way across the country to New Hampshire for Ginny Wilson's Mushing Boot Camp. Any chance you'd be interested in going? It's from October 4 through October 6. This is the boot camp we normally attend, but we haven't driven this far before. It will be worth it. Ginny's my hero <smile>, definitely the "been there and done that but not gonna brag about it" sort. You'd learn a lot and love it. I'll have all eight dogs with me. I never go anywhere without North, and rarely do I attend dog-related functions without everyone. But you'd have fun with just your two. Think about it!

Twila

From: HollyWinter@amrone.org
To: TwilaBaker@QuinaultMals.net
Subj: Re: Mushing Boot Camp

Hi Twila,

Camp sounds like fun, but I can't go this year. Steve and I will be in Paris on our honeymoon! But I have a plan. We're getting married on September 29, the Sunday before camp. Could I persuade you to come to our wedding? You could stay here in Cambridge until camp. My house has three apartments. You could have the one on the third floor. My father and stepmother (she's anything but wicked) will be there from Friday through Sunday, but they'll leave right after the wedding, and you'd have it to yourself after that. My yard is small, but it's fenced, and you and the dogs would be more than welcome. In fact, would North like to attend the wedding? He's so beautiful that he'd be an ornament to the occasion.

In fact, you and North could do me a big favor. My father is very devoted to me and very generous, and he's wonderful with dogs, but he's far from the easiest person with other people, especially, alas, Steve. North would be the perfect father-sitter. With North around, my father might totally forget about the wedding!

Holly

From: AskDrMacMcCloud@aol.com
To: HollyWinter@amrone.org
Subj: Promotion

Dear Holly,
In the spirit of taking an assertive approach to promotion, I have given your name to a shameless number of people who will ask you to donate autographed copies of your book to Sundry Good Causes — Yankee Golden Retriever Rescue's auction, a couple of literacy groups, and an AIDS charity. All are excellent opportunities for you.

With warm regards,
Mac

Chapter 13

Public fear of the so-called Cambridge Killer arose not on Saturday, immediately after the murder of Victoria Trotter, but on Sunday, September 1, a day that Steve and I spent hiking with our dogs in an area of Gloucester known as Dogtown. As we hiked, we made some decisions about our marriage and our wedding. In the manner of a purebred registered dog, I was keeping the kennel name I'd started with. Anita the Fiend had hyphenated her name, by which I mean, of course, that she'd been Fairley-Delaney and not that she'd asked people to call her Anita-the-Fiend. I had no desire to copy her. Cambridge being Cambridge, substituting *Delaney* for *Winter* was out. If you think that the breakfast-food consumption ordinance is fierce, you should see the penalties for female nomenclatural submission to the patriarchy!

We also debriefed the previous evening, which we'd spent at a South End bistro with Rita and Artie.

"Artie seems crazy about Rita," I said. "Did you notice what he said when she was on her way back from the ladies' room? He said, 'Isn't Rita wonderful! I just adore her!'"

Steve was silent.

"It evidently didn't make a big impression on you," I finally said.

"Actually, it did. I didn't like it."

"Because you wouldn't say something like that? Even if you thought it? You wouldn't. I agree. But I think it's just a difference of style."

He shrugged. We dropped the topic.

We returned home from the hike to find that the Boston papers had compensated for the dullness of other people's Labor Day weekends by playing up the similarities between the murders of Laura Skipcliff and Victoria Trotter. The papers couldn't be expected to present as fresh and exciting the information that authorities were still investigating two homicides that might well turn out to be entirely unconnected. In contrast, warnings about a serial killer were newsworthy.

It was true that both Laura Skipcliff and Victoria Trotter had been bludgeoned to death in Cambridge. Both murders had occurred in the evening, the first in the garage of the victim's hotel, the second on the porch of the victim's house. Both victims were, of course, women in their mid-fifties. The only truly new information in the Sunday papers was a weird feature of Victoria Trotter's killing. In addition to showing a high blood-alcohol level, postmortem examination had revealed that immediately after death, she had been injected with a large dose of insulin.

Steve and I ate pizza and watched the evening news in the living room. According to the television report, a search of Victoria's house had uncovered neither insulin nor syringes nor glucose-monitoring supplies. Victoria had not been diabetic. Furthermore, neither of her dogs was diabetic. The segment closed with a few seconds of footage showing Victoria's whippets with their breeder, who had reclaimed them. The dogs looked clean and happy. I'd have bet that the breeder was anything but happy about the condition they'd been in when the police had taken charge of them.

After swallowing a bite of pizza, Steve the Rational said, "Insulin. That's irrational. She was already dead."

"The murderer didn't necessarily know that. Maybe he was making sure. Or maybe he intended to knock her out so he could inject her."

Steve shrugged. Although the television story had ended, Steve stayed with it. "Those warnings in the papers didn't seem to get to you."

"I didn't do more than skim them. They say the same things that Kevin is always preaching. But it did occur to me that we could use a few extra outside lights. Not that I believe that there's necessarily a 'Cambridge Killer.' And Rita's no more likely than I am to loll around on the front porch drinking gin. But she does sometimes drive home alone after dark, and she runs Willie out for a minute before she goes to bed. A few more outside lights might make her feel secure."

"She should call you from her car when she gets near home. And come through here with Willie and let him use the yard."

"Steve, this idea of a serial killer is almost certainly a media invention. Like the Boston Strangler. According to just about everything I've read, there was no Boston Strangler. Those were not serial murders. And that's what Kevin says, too. But I'll get more lights just as a general precaution. I'll call an electrician."

"I'll do it. We've got light fixtures at work," Steve said. "They've been sitting on a shelf for years."

The next afternoon, Labor Day, he made a trip to the clinic and returned with six outdoor lights that he spent hours installing. Although I do a lot of home repair and maintenance, I won't risk electrocution. I kept reminding Steve that the forecast was for rain and that I had no intention of watching him handle electrical wires in a downpour. Furthermore, I said, the Wayside Wildlife Refuge was open to visitors only until five o'clock. We absolutely had to find a place for our wedding, and if we didn't hurry up, we'd have to rush through our visit to the refuge and would see the place only in dismal weather.

Steve wouldn't be hurried. Although the Wayside Wildlife Refuge was fairly nearby, in Lexington, it was four o'clock when we pulled into its deserted parking lot. By then, the promised rain was pelting down. The maples and oaks that lined the narrow, rutted access road and surrounded the parking lot had suffered in the August heat. In the rain, their leaves were simultaneously desiccated and drenched. Not a single light shone in the big, shabby brown-shingled building next to the flooded parking lot.

"On a nice day —" Steve began. He didn't bother to finish.

"No wonder it's available at this late date," I said. "And no wonder it's not an Audubon sanctuary. I'm surprised that Judith and Olivia even suggested it."

Mac's wife and daughter had done us the favor of making a few phone calls to places they thought might still be available.

I added, "Maybe neither of them has actually been here. It's really quite gruesome."

111

"Don't Mac and Judith live in Lexington?"

"Yes," I said.

"The roof is sagging. Probably leaks. You want to bother getting out?"

"We're desperate. Gabrielle can't do the invitations until we find a place. We'd better take a look. For all we know, the front is unpromising but there's a beautiful garden in the back with glass doors all along that side of the . . ."

". . . dump," Steve finished.

"At least it's a big dump."

We pulled up the hoods of our rain gear and splashed our way to the building's entrance. Peering through the dirty glass panes of the front door, we saw a nearly vacant room that wasn't even all that spacious.

"There's supposed to be a ballroom," I said. "Maybe this is just the front hall. Look, since we're here, let's take a look in back before we write it off."

"Write it off? I haven't written it off. The next time I want to throw a funeral for my worst enemy, it'll be my first choice."

Following a weedy flagstone path, we trudged to the rear of the building, which did, indeed, have glass doors and where there was, in fact, a garden — or the remains of one. The dominant plant was crabgrass, which flourished in flowerless flowerbeds and spread over the patio-block terrace that ran up to the back of the building. We could have looked through the doors, but did not because neatly laid out next to one of them was the dead body of a large rat.

"You're psychic," I told Steve. "The funeral? Yuck! Dismal was bad enough, but this is disgusting. Not only is there this rat, but it hasn't been removed."

"It's been here awhile."

"No one asked for an autopsy."

Steve said, "There are flakes of paint on the body. From what's peeling off the doors."

"Sherlock Holmes! Althea will be so pleased! We can tell her that we found the Giant Rat of Sumatra and that you made a genuine Holmesian deduction."

Althea Battlefield, the elder sister of Ceci Love, was a Holmes fanatic, a member of the elite Baker Street Irregulars and an Adventuress of Sherlock Holmes. If Althea alone had chosen the cake that my honorary aunts had provided for the launch party at The Wordsmythe, Althea would have made sure the decorations reflected what she'd have called "Canonical motifs." The dog would have worn a deerstalker hat and carried a magnifying glass or a pipe. Somewhere on the cake would've been an obscure Holmesian object, a gasogene perhaps, and there'd have been portraits of Holmes, Watson, Moriarty, and Irene Adler. Anyway, the presence of the decomposing Giant Rat of Sumatra sent us directly back to the car.

The rain was now falling in drops so big that they made expanding pools in the parking lot, as if the Wayside Wildlife Refuge were a fish hatchery with schools of minnows surfacing to feed. In a doomed attempt to preserve the newness of my car, I'd lined the back with frayed sheets, which lay under my dogs' crates. Inside the crates were old blankets. In the household of a real dog person, linens do not make an ignoble exit from human-use existence by being turned into dust rags; rather, they are honorably reborn as valued dog linens. Thus it was that in addition to born-again sheets and blankets, my car contained a stack of clean, if threadbare, towels, one of which Steve spread on the passenger seat before he climbed in. I put another towel on the driver's seat, and Steve used a third to mop our faces. By then, we were laughing at the horrors of the Wayside.

It's worth noting that during our brief visit there, we'd seen no sign of other human beings: no employees, no volunteers, no visitors. Driving out of the parking lot, we left it as we'd found it: empty.

"Did you so much as hear a bird?" I asked.

"The closest thing to life was the dead rat. The place must belong to some private society with no money. And that's why they allow dogs at weddings."

"Going to the dogs would be a major improvement," I said.

A second later, we did, however, see a sign of life, namely, a black sedan parked under some trees in a little turnout. Even I, an automotive ignoramus, was able to identify the vehicle as Artie Spicer's Citroën. Citroëns are, of course, distinctive, and who but an ornithological zealot like Artie would go birding at this bleak sanctuary during a deluge?

Steve said the obvious: "That's Artie's car."

I slowed down and pulled to the side of the lane. "He must've dragged Rita here to add some rain-loving migrant to her life list. We'd better try to rescue her. We can all go and get sushi somewhere."

Steve tried to stop me. As I opened my door, he said, "The motor's running."

"Rita's probably making Artie wait for the rain to let up."

"Holly —"

What failed to register on me was that although the motor was, indeed, running, and although the windows were defogged, no one was sitting in the car. Did I imagine that Artie and Rita had left the engine going as they wandered nearby in search of a rara avis? No, I did not. I imagined nothing whatever. Fool that I was, I pulled up my hood and ran through the downpour to Artie's car.

Fate was smarter than I was and more effective than Steve had been. Fate and nothing else prevented me from rapping on the glass before I looked in the car. Stretched out on the rear seat, wearing a black merry widow I'd last seen in her hand, was Francie Julong, the dowdy birding buddy of Rita's we'd met at the mall. Francie didn't see me; her eyes were closed, and her attention was elsewhere. Specifically, it was on the man whose face I couldn't see.

Rara avis was the wrong Latin phrase. The right one was *in flagrante delicto.*

Chapter 14

My first word was dog. I spoke it at the age of nine months and — yes — haven't shut up since. Now, for once, I was not only silent on the subject of dogs, but shocked into utter speechlessness. *Utter.* Sorry. Victim that I am of anxiety-driven punning, I could serve as a case study in the verbal psychopathology of everyday life. The Viennese Dog Man would have understood. Now, he'd have been quick to remark that the source of my tension was sex. While I'm on the subject of Freud, let me digress briefly by guessing that little Sigmund's first word was almost certainly *Hund.*

Anyway, after tiptoeing away from Artie Spicer's car and hastening to my own, I got in and drove slowly away without so much as swearing or groaning.

Steve refrained from saying that he'd told me so. Actually, he hadn't. Not outright. What he said, with maddening equanimity, was, "Not Rita, I take it."

117

I exhaled noisily. "Steve, the worst of it is that I'm not sure it was Artie. And whether it was Artie or someone else, if you want to say 'I told you so,' that's okay. Except that you didn't. Not exactly. And why should you have had to? Who'd've thought that I could be so stupid? Here's this nowhere place with a car pulled in at what any idiot would recognize as a lover's lane, and the engine's running, and when I don't see anyone sitting in the car, do I reach the obvious conclusion? I do not. And why not? Because it never crosses my feeble excuse for a mind that Artie Spicer, *nice* Artie Spicer, Artie the birdwatcher, is a lying, two-timing bastard who isn't just cheating on Rita, but is doing it in the backseat of his car like some teenager, for God's sake, in daylight! If it was Artie. And with that smarmy little hypocrite, who, I have to tell you, had the nerve to fall all over Rita! But it's possible, remotely possible, that she borrowed Artie's car. Anyway, I saw *her* clearly. Maybe I should've tapped on the window! That way, I'd know for sure whether it was Artie or not."

"You want to go back?"

"No! Of course not. And we're not lurking around until they drive out, either. You know what's amazing? Steve, I literally can hardly believe it! I saw it myself about two minutes ago, and I am having trouble convincing myself that I saw what, believe me, I really did see. Incredible!"

With the calmness I love so deeply, Steve said, "Holly, you need to slow down. Slow it all down. For a start, you need to pull over and let me drive."

I had the sense to realize that he was right. With my foot safely off the gas pedal and Steve at the wheel, we headed for Route 2 and then toward Cambridge.

"The woman was someone you know," Steve said.

"Francie Julong. I met her on Friday when Rita and I went to the Chestnut Hill Mall, and let me tell you, Steve, she greeted Rita like a dear friend. She gushed. And kow-towed. She's a member of Rita's birding group. In other words, Artie Spicer's birding group. That's what makes me wonder. It's possible that Francie borrowed his car. The problem is that seen from . . . seen from the perspective . . . the problem is that Artie isn't all that distinctive. From that angle. But one thing I can promise you is that if it was Artie, Rita has *no* idea. None. None!"

"Take a slow, deep breath."

"Stop sounding like Rita! I don't need to take a deep breath!" But I did pause for a second to collect myself. "I'm sorry. I am so stunned that I'm incoherent. Thank God that Rita hasn't married him! Steve, if this is true, she is going to be devastated. Heartbroken. If it was Artie, how could he do this to her? If he wants other women, lots of them, any of them, okay! But there he was on Saturday night at the restaurant saying how he, quote, adores Rita, unquote, and here he is two days later sneaking around having sex in a damned car with that corset-wearing tramp? So maybe it was someone else. But you wondered about him. When he said that he adored Rita? You wondered."

"Corset?"

"That's what Francie was buying when we met her. Black lace underwear. A thing called a merry widow." I managed not to mention that we'd been in Victoria's Secret, and I especially managed not to report that his ex-wife had been there, too. "Steve, if that was Artie, he must be insane. This woman, Francie, is . . . any sane man who could choose between her and Rita would choose Rita. On all counts. This whole thing is so squalid! My God! Rita deserves the best. You know that! She is the best friend in existence, and the finest human being in the world. She is kind, intelligent, pretty, funny . . . and if this is true, she is going to be so sick and so crushed. I just can't stand it."

"You're going to tell her."

"I have no idea. Among other things, there's . . ."

"HIV," he said. "In the long run, there's one big issue. And that's what it is."

120

"If that was Artie Spicer, I could kill him. I could happily kill him for this."

I talked pretty much nonstop throughout the short ride home. As we drove up Appleton Street, Steve said, "One thing is, Holly, it'd be a bad idea just to blurt all this out to Rita."

"I won't. Of course not! Why would I do that? Damn it! I have no idea what to do!"

"If you're going to tell her, you've got to think about what you're going to say. How you're going to say it."

"I'm not telling her anything right now. First of all, we have to think this through. Also, she's got some cousin here, the daughter of a cousin, a girl who's looking at colleges. One of them is MIT. She's staying with Rita. And Rita has moved some of her regular Monday patients to Tuesday, because of Labor Day. So she's got a heavy day tomorrow. Ten hours, she said. I can't break this news to her when she has to face ten patients. If it is news. I mean, if it's true. And if it isn't, what a horrible way to treat Artie!"

When we pulled into the driveway, Rita's car was there. For the first time I could remember, I was sorry to see a sign that she was home; my strong suspicion created a barrier I'd never felt before. As Steve and I ate dinner, fed and walked our dogs, checked our E-mail, and went about our ordinary business, it seemed to me that the ceiling

121

overhead had somehow thickened; even though I could occasionally hear sounds from Rita's apartment — a bark from Willie, the muffled voices of a radio program — she and I now lived far away from each other instead of comfortingly close. If the incident at Wayside hadn't occurred, I'd probably have gone upstairs just to say hello and to meet the visiting cousin. As it was, I fought a sense of shame about wanting to concoct innocuous excuses to dash up and have a word with Rita: I could pop in to tell her about the new outside lights. As if I needed an excuse! But I didn't run upstairs. In fact, I just couldn't face Rita. And when Steve and I discussed what I'd seen and what we should do, we abided by an unspoken agreement to talk in low tones, as if our voices and words might magically rise upward and break Rita's heart. But talk we did — and clung to each other and to our dogs almost as if Artie's probable falsehood were a contagious disease that would afflict us unless we warded it off with little rites and incantations of love. During the night, I awoke several times to find myself reaching for Steve.

Over breakfast, I said, "All along, you didn't trust him."

"In dogs we trust," he said. "And in each other. Holly, I love you. And it isn't as if you knew for sure it was Artie."

After Steve left for work, I tried to distract

122

myself by bathing and grooming Kimi so she'd look her best at a signing that Mac McCloud and I were doing at a bookstore that evening. Both dogs, of course, would've made a more spectacular PR statement than either dog could achieve alone, but any two malamutes, even two as well trained as mine, might go so far as to make a spectacle of themselves by raiding any food the bookstore offered or by unintentionally frightening customers who had the misfortune not to love dogs: I did not intend to handle both Rowdy and Kimi while I simultaneously signed books. Consequently, my plan was to let Rowdy and Kimi share the role of PR dog by taking turns. Tonight was to be Kimi's turn.

The weather was warm enough to allow me to cut down on housework by washing and grooming her outside. My plumber, Ron, had rigged an outdoor faucet that sent warm water through the hose, and I moved a grooming table and my powerful dryer into the yard. Kimi didn't share Rowdy's conviction, common among malamutes, that a bath was a dangerous prelude to death from hypothermia. She cooperated as I shampooed and rinsed her, and stood happily on the grooming table as I blew her dry and brushed her out. Ordinarily, I enjoy being outdoors, and with a dog who likes being groomed, I let the repetitive motion of brushing and the familiar feel of the dog's body draw me into a meditative trance. Today, the weather interfered. Despite the previous day's rain, the sky had a bloated, jaundiced look, as if the atmosphere suffered from hepatitis, and the air was thick and polluted. My thoughts, too, felt ugly, and my bewilderment kept me from losing myself in my simple love for Kimi and my pleasure in taking care of her. When I'd finished, Kimi looked as beautiful as a malamute can look when she's shed most of her old coat and is waiting for the new one to come in. The bookstore, however, wasn't a show ring. A lot of people would probably admire my "husky" or ask whether Kimi was part wolf. Furthermore, no one but me would notice how shiny and perfect she was. But especially now, it felt important to have acted on my love for Kimi and my pride in her by seeing to it that in this jaundiced and corrupt world, one creature was clean and sweet.

When Kimi and I were back inside, I continued to sense the new and unwelcome barrier that separated me from Rita. Although my main concern was for Rita, it also irked me to realize that I was now without my principal confidante and advisor; had my concerns been about anyone but Rita, I'd have consulted her. I thought about discussing the matter with my stepmother, but realized that she'd immediately guess who it was I was talking about; to tell Gabrielle felt like a betrayal. As to Steve, we'd already talked everything over. Besides, I wanted to talk to a woman, preferably a wise one.

Consequently, I called Althea Battlefield, to whom I intended to give a somewhat general account, with names deleted and graphic details expurgated. Althea was a strange choice in that she was one of the most rational people I'd ever known, the opposite of the sort of emotion-driven earth-mother type to whom I could pour out my rage and confusion. She was, however, ethics incarnate. What's more, she was generous about sharing her wonderful intelligence and always interested in dilemmas of the human condition. Unfortunately, when I phoned, I reached her sister, Ceci, who informed me that Althea was asleep and then went on in her usual garrulous fashion to question me about my wedding plans and talk about Nina Kerkel, the ex-daughter-in-law of her friend Greta.

"Naturally," Ceci said, "I had to tell Greta that that Nina had died, because for all we know, Hal, that's Greta's son, the one who was married to this Nina, might not have heard, and after all, they were married once and even though that Nina was anything but my idea of a wife, or Greta's, for that matter, she was Hal's . . . well, probably not his idea of a wife, either, but he did marry her, and the wedding was very nice, although that Nina was ungrateful for everything Greta did.

Have you thought about a champagne fountain?"

"A champagne fountain?"

"I thought of it because Greta offered to have one, and that Nina did nothing but sneer at her, and it might not have been to Nina's taste, not that she had any, the truth is, not to be snobbish, but she was something out of the gutter, I don't know where Hal found her, her family simply devoted itself to producing illegitimate children and nothing else . . . but generosity is generosity, and Greta was making what was meant as a nice offer, and all this Nina did was make fun of Greta for it, and if you ask me, Greta would've done better to offer her a keg of beer instead of a champagne fountain. Of course, she was quite pretty, that must've been the attraction, drugstore blond, not that there's anything objectionable about helping nature along if it's done well, but she had no bosom and very chapped lips and I remember that she wore one of those . . . what do you call them? Those wide bracelets. Way up on her arm."

"A slave bracelet."

"That's it! But in her own way, although Greta doesn't like to admit it, Nina was quite pretty, like a child really, very young, almost like a young boy, really, but with long blond hair, you don't suppose . . . where was I? The champagne fountain!

Have you thought of one?"

"You're way ahead of us. So far, we don't have a place for a champagne fountain or anything else. We don't have a place to get married. But we're looking. The prospects aren't good." In part to keep Ceci from returning to her obsession with Greta Kerkel and the regrettable Nina, I related the story of our visit to the Wayside Wildlife Refuge. In a fashion intended to distract and entertain Ceci, I described the dismal building with its sagging roof and the finding of the dead rat, but I said nothing, of course, about Artie's Citroën, Francie, or wildlife I'd accidentally witnessed at the refuge. In a peculiar way, I loved Ceci, but my primary attachment, as Rita would say, was to her sister, Althea, whom I'd met when she was in a nursing home where I took Rowdy for therapy-dog visits. Our friendship had continued and deepened after Althea had moved in with Ceci. Rowdy, Kimi, and I made social rather than therapeutic visits to the elderly sisters, who shared Ceci's lavish suburban house with Ceci's Newfoundland, Quest. Ceci and I shared a passion for dogs, but she was not someone whose advice I ever sought about important questions.

Indeed, when Ceci ended our phone conversation with entirely uncharacteristic abruptness, I wondered whether she'd sensed my desire to consult with Althea and had felt slighted. I was wrong. About a half hour later, Ceci called back with what might be termed a marriage proposal. After we'd hung up, Ceci had awakened Althea from her nap, and my honorary aunts had swiftly resolved to pop the question: Would Steve and I do them the honor of holding our wedding and reception at their house?

Would we ever!

Chapter 15

Partnership with a good dog has millions of advantages over partnership with even the best human being. If a generous friend, Ceci, for instance, had extended an invitation to my dogs and me, I'd have been free to accept without quizzing Rowdy and Kimi about their feelings. As it was, although I was almost positive that Steve would be as relieved as I was to have secured a suitable site for our nuptial show, I couldn't give Ceci a definite yes until I'd checked with him, as I dutifully did on the way to my Tuesday evening signing. Mac McCloud, I might mention, had a habit of dragging his friends to his signings and talks whenever he suspected that attendance would be sparse. He'd recommended the practice to me. It was one piece of advice from Mac that I meant to reject. For one thing, I had no intention of going to any book event without Rowdy or Kimi, so I felt assured of always having a devoted and attentive audience. The prospect of having no human audience and no book buyers didn't bother me as it did Mac. In other words, I was the real dog person. If Mac had sat alone in a bookstore with no one but Uli, his Bernese mountain dog, he'd have felt all alone, in part because Uli's deep allegiance was to Judith rather than to Mac. With Kimi, I, in contrast, would be in excellent company. I'd thus planned to go to the signing with Kimi and hadn't intended to haul Steve along. He'd insisted. I'd said that he'd be bored. He'd countered that on the contrary, he'd enjoy himself. He'd also mentioned the two murders and my safety.

As it turned out, the drive to the bookstore was a lot more fun with Steve than it would've been without him, and it gave us the chance to talk about Ceci's offer. As I expected, he had to think through every aspect of it.

"Did you discuss costs with Ceci?" he asked. For once, he was driving my new Blazer, a vehicle he objected to because of its source. Enzio Guarini had gotten me a good deal on it. Steve, who wanted nothing to do with my Mob-boss dog-training client, had decided that the car must therefore have been stolen. The conviction was ridiculous and atypical of Steve, who was almost always logical.

"No. There's nothing to discuss, is there? We'd want a tent, and Ceci obviously shouldn't pay for that. Otherwise, the costs would be the same as they'd be at some historic house or anywhere else, wouldn't they?"

"Cleaning up afterward?"

"I hadn't thought of that. But that wouldn't be Ceci's responsibility, either."

"What about the stress on Althea?"

"For someone in her nineties, Althea is apparently in decent shape. Except for her eyesight, of course. And she uses a wheelchair because of mobility problems. But there's nothing wrong with her general health. Heart and lungs and so on. Althea looks frail, and she rests a lot, but I don't think the excitement would do her any harm. And Ceci just had a checkup. According to her, the doctor said that she could pass for thirty. That's probably an exaggeration. Well, knowing Ceci, it *is* an exaggeration. But she thrives on activity. And she has more common sense than you might imagine. If she couldn't manage a wedding, she wouldn't have offered. And, Steve, her house is so beautiful! You'll love it, too. It's big. So is the yard. It slopes down pretty sharply in back, but the part right next to the house is level. Or maybe the tent should go in front of the house. If the weather is good, we could get married outdoors on the terrace in the back, and then have the reception inside and in the tent, and outdoors, too. And the neighborhood would be perfect."

Ceci's house was a big white colonial in Newton, a suburb just west of Boston. She lived on a hill in a charming area with winding streets and, remarkably, gas streetlights.

Looking horribly serious, as if he intended to decline, Steve said, "You're the closest they have to a relative. They really think of you as their niece. Is this what you want?"

"Yes. Don't you?"

"Me? I think it'd be great. Now all we need is someone to marry us. I've been wondering. What would you think about Althea?"

"Althea?" I asked casually, thinking, *Yes, yes, yes! Althea! And not my father!*

"You might not know, but it's legal. She could a get a special permit, good for one day."

"Oh," I said innocently, "is that right?"

"Yeah. I'd like it. Althea is a great lady. If it'd be okay with you."

"It would be wonderful."

"Good."

So, we agreed to offer our hands in marriage to Althea Battlefield. We felt confident that she'd accept. I silently vowed to delegate to Gabrielle the task of informing Buck that his only role in the wedding would be as father of the bride. Hurrah!

I gloated for the remainder of the ride to the bookstore, which belonged to a national chain and was located in a distant suburb that I'll leave unnamed lest the store or the chain take offense and never again order *101 Ways to Cook Liver* or any other book I may ever write. Not that the store was exactly promoting my current book with unbridled enthusiasm. Not a single copy was displayed in the window. Mac's books weren't there, either. As I was wondering aloud whether I had the date wrong, however, Steve spotted a sheet of white computer paper taped to the door. Printed in felt marker on the piece of paper were Mac's name and mine, together with the titles of our books and a bald "7:00."

"Don't let stardom go to your head," Steve said.

Inside, the store was bright, cheerful, and so gigantic that Steve, Kimi, and I had to wander around for a while before we happened on a podium that faced three rows of folding chairs with three chairs per row. The podium sat on a table that also held piles of *101 Ways to Cook Liver* and *Ask Dr. Mac.* As we were about to greet Mac, Judith, and Uli, who stood nearby, an angry-looking blond man bustled up to me and said, "I'm sorry, but dogs aren't allowed." He pointed to Uli. "That one's an exception."

Kimi's exceptionality had been recognized and rewarded by numerous American Kennel Club conformation and obedience judges as well as by her doting owner. At the moment, her exceptionality was evident in her response to the officious man, whose plastic badge identified him as an assistant manager. Ignoring him, my lovely Kimi turned her attention to the only person occupying any of the nine chairs, a long-haired guy in jeans who obligingly grasped her head in his hands and let her lick his face. The dignity of Kimi's response reminded me of Eleanor Roosevelt's famous statement that no one can make you feel small without your permission, not that Mrs. Roosevelt translated her belief into action by lapping the countenances of strangers . . . so far as I know, anyway. But in her own way, of course, Mrs. Roosevelt, too, was exceptional.

In any case, instead of delivering a tirade to the dog cop, I introduced myself and went on to say, "I'm here to sign books. My dog has permission to be here. Her name is Kimi." Nodding toward Steve, I added, "Kimi has brought along her own personal veterinarian just in case anyone decides to bite her. Steve Delaney."

The assistant manager apparently decided that I was joking. He gave Steve a nod of acknowledgment and was beginning to speak to me when Mac approached, smiled at everyone, and said, "We're early. Steve, good to see you." He kissed my cheek. After glancing at the assistant manager's badge, he said, "Sidney, Mac McCloud. And the literary figure in the family, my wife, Judith Esterhazy."

Sidney's expression made an abrupt shift from bored condescension to awed shyness. "This is truly an honor," he told Judith, who wore black and looked even slimmer and more awe-inspiring than usual.

Judith thanked him modestly and said, "Holly, I don't think you've met Ian. Our son."

The object of Kimi's affection rose to his feet. I had the puzzling sense that Ian McCloud looked damp. Kimi had, in fact, licked Ian's face, but he was otherwise perfectly dry; his forehead wasn't beaded in sweat, and his long brown ponytail, brown cotton sweater, faded jeans, and well-worn hiking boots showed no signs of moisture. In trying to figure out how a dry person can somehow look as if he's just emerged fully clothed from a lake, I discounted the dog saliva, which I saw so often that I took it for granted. I finally settled on the watery blueness of Ian's eyes. In any case, far from holding Ian's slightly peculiar appearance against him, I felt prepared to like him, not only because Kimi did, but because he'd returned her exuberant affection with warmth and good humor. "I'm happy to meet you," I said. "You're a musician, aren't you?" His sister, Olivia, had said that he played a variety of instruments. She'd suggested that her brother might do the music for our wedding, but it would've sounded brash and opportunistic to try to hire Ian within seconds of meeting him. Furthermore, for all I knew, Steve and I would hate every note that Ian played.

"Ian went to Berklee," Judith said.

"The Berklee College of Music," Mac added. "Not UC Berkeley."

"Bruce," Judith said, "in Boston, *Berklee* means Berklee." Mac's wife was the only person I'd ever heard call Mac by his real first name. Neither Mac nor anyone else ever called Judith anything except Judith. "Ian," she went on, "plays in an early-music group and a jazz band, and he's the best country fiddler in the world."

Steve looked as interested as I felt. Before Steve had the chance to say anything, Sidney, the assistant manager, announced that it was time to begin. Four strangers had taken seats. Ian sat down, as did Steve, with Kimi next to him, but before Judith could join the audience, Sidney beckoned to her and drew her aside. He didn't bother to introduce Mac and me, but led Judith away. She held Uli's leash, and the old dog followed her. Neither Sidney's rudeness nor the sparse attendance fazed Mac, who looked so healthy and vigorous that he could easily have been mistaken for the author of an exercise book or a how-to book about the secrets for staying young forever. Taking my arm and escorting me to the podium, he faced our little audience and self-confidently presented himself and me. To my relief, he said, "And since we're a small group tonight, we'll keep things informal. I'll read a little from *Ask Dr. Mac*, and then Holly will tell us everything about the magic of training with good homemade food. After that, we'll answer questions, and we'll both be glad to sign *Ask Dr. Mac* and *101 Ways to Cook Liver* or anything else you want, preferably, but not necessarily, books we've written ourselves."

As people chuckled, Mac picked up a copy of his book — pardon me, a copy of *Ask Dr. Mac* — that he'd brought with him. The jacket bore a ring left by a coffee cup, and slips of papers stuck out where he'd marked passages. I felt like a dope standing there with nothing to do, so I took a seat in the first row, directly in front of Steve and Kimi. As Mac began to read a charming and funny account of a Siberian husky whose indulgent owners had allowed him to eat five love seats before they'd called for professional help, a latecomer arrived, a fellow dog writer named Elspeth Jantzen, who took the seat next to mine, elbowed me gently, and whispered, "Sorry I'm late."

Elspeth was the reddest person I've ever known. She had tomato hair, crimson freckles, and rosy cheeks. Red hair runs in my family, and to a person, every red-headed relative of mine avoids red clothing. My cousin Leah, with her masses of red-gold curls, actually looks good in red, but it is almost impossible to convince her to wear it. Elspeth, however, who looked ghastly in red, favored the color almost to the exclusion of all others. Tonight, she had on a red sweater and red jeans. At thirty-eight, she was a little too old for the jeans. I knew her age because she'd told me. It was sadly typical of her to have given me a piece of personal information in which I had no interest. Indeed, honesty forces me to characterize her as a nice pest. I'd learned to count on Elspeth always to be warm, friendly, and confiding. Just as reliably, she always needed a favor. On Dogwriters-L, the E-mail list for members of our profession, she was forever posting requests for information that she could easily have looked up herself — for example, definitions of veterinary terms and lists of diseases to which certain breeds are prone. She did, however, join other list members in enthusiastically congratulating anyone who'd just published a book, received an award, or put a new title on a dog. In other words, in cyberspace, too, she was a nice pest. Tonight, having seated herself next to me and muttered her apology for arriving late, she dropped her eyes to a manila envelope on her lap, and I absolutely, positively knew that she'd brought a manuscript that she'd ask me to read, edit, or send to my agent or editor. What's more, I had a vivid premonition that once Elspeth heard of my engagement, she'd try to wangle an invitation to the wedding and, with it, introductions to all the marriageable men who'd be attending.

At the moment, she had eyes only for Mac, who was reading the happy ending of the story of the delinquent Sibe, whose owners had learned to confine the dog to a crate instead of giving him the freedom to destroy furniture. Behind me, I felt Steve stir and knew that he and I were sharing the thought that a Siberian who's devouring love seats is a dog who's begging for exercise; crate training was a short-term measure that ignored the cause of the problem and, in a breed born to run, was doomed to produce some new and different form of misbehavior.

No one in the small audience voiced the objection. Rather, everyone applauded Mac and then applauded me as Mac introduced me as "*Dog's Life*'s favorite columnist and legendary dog guru, Holly Winter." As I took my place at the podium, Mac briefly brushed his hand against my arm in a gesture of encouragement and support. For a second, I was glad that it happened to be Kimi's turn to accompany me and not Rowdy's. Then my eyes found Steve's face, where I saw the same watchful expression I'd have seen on

Rowdy's. It was flattering to realize that neither of my big males liked to see another man touch me. Basking in the warmth of Steve and Rowdy's loyalty, I gave my little talk about training with food. I started with my late mother's extreme prejudice against "bribing" dogs, as she called it, and touched lightly on what had, in actuality, been my parents' monumental fights about Buck's persistence in using food to teach tricks to our dogs. I blathered on for a while and finished by giving a simple recipe for the liver bait that handlers use in the show ring. Secrets of the stars! Steve's loud clapping and Kimi's *woo-woo*ing accounted for a lot of the noise that followed, but I still felt pleased to have done anything even remotely like a reading from *101 Ways to Cook Liver*.

While I'd held the center of the minuscule stage, Mac had stood off to the side. He joined me now and invited questions and comments. Elspeth's hand popped up, and when Mac pointed to her, she said, "Hi, Mac! Nice to see you. You, too, Holly. I just want to say that I loved both of your books. You two are the best."

Glancing at Mac, I saw no indication that he recognized Elspeth. Knowing her as I did, I assumed that she was claiming acquaintance to ask Mac a favor. Mac's blank look vanished in a second, we both thanked Elspeth, and then a stranger asked how we'd gotten published.

"Luck," I blurted out.

Mac recommended web sites and books. He emphasized the need for persistence. He was terrific. No one would've guessed that he'd taken no initiative whatever about finding a publisher; on the contrary, he'd been approached by his publisher and asked to do his first book, and his second one was a follow-up to the first. After a few more questions, someone who liked my column asked where Rowdy was and then asked Mac about the Bernese mountain dog on the cover of his book. As Mac was answering, Sidney returned with Judith and Uli. After that, our little audience ignored us, fell all over the dogs, and even I, the author of *101 Ways to Cook Liver*, have to admit that we couldn't have liver-bribed Uli and Kimi to act any sweeter than they did all on their own. The black, rust, and white of Bernese mountain dogs is striking, and to his breed's beauty, Uli added the engaging habit of smiling. Do dogs really smile? Uli did. He also wagged his white-tipped tail over his big back and, with grace and nobility, accepted the petting of strangers. Uli was perfectly groomed and unmistakably ancient. My heart went out to Judith. In contrast to the sedate Uli, Kimi staged a Rowdy-worthy performance by singing Arctic carols, flinging herself onto the floor, rolling over, wiggling her legs in the air, and then tucking in her forepaws and directing big-brown-eyed pleas for tummy rubs at five potential book buyers, all of whom complied with her demands by administering thumps and scratches, and four of whom had me sign books.

As I was sitting at the table penning the final inscription ("To Frodo, Bilbo, Merry, Pippin, and Evelyn, and with special congratulations to AM/CAN CH Galadriel's Entwife . . ."), Elspeth's red glow shone in the corner of my eye, and I heard her address Mac, who sat next to me. "Hey, Mac, it's been a long time," she said.

As smoothly as usual, Mac said, "I guess it has."

A quick peek showed me that Elspeth was presenting him with a copy of *Ask Dr. Mac.*

"How'd you like this signed? Is it a Christmas present for someone?"

"Just make it to me," Elspeth said. " 'For old times' sake.' "

Mac shifted almost imperceptibly.

I took pity on him. *"Elspeth,"* I said with admirable clarity and a special emphasis on the *p,* "it was very nice of you to come tonight."

"My pleasure. Actually, there's something I want to talk to both of you about."

I now saw that she held not one manila envelope but two. A smiling couple rescued Mac by asking him to sign a book. No one rescued me. "My editor," Elspeth said, "was so happy when I told her that you and Mac might do blurbs for my book." Thrusting one of the envelopes at me, she added, "I've brought you the first two chapters, and there's a form for you to send an advance quote to my publisher."

"My time is really short right now," I said, carefully avoiding using my wedding plans as an excuse.

"You're always so busy. That's why I didn't bring the whole book. Not that it's very long."

"What's it about?" I hoped, of course, that the topic would be one I was unqualified to comment on.

"Kindness to animals. It's for parents and teachers. It has a companion story for children. It's about how to teach kindness to children."

I could hardly object. "I'll be glad to read it. But I'll need to see the whole book." I was, I might mention, going against Mac's advice. He'd told me to write every cover quote I had the chance to do. But I was simply incapable of pretending to have read, never mind liked, a book I hadn't gone through in its entirety. Worse, I knew myself to be equally incapable of saying in print that I recommended a book that I'd hated.

"That's great. I'll get you the manuscript. Thank you!"

Score: Elspeth, one. Holly, zero. Or so it seemed.

Elspeth turned to Mac and said, "Hey, Mac, how'd you like to blurb my book?"

"Delighted," he said.

Chapter 16

The first item in the dossier on Bonny Carr came from the web site of a Girl Scout camp in Vermont. The page listed the names of Camp Tecumseh alumnae whose last names began with *C*. Carr, Bonny appeared near the top, together with an address: 89 Glenn Street, Nashua, NH. I felt oddly relieved and weirdly grateful to my parents, whose need for unpaid kennel help had made me ineligible for any such online list. I'd spent my childhood summers at Buck and Marissa Winter's Show-Dog Boot Camp, where I'd scooped and disinfected kennels, and trimmed the nails of our golden retrievers. But the field trips had been frequent and fabulous; all had, of course, been to dog shows. If, like Bonny Carr, I'd gone to an ordinary camp, my name, too, might appear on a camp web site, together with my childhood address.

The second page gave the results of an online reverse search of 89 Glenn Street in

Nashua. According to result 1–1 of 1, as the page actually read, the current resident was Lafayette, G.; Bonny Carr's family had evidently moved since she'd attended Camp Tecumseh. They'd had plenty of time; AnyBirthday.com gave her age as forty-five. The next page of the dossier showed where Mr. and Mrs. Carr had gone. It was not principally about them, but about a man named Charles H. McDonough, who had lived and, more to the point, died three years earlier in Manchester, New Hampshire. This item in the dossier was a copy of his obituary as it had been printed in the *Manchester Union-Leader.* He had left, among many other survivors, a daughter, Helen Carr, and her husband, John Carr, of Sarasota, Florida. Among McDonough's grandchildren was Bonny Carr, of Brookline, Massachusetts.

Next came detailed material about exactly where in Brookline, Massachusetts, Bonny Carr lived. The Brookline Assessors Property Database had supplied four pages of facts about a condominium on Kent Street. Owner: Carr, Bonny G. Residential Exemption: Y. Usage: 102-RESDNL CONDOMINIUM. Land Area: 0. Unit Number: 4. Building Style: LOW-RISE. The facts went on and on. Bonny Carr had bought her condo two years earlier. The building was three stories high and had been built in 1930. Her unit had a living area of 625 square feet. Its four rooms included two bedrooms. There was one full bath. Bath Quality was TYPICAL. So was Kitchen Quality. The building had hot-water heating, no elevator, no central air conditioning, and no fireplaces. The basement was unfinished. The parking was "open" rather than "covered." Just in case all the numbers about Parcel-ID, Deed Book, sale price, residential values, beneficial interest, and so on failed to give a complete picture, the database had also provided a photograph of an unprepossessing three-story brick apartment building. One of these years, I suppose, web surfers will easily find interior photographs of every room in everyone's house. For all I know, some databases already offer shots of people's "typical"-quality kitchens, their living rooms with or without fireplaces, and their bedrooms, presumably with beds rated "made" or "unmade."

Next were pages from the database of Massachusetts corporations maintained by the Secretary of the Commonwealth. Bonny Carr was president, treasurer, and everything else of a domestic profit corporation with the "exact name" of HealADog; if she'd incorporated using an inexact, vague, or perhaps even fishy name, it wasn't listed. In any case, although I'd never before heard or seen the name *HealADog*, Bonny Carr's career as a practitioner of healing touch was how I'd known her. She'd published a book about using touch to relieve anxiety and pain in physically and emotionally traumatized animals, especially dogs. The web sites of the United States Copyright Office, the Library of Congress, and two major online booksellers agreed that the book had been published the previous year and that its title was *Magical Fingers: Ideas Immediately Applicable to Using Human Touch to Treat Traumatized Animals.*

Bonny Carr also gave seminars, workshops, and lectures on the topic. Rowdy and I had attended one of her workshops about two years earlier. You won't find my opinion of the workshop anywhere on the web. I'd intended to write about it in my *Dog's Life* column, but I prefer to keep my column positive, and I always keep it truthful. In truth, Bonny Carr's "healing touch" seemed to me identical to everything I already did in hugging, grooming, stroking, and otherwise making physical contact with my dogs. Furthermore, her supposed system was far less systematic than the well-known TTouch approach of Linda Tellington-Jones. But the real reason I couldn't write about the workshop was Rowdy, who had always been a total hedonist about being held, brushed, massaged, or just plain patted. Here was a dog who adored everything from gentle little finger circles on his ears to vigorous thumps on the rib cage. And exactly what did the big boy do in public at Bonny Carr's workshop on healing touch? Refused to rest on the floor. Sprang to his feet. *Woo-woo*ed in an apparent effort to drown her out. Embarrassed the daylights out of me. Oh, and while he was at it? Wordlessly informed me that he'd spotted Bonny Carr for the phony that I, too, thought she was. My experience with her at the workshop was quite unpleasant. Instead of sensibly saying that my untraumatized Rowdy was an unsuitable test case for her "healing touch," she announced that the method required time and patience with severely abused animals. Her implication, as was clear to everyone in the workshop, was that I, Holly Winter, was the perpetrator of the abuse. So, I wrote nothing about Bonny Carr. But I was tempted. Severely so.

Next in the dossier came twenty or thirty web pages that documented, with tedious repetition, the seminars, workshops, and lectures Bonny Carr had given and was scheduled to give. Her older presentations had been like the one I'd attended; she'd focused on teaching pet owners, shelter workers, and veterinary professionals to use touch on dogs and cats in their care. In the recent past, she'd shifted to teaching people to teach her methods, what she called "training trainers." It's worth noting that this section of the dossier presented many pages that listed events of interest to veterinary professionals. On those pages, only a few lines were about a workshop, seminar, or lecture given by Bonny Carr. For example, on a web site about a veterinary conference held the previous winter in New Orleans, she'd been one of forty or fifty presenters; it was difficult for me even to find her name. It seemed to me that this portion of the dossier must represent an obsessive determination to record every reference to Bonny Carr on the entire World Wide Web.

The final pages showed different versions of the same photograph of Bonny Carr. The first of those pages showed a small black-and-white photo next to a paragraph about a seminar she'd done on training trainers in treating animal trauma. On the following page, the same picture appeared alone. It could have been, and maybe was, a passport picture: accurate and unflattering. In it, Bonny Carr looked as I remembered her. She was coarse and exotic, with masses of dark Medusa curls. Her face was strikingly asymmetric, her eyebrows so thoroughly plucked that they almost looked as if they'd been burned off. She had full lips and a long neck with a peculiarly ribbed appearance, as if the skin were stretched over the bones of her throat with no tissue in between. Neither smiling nor frowning, she stared boldly at the camera, squarely meeting its eye. Next was an enlargement of the same picture that took up perhaps half the page. The photo was now blurred and grainy. Finally, there was a full-page blowup that broke Bonny Carr's face, neck, and hair into tiny squares. Although Bonny Carr retained her brazen expression, the result was fractured and grotesque. She looked like a fiend. It was impossible to see the effect as anything but deliberate.

Chapter 17

On Thursday evening, while Steve and I, together with the other members of the Cambridge Dog Training Club, peacefully worked with our dogs in the brightness and safety of the armory near the Fresh Pond rotary, Bonny Carr was bludgeoned to death in the parking lot behind her condo building in Brookline. She must have died shortly before Steve and I returned home with Sammy and Rowdy. The evening was mild, and we'd gone to dog training on foot and paw. We finished at about nine, helped to put away the equipment, spent a few minutes talking with friends, escorted two women with small dogs to their cars, and walked back up Concord Avenue. On the way home, neither of us mentioned the murders of Laura Skipcliff and Victoria Trotter. It never occurred to me to feel afraid; I took security for granted.

As we were about to turn the corner from Concord Avenue to Appleton Street, a car pulled to the curb in front of my house. The driver emerged and called out, "Holly? Steve? Olivia Berkowitz. I'm glad I caught you. I was going to drop off these CDs of Ian's so you'd have a chance to listen to them."

"Mac and Judith's daughter," I whispered to Steve, who'd met Olivia at the launch party at The Wordsmythe, where he'd also met dozens of other new people. At normal volume, I greeted Olivia, and then Steve did, too. On our own, neither Steve nor I would've invited Olivia in, but Rowdy and Sammy teamed up to stage a performance of effusive malamute hospitality, and because of the newly installed lights on the outside of the house, Olivia got a fine look at the father-and-son big-brown-eyes routine and ended up exclaiming about how beautiful the dogs were and how much they looked alike. Since she was awkwardly clutching the CDs in one hand, patting the dogs with other, trying to keep her shoulder bag from tumbling down her arm, and asking questions about Rowdy and Sammy, it seemed discourteous just to grab the music and vanish indoors. Consequently, we ended up in the kitchen, where Olivia accepted my offer of a drink by requesting decaf coffee.

As I was putting on the kettle, getting out a filter, and so on, Olivia talked nonstop about Ian, who, according to his sister, underrated himself. "Daddy belittles Ian's accomplishments," Olivia said. "Mommy and I try to compensate." The childish terms for her parents suited her appearance. Her light brown hair was in pigtails, and her loose blue-checked dress could've been a giant version of a baby outfit. I had to remind myself that Olivia was a married woman in her late twenties, old enough to drink the coffee I was making. It would've felt natural to prepare a children's drink for her — say, hot cocoa with miniature marshmallows.

"Mommy was happy that Ian showed up the other night," Olivia said. "He and Daddy are both making an effort these days, and it's good that Ian's doing his part. Mostly, Ian just has the great original *thing* about his mother. Daddy just doesn't appreciate . . . well, you'll hear." She patted the CDs. "There isn't a stringed instrument that Ian can't play better than everyone else who was ever born, and he has a pretty good voice, too, and he doesn't even work at that."

"Your mother said he was real versatile," Steve said.

"Does he actually do weddings?" I asked.

"Musicians have to take what they can get," Olivia said. "Not that *your* wedding . . . really, he'd love to do it. He's a gentle soul, and he could do anything you wanted if you just gave him a general idea, maybe early music before and during the service, and then bluegrass or Motown for the reception, if you want dancing. Or jazz?"

"All this by himself?" I poured coffee. In my eagerness to hasten Olivia's visit, I'd filled the kettle with hot tap water.

"No, of course not, and his groups are almost as good as he is." She tapped the CDs and sipped her coffee. I wished that she'd gulp it down and flee. Steve and I had dogs to take care of, and we wanted some time together. Alone! Olivia said again, "You'll hear." She took another sip of coffee and said, "So, Mommy says you're making progress with your wedding."

"Excellent progress." I tried to make the statement definitive, as if the matter required no discussion.

"Mommy says you're having it at someone's house."

Steve laughed.

I felt defensive. "It's not just any old house. It's on Norwood Hill in Newton. It belongs to two elderly sisters who are friends of ours. You must've met one of them, Ceci, at The Wordsmythe. Their house is beautiful, and it's generous of them to open it to us. The caterer we want to use is a client of Steve's, and some of the historic houses and so forth make you pick from a short list of approved caterers. And a lot of places don't allow dogs. The Wayside Wildlife Refuge didn't work out. Ceci's house is big, and so is her yard, and we can use our caterer, and Ceci is crazy about dogs. It's perfect."

155

You'd have to have known Steve to spot the subtle signs of restlessness. His eyes were only slightly glazed. He swallowed a yawn.

"Thank you for the CDs," I said. "We enjoyed meeting Ian."

"He's so modest," Olivia said. "He doesn't promote himself. Obviously, Daddy's gene didn't triumph there. Ian is so much like Mommy. He practically models himself on her, including her dog thing. Uli just worships Ian. Dogs do. But when it comes to people . . . But his music is incredible. You'll love it."

Having outstayed her welcome, Olivia finally left — and left us convinced that far from loving Ian McCloud's music, we'd detest it. The main reason we decided to put on one of his homemade CDs right away was, as Steve remarked, "to get this over with."

As Steve loaded the coffee mugs into the dishwasher, I shuffled through the discs. "Country and bluegrass? Or jazz? Or early music."

"Country," Steve said.

We shared the unspoken assumption that Ian's music would serve as the background for the nightly routine of letting the dogs into the yard to relieve themselves. We also shared, I confess, the expectation that the music would be all too appropriate to the activity. I popped a CD into the boom box, and within seconds, Steve and I were wide-eyed. The tune was "Wabash Cannonball," a standard I'd heard thousands of times in hundreds of versions, none of which, including Doc Watson's, was better than this instrumental on guitar, banjo, mandolin, and bass. For the duration of the song, we stood there grinning and tapping our feet and feeling like fools to have judged Ian's music by his faded appearance and his sister's over-sell. Poring over the CD cases, Steve said, "That's Ian on guitar. He's another Doc Watson. He's another Norman Blake."

And Ian could sing. He sang one of the best versions of "You Win Again" that I'd ever heard, different from the Ray Charles classic, but extraordinary and heartbreaking. Steve made a quick phone call to Ian, who was free on the twenty-ninth and agreed to play. We were so elated that we took the boom box and all five dogs out to the yard, where we just about couldn't stop listening and exclaiming about what a genius Ian was and how incredible his groups were and how lucky we were that he'd do the music for our wedding. Rowdy, the most melodious of our five dogs, contributed accompaniments, and Kimi danced around with Sammy, whom she liked, instead of provoking India or bullying poor Lady.

Except for the mild tediousness of Olivia's visit — I'd now forgiven her — the evening was perfect: harmony in our pack and music that somehow made the wedding real for us as nothing else had done. With Steve's dogs in the third-floor apartment and my two crated in my guest room, Steve and I had the bedroom to ourselves and took long, satisfying advantage of our privacy.

As I often do as I fall asleep, I silently counted my blessings. I took nothing for granted, or so I imagined. I was grateful to be well fed and healthy. Nearby, in and around Harvard Square, homeless people slept in doorways and parks; I was in my own house. Millions of daughters were cursed with hostile, unloving, or boring stepmothers; in marrying Gabrielle, my father had blessed me. Judith Esterhazy's literary fiction sold poorly, and Ian's talent hadn't yet brought him the success he deserved; by comparison, my career was thriving. Judith had only one dog, Uli, a wonderful old dog, but a dog horribly close to the end of his life; I had Rowdy and Kimi as well as Steve's Lady, India, and Sammy. Sammy! Rowdy's son! God receives odd thanks from fanciers of purebred dogs: All three malamutes had dark brown, almond-shaped eyes, warm expressions, blocky muzzles, heavy bone, and correct coats. As to my cat, Tracker, I was fortunate to have the resources and, yes, damn it, the moral fiber to give a good home to an animal no one else would want. I had dozens of friends. My cousin Leah went to college right down the street. Upstairs slept Rita, the best of friends, who was almost certainly being deceived and betrayed; next to me slept Steve, my love, my husband-to-be.

Oh, yes, I was alive. It was a blessing I neglected to count.

Chapter 18

"Amitriptyline," Steve informed Ceci. "Elavil. It's a tricyclic antidepressant."

"*That,*" Ceci said, "explains everything!"

Althea said, "My sister is flirtatiously requesting explication."

It was Friday evening. Ceci and Althea had invited us to dinner to plan the wedding. Amitriptyline was not scheduled to play a role in the festivities, nor did it appear on the table around which we now sat. The food prepared and served by Ceci's new maid, Ellen, was conventional: green beans, mashed potatoes, a salad, Yorkshire pudding, and prime rib, which Steve was carving with surgical care. So far, Ceci had allowed little opportunity to discuss the wedding at all. Rather, like many other people in Greater Boston, she was obsessed with the murder of Bonny Carr, who, I should explain, had been bludgeoned to death and then injected with amitriptyline, hence Ceci's interest in the drug and her interrogation of Steve, which began over drinks in the living room and now continued over dinner. In general, Ceci suffered from a tendency to latch onto topics that she blathered on about at great length; or maybe it's more accurate to say that she herself enjoyed the tendency, thereby inflicting conversational suffering on others, especially Althea. By the way, when I refer to the big gabled white house on Norwood Hill as Ceci and Althea's, I do so out of deference to Althea, who was, in reality, a permanent guest. Although I never knew Ceci's late husband, Ellis Love, I always regarded him with tenderness, mainly because the principal feature of Ceci's spacious living room was a monumental oil painting of a Newfoundland dog of hers that hung over the fireplace, whereas the only visible tribute to Love was a small framed photograph that sat on a side table among six or eight crystal and china knickknacks. For all I knew, Ceci hadn't even displayed the little photo until after the tolerant Mr. Love's death. Like Althea, he had been a Sherlock Holmes fanatic rather than a dog zealot. Of course, for all I knew, when he'd been alive, the place of honor had been occupied by a monumental oil painting of Sir Arthur Conan Doyle.

Anyway, Althea was right about Ceci's flirtatiousness. In contrast to her petite sister, Althea was immensely tall, with large hands and feet, and she made no effort to disguise her keen intellect. Ceci was, as Althea said, "the pretty one," but by modern standards, Althea had a peculiar beauty. Age had given her skin and her blue eyes an otherworldly translucence, and her short, thin, curly hair hovered over her scalp like a white halo.

"Holly is not offended," Ceci said. "Are you? She knows I'm only joking, except that I have no idea what this amitriptyline is beyond being an antidepressant, but as a matter of fact, I have heard of Elavil because I knew someone whose dog was supposed to be taking Prozac because it shook all the time and hid under the bed, and Prozac was terribly expensive, so she tried Elavil instead, and it worked just fine, but now Prozac is generic, so why would someone take whatever it is instead?"

Inadvertently echoing Ceci, Steve said, "As a matter of fact, I wondered about amitriptyline, too." With his usual deliberation, he paused to serve the beef he'd been carving. Then he resumed. "I was curious. I looked it up. It turns out that there's an injectable version of amitriptyline available for veterinary use. Not widely used, as far as I know. So, it was an odd choice. The injection itself was odd, too, of course."

"Singular," said Althea. " 'The most distinctive and suggestive point in the case.' " In quoting the Canon, she was quizzing me.

Before I could take a guess about the

Sherlock Holmes story in which the phrase appeared, Ceci said, "Suggestive? What on earth is suggestive about it? It's weird and senseless to go around beating people to death and then drugging them when it's too late to do any good, so to speak — any bad, really — but there's nothing in the least bit off-color about it that I can see, but maybe I'm terribly naive. Am I missing something? These women were not . . . assaulted, unless they *were,* and the police are keeping it a secret, possibly for their own good reasons, I assume. Holly, has Lieutenant Dennehy said anything to you about whether they were . . . ?"

"Yes," I said. "I mean, yes, I've talked to Kevin, and no, the women weren't, uh, assaulted. Althea, 'The Crooked Man'?"

"That's one of *their* stories," Ceci told Steve. By now, she'd somehow managed to surround his plate with the salad bowl and the serving dishes of green beans, Yorkshire pudding, and mashed potatoes. The carving board was still within his reach.

"Indeed," said Althea.

"It's impossible to follow what they're saying," Ceci said. "They make no effort to make any sense, crooked men, I ask you! As if Lieutenant Dennehy were crooked, when he's perfectly upright, I'm sure, although how does he know about this latest horror when it happened in Brookline, which is, as I was going to say, alarmingly close to Newton, and

163

when I got out of my car this afternoon, well, before I opened the door, I checked carefully all around even though Quest was with me, but in the back, which is where Bonny Carr's dog was, in her car and helpless to come to her rescue, but perhaps a small dog, the paper didn't say."

"Big. Bonny Carr had a big dog," I said. "An Airedale mix, I guess. That's what he looked like."

Ceci was elated. "You knew her?"

"Not really. I went to a workshop of hers. But I didn't really know her." And didn't want to.

"And you knew that tarot woman, too."

Steve laughed. "I'm Holly's alibi. She was with me."

"Ceci, you may relax," Althea said. "Dr. Skipcliff was fifty-seven. Victoria Trotter was fifty-six. Bonny Carr was only forty-five. And you are —"

"A dog owner!" Ceci hastened to exclaim. "A woman! A woman known to Holly. Who was returning home."

"You were returning home in daylight," Althea pointed out. Both sisters followed the television news closely. Althea's eyesight didn't allow her to read, but her Sherlockian admirers, Hugh and Robert, read newspapers to her. "Holly, you didn't know Laura Skipcliff, did you?"

My mouth was full. I shook my head, swal-

164

lowed, and said, "No, I didn't. She seems to have been a nice woman."

If my Kimi had been next to the table with a clear shot at the prime rib, she wouldn't have pounced any more swiftly than Ceci did. "And the others weren't! You're just too nice to say so."

"I barely knew Bonny Carr. And I didn't know Victoria Trotter well, either. I interviewed her for a couple of articles. That's all. We weren't friends."

"If either of you uses the word *nice* again —" Althea began to threaten.

"Althea," Ceci said, "you retired from teaching quite a few years ago, and we are not writing essays to hand in to you, we are at the dinner table discussing a subject of common interest, and . . ." For once, Ceci paused.

I pounced. "Speaking of a subject of interest *and* writing, we need to talk about the ceremony. Althea, what are your thoughts about your part? Is there something you particularly want to include?"

"Whoever would have thought that Althea would be allowed to marry people," said Ceci, as if to herself.

"The Office of Solemnizations," Steve replied. "I have the forms."

"What if this monster is still at large?" Ceci exclaimed.

"He's not invited," Althea murmured.

Steve said, "We're getting married no matter what."

Have I mentioned that I am crazy about this man?

"As the Jewish ladies in Newton say," Ceci told me, "when you got him, you got gold. One of those awnings you see at Jewish weddings would be nice, what are they called? A hoopla? And I always like that part when they step on the wineglass, and everyone says mazel tov."

Simultaneously, Althea said, "Huppah," while I said, "An arch with flowers would be lovely," and Steve said, "Whatever Holly wants."

Before Ceci could return to her plans to unite two gentiles in a Jewish ceremony conducted by her gentile sister, and before she could return to her obsession with the serial killer, Althea began to question us about precisely what we wanted her to say.

"The one that starts 'Dearly beloved,'" Steve said.

"No obeying," I said.

"Of course not," Althea said. "Perhaps something from the Bible, with a few words of my own."

I was sitting close enough to Althea for her to see the expression on my face. Or maybe she heard me catch my breath. In any case, her laughter burbled out, and when she recovered from the exertion, she said, "The

King James, my dear! Did you truly imagine that I intended to string together nuptial passages from Dr. Watson?"

To the best of my recollection, Althea's Canon contained a brief reference or two to Dr. Watson's conjugal bliss and almost nothing else that could be construed as any sort of paean to marriage. "We trust you completely," I said. "We hope you'll say anything you want. And Ceci, Steve and I wondered whether you might be willing to read a poem. But you don't have to. We know how much work it will be for you to have the wedding here, and we're so happy about it and so grateful. So if you'd rather not read during the ceremony, just say so. You could choose any poem you wanted." Steve and I had wanted to make sure that Ceci wouldn't feel left out. We'd toyed with the possibility of making a secret wager about the nature of Ceci's selection, but somewhat to our disappointment, we'd found ourselves with nothing to bet on: Both of us were certain that she'd choose a poem involving love and the moon.

Ceci was beaming. "I would adore it!" With that, she leaped from her seat and hugged Steve and then me. Having finished our main course, we moved to the living room for coffee and chocolate cake iced with whipped cream. Now that Ceci's house had become the site of our wedding, I regarded it with a new and proprietary interest. The living room ran all the way from the front of the house to the rear, where it became a small conservatory with a tiled floor, wicker furniture, and potted palms. As I was envisioning our wedding guests strolling around in their finery while sipping champagne and listening to Ian McCloud's music, Ceci excused herself and immediately returned with a stack of manila folders that turned out to contain thorough and sensible plans for the wedding. Her principal concern, a reasonable one, was the question of a tent or tents. Late September weather in New England being as variable as it was, we'd need heaters. But would we want a dance floor? Although Steve and I were equally capable of making good choices about the arrangements, Ceci addressed Steve, who told her about Ian McCloud, the caterer, and our ideas about a menu. The food was Steve's responsibility, in part because the caterer was a client of his and in part because Steve cared more about the particulars of the wedding feast than I did. After Steve had consumed two big pieces of cake, Ceci decided that he needed to go outdoors with her to examine the proposed tent sites and also to check on Quest, her Newfoundland, and Lady, who had been invited to play with the big black bear of a dog while we had dinner. At home, in our own pack, the anxious pointer seldom had the self-confidence to initiate play with another dog. India guided and protected her, Kimi bossed her around, Rowdy coexisted with her, and Sammy jumped over her lengthwise, but rarely was she sought as a playmate. Quest, however, had been startlingly and touchingly smitten with Lady from the moment they'd first been introduced. Despite his great size, he romped gently with her, and she, in turn, perhaps sensing his advanced age and the joint disease that plagues giant breeds, toned down her nervous energy to become as relaxed as I'd ever seen her.

Alone with Althea, I was surprised to notice a marked change in her demeanor. Her ancient face was serious, and her voice, never loud, was so low that she nearly whispered. "I'm glad to have the opportunity to speak to you out of my sister's hearing," she said. "I'll be brief. Ceci is, as you've no doubt observed, in a state of considerable hysteria about these murders, which are, of course, horrific and frightening, but constitute no personal threat to her. You, Holly, are another matter. Hugh and Robert share my concern, and I have promised them that I would speak to you, as I'd have done even without their prompting. The case that concerns us most is this recent one. I find it all too easy to see what happened. The victim, Bonny Carr, drove to her home at night. She pulled into a parking space behind her building and got out — with the intention of immediately getting her dog from a crate in the back of the car. Before she could do so, the murderer struck. What alarms me is that I can easily envision you in precisely that vulnerable situation. You go somewhere with one or both of your dogs. You arrive home. You get out of your car. You feel neither alone nor vulnerable because, in seconds, you'll have a powerful dog at your side. For those few seconds, however, you are unprotected."

"Althea, I'm grateful for your concern. Steve has installed new outdoor lights, as much for Rita's safety as for mine. Kevin Dennehy lives next door. I'm sure that he has cruisers checking our neighborhood all the time. As of yesterday, Rita and I have a buddy system. She calls me when she leaves her office, and I watch for her to get home. She's carrying a personal alarm device. I don't go out without a dog. Even if I'm just getting something from my car, I take a dog with me, and not Lady or Sammy, either. I take Rowdy or Kimi or India."

"These last two women were in professions similar to yours."

"Every woman who works with animals is worried. Steve had a meeting with all his staff yesterday afternoon. No woman leaves there without an escort. He's checking on security services and off-duty cops. And I'm concerned for Leah the way you're concerned for me. She isn't a dog professional, but she trains and handles Kimi, and for all we know, maybe that's close enough. That is, if dogs really have anything to do with the motivation. Maybe they don't. Harvard has set up extra shuttle buses and taken all kinds of precautions. Leah has sworn to me that she won't go out alone after dark."

"You are very dear to me," Althea said.

"I'll be careful," I said. "I promise. After all, I'm fairly dear to myself, too."

Chapter 19

At four o'clock on Sunday morning, Steve, Lady, India, and Sammy left for a little town west of Worcester. In an act of noble self-sacrifice, Steve had volunteered to play the role known as "subject" in the crucial forty-acre test that a prospective Search and Rescue dog had to pass to achieve certification for daytime searches. This Search and Rescue group shunned the all-too-accurate term *victim* for the person who, in the aforementioned act of noble self-sacrifice, agreed to get up before dawn, drive a long distance, hide in a forty-acre wilderness, and sit on the cold ground with nothing to do except wait to be discovered by the dog taking the test. I'd refused Steve's invitation to accompany him to the test and on the hike he intended to take with his dogs once he'd been found. Rita, Leah, and I were scheduled to shop for wedding apparel at two o'clock, and if the canine searcher dallied, there'd be insufficient time after the test to hike and get back to Cambridge on time.

I slept until what was for me the luxuriously late hour of eight. I fed Rowdy and Kimi, let them into the yard, had breakfast, and, over coffee, checked my E-mail. Instead of leaving a note on my door, Rita had E-mailed me to say that she and Artie were leaving at 5:30 a.m. to go to Plum Island, where someone had spotted a rare bird. They were taking Willie with them — why, I couldn't imagine, since Willie would scare off birds, rare or otherwise. Rita promised to be back in time for our dress-shopping trip. My stepmother, Gabrielle, had sent a brief message to say that she and Buck had mailed the wedding invitations on Friday. My father had made a spectacle of himself at the post office by bragging about me. She'd call soon. I scanned the messages on Dogwriters-L, Malamute-L, and the other lists to which I subscribed. Then I visited one of the online booksellers, where I was irked to see that one reader's sour review had lowered the rating of *101 Ways to Cook Liver* from five stars to four and a half. The sourpuss who'd given my book a rotten rating had written, incredibly, "This book is about cooking for dogs! What a waste of time! Why would anyone bother?"

In an effort to scrub off my resentment at the unfair treatment of my work, I took a shower. As I was toweling off, it finally occurred to me that the same mean-spirited reader had probably written almost the same thing about *The Joy of Cooking*: "This book is about cooking! What a waste of time! Why would anyone bother?" The realization brought me only a little consolation. To battle my sense of mistreatment, I dug two liver brownies out of the depths of the freezer and fed them to Rowdy and Kimi, who gobbled them with gusto. Yet one more reason to worship the Sacred Animal! No dog has ever given me anything but a rave review.

I made a fresh pot of coffee and settled in with the Sunday paper, which had two articles and a long sidebar about the serial murders. The first article recapped old news about the slayings of Dr. Laura Skipcliff, Victoria Trotter, and Bonny Carr. It pointed out that the three victims were dark-haired women in their forties or fifties. The murders had taken place in the evening. All three victims had been bludgeoned to death. The weapon or weapons had not been identified. Victoria Trotter had been injected with insulin, Bonny Carr with amitriptyline. Dr. Laura Skipcliff had been a noted anesthesiologist. Victoria Trotter had published a tarot deck with illustrations of dogs and a companion book to be used in what the paper called "fortune telling." Bonny Carr had been an expert on treating trauma in dogs. And so on. The police were, as usual, pursuing their investigations.

The second article was more interesting than the first. Its material had been provided by a panel of local mental-health professionals assembled to advise Massachusetts law enforcement personnel and the general public about serial murderers. So far, the panel's work seemed to have consisted of providing psychosocial profiles. According to the article, the typical serial killer was a white male between twenty and forty years of age who came from a dysfunctional family and had a history of abuse. He usually killed his victims near their homes or workplaces. In most cases, there was a cooling-off period between homicides. Serial killers were socially isolated men given to daydreaming and compulsive masturbation. They experienced delusions of grandeur, depression, and feelings of failure, as well as — gulp — difficulty in accepting criticism and a sense of mistreatment. I was chagrined to realize that with regard to such experiences, published writers had an awful lot in common with serial murderers.

The sidebar consisted of reasonable advice that most of us, especially women, had already taken. Throughout Greater Boston, women had installed new outside lights, set up buddy systems and phone checks with friends, and made arrangements never to be outside alone at night. I didn't own a personal alarm device, but a lot of other women had bought them. As to the recommendation about getting a big dog, I'd done that in duplicate long before the murders. Attitude was said to be important: Like other women, especially women whose work had anything to do with dogs, I was trying to remain calm but alert. Morale mattered, too: Unlike some other women, I had not been terrorized into locking myself up in the protective custody of my house.

Just as I was reminding myself of reasons to feel optimistic about the capture of the serial killer, the principal such reason, Kevin Dennehy, showed up at my back door. He looked tired, but issued his invariable greeting: "Hey, Holly, how ya doin'?"

"Fine, Kevin. I've been reading the papers, and there's something I want to ask you. So, how do these experts know that serial murderers engage in compulsive masturbation?"

Kevin's face turned as violently red as his hair, but he made a grand recovery. "They get acne," he said, "and then they go blind. Give me a cup of coffee, and I'll tell you all about it. It's wicked technical. The first thing we do is look for guys with zits. And then —"

Five minutes later, Kevin was seated at my kitchen table drinking the promised coffee and fooling around with Rowdy and Kimi. Although his professional life was devoted to enforcing the public law, he was chronically guilty of breaking my personal laws pertaining to behavior with my dogs. I knew of his crimes not only because I'd caught him perpetrating them a few times, but because Rowdy and Kimi unintentionally snitched on him by begging him for food and drink, and by knocking up against him and issuing playgrowl invitations to engage in rough games. Never, ever would the dogs have deliberately betrayed Kevin. Being dogs, they were incapable of lying, but if they'd suspected that their truth-telling would get Kevin in trouble, they'd have done their best to prevaricate. They simply adored him.

"I knew Bonny Carr," I told Kevin. "Not well. She gave workshops about treating traumatized dogs. I went to one a few years ago."

"Is there a dog owner in the Commonwealth that you don't know?"

"There are thousands. But I do know a lot of people who work with dogs. Or write about dogs. Or show. Train. Do agility. But Bonny Carr wasn't really a dog trainer, and she didn't show. I went to the workshop because I thought I might write about it."

"And did you?"

"No."

"For no good reason."

"On the contrary. For an excellent reason."

"I gotta drag this out of you?"

I drank some coffee. "No. It's . . . I'm embarrassed. And kind of ashamed. Because I told you that I really didn't like Victoria Trotter."

"And you didn't like Ms. Carr any better."

"There's more to it than that."

Kevin looked at Rowdy and Kimi, who'd thrown themselves at his big feet. "I gotta ask you guys?"

"Rowdy's the one to ask. He went with me to Bonny Carr's workshop. He acted horrible. Her method had to do with relieving anxiety by touching the dog. Massaging. And you know how Rowdy loves anything like that. And he would *not* cooperate. She'd say something about applying gentle pressure to the dog's ears, and Rowdy would bounce up and start yelping. It was humiliating. But what I realized, belatedly, was that Rowdy was right. What he didn't like was being there at all. And the reason was that he didn't like Bonny Carr. He spotted something wrong. Something fake."

Kevin wrapped his giant hands around Rowdy's muzzle and moved the big dog's head back and forth. "You got a nose for a phony, huh?"

"He did this time. Kevin, something about that woman just didn't ring true. Supposedly, she was devoted to relieving trauma. But as I thought it over afterward, it seemed to me that what she was actually devoted to was presenting herself as a sort of savior. Her strong emphasis, her real energy, was directed at how she came across. I had the feeling that we were meant to leave there with the image of Saint Bonny. And that the dogs she was talking about didn't matter much to her at all. Also, she more than suggested that Rowdy was acting wild because I'd abused him!"

"Any connection between her and Victoria Trotter?"

"Not that I know of. I don't see why there should have been. Victoria had no interest in shelter dogs or rescue or anything like that. And what Bonny Carr did had no connection with the tarot or mysticism or anything remotely like that. In the world of dogs, they moved in completely different circles. The only possible connection I could think of was that both of them might've belonged to DWAA." I refilled Kevin's cup. "The Dog Writers Association of America. But I checked the DWAA directory, and neither of them belonged. You know, though, there's one thing I've wondered. Kevin, do you know whether Laura Skipcliff owned a dog?"

"No pets," he said. "Not so much as an ant farm."

"Do you have any idea what the murder weapon was? Or what the weapons were?"

What I heard him say was, "Heavy metal."

I must've looked bewildered.

"Metal object. Heavy. Probably new. Clean.

179

Probably with a wooden handle. All along, I've been guessing a sledge hammer. Like they say, a blunt instrument. Not an ax."

"I have to tell you," I said, "and I'm not the only person who feels this way — I really hope that all the people investigating these murders know a lot more than anyone is saying."

"You and me both."

"That's why I was honest with you about Bonny Carr. And Victoria. Maybe my dislike wasn't just a personal matter. Maybe it's information. I'd like to say that they were both beautiful human beings, and it's perfectly possible that lots of people thought so. But I didn't."

"Hey, if it's any consolation, someone agreed with you."

"It's no consolation," I said.

Chapter 20

As promised, Rita arrived home in time for our shopping trip, which was to be no ordinary outing, but a ritual quest for nuptial finery. Consequently, two o'clock on Sunday afternoon found Rita, Leah, and me in Maurice's Bridal Shop, a vast suburban strip-mall emporium recommended by Olivia Berkowitz. I almost wish that I'd counted the number of white gowns jammed into the miles of extralong racks, but if I'd started the task, I wouldn't be done with it yet. There were trillions, each more elaborate than the others, or so it seemed to me.

Yanking a heavy satin, lace, and seed-pearl garment from an overstuffed rack, my cousin Leah said, much too loudly, "Yuck! Holly, is this ever not you! What are we doing in this awful place? This thing looks like a Halloween costume for someone who wants to go as the pope."

"Leah, keep your voice down," I whispered. "You may not care for the dress or the store,

181

but for all you know, some woman in the next aisle just bought that exact dress and is thrilled with it. Or was until you opened your mouth."

Thereafter, Leah modulated her volume. Her opinions, however, remained unchanged, and she continued to claim that one dress looked like a mammoth christening gown, another like a First Communion outfit, and another like a nurse's uniform. Rita, who also found nothing to her liking, nonetheless insisted that we try on a few bridal gowns for me and pastel atrocities (or so I thought) for herself and Leah. Our arms laden with Rita's selections, we staggered to the dressing rooms at the back of Maurice's and dutifully enrobed ourselves. At the urging of a salesperson, we then paraded out to a small, low stage backed by mirrors, where I examined us and thought that we looked dandy — but only when I managed to keep my eyes exclusively on our heads. Leah's red-gold curls spilled from a becoming top knot. Rita's morning walk with Artie and Willie had given her cheeks a healthy, ruddy glow. In evaluating myself, I tried to filter out my resemblance to a golden retriever.

Just as I was succeeding in seeing the three of us as a lovely bridal party, two minor events ruined the perspective. The first was that Leah pointed a finger at Rita's dress, a cocktail-length pale green affair, and said, admittedly in a hushed tone, "That thing looks like a high school prom dress, and it's the exact same color as a lime Popsicle."

The second event was that I glanced toward the front of the store and spotted a tall, slim woman with long, silky blond hair identical to Anita Fairley's. The next moment, the woman turned, and I saw that her face looked nothing like Anita's. Still, the pangs of jealousy and envy soured my mood. Or maybe what hurt was the sharp realization that even on my wedding day, when I'd presumably glow with ephemeral bridal loveliness, even when I was wearing a gracious, simple, elegant, and flattering gown entirely unlike the one I now wore, I'd still never be half as beautiful as Anita at her very worst.

"This place isn't for us," I said abruptly. "We have to go somewhere else."

New Yorker that she was, Rita decided that the somewhere else should, of course, be Bloomingdale's. Wise counselor that she was, she turned out to be right. Indeed, the second we entered the Bloomie's on Route 9, I felt myself catch Rita's spirit of optimism and happily glued myself to her in the attentive manner of a well-trained dog heeling beside a trusted, capable handler. In a small, uncrowded department on the second floor, we immediately found a long, absolutely simple, and simply perfect silky white dress and, miraculously, short dresses for Rita and

Leah in the same style and fabric, but tinted a pale apricot.

When I tried on my dress, Leah, instead of announcing in her usual manner that it made me look like a monstrous infant or a nun about to take vows, said, "It's so romantic! Holly, it's perfect."

And it was, too. Even the fit was perfect. Leah's apricot dress was, however, too tight, and Rita's had a greasy spot on the bosom. Consequently, I was left alone in a cubicle of the dressing area while Leah and Rita went in search of replacements. Having succumbed to the temptation to admire myself in the mirror, I was enjoying the sight of my very bridal and decidedly undoglike image when I heard the voices of two women and the rustle of the clothing they obviously intended to try on. But they were not discussing their proposed purchases. Rather, they were talking about the murder of Bonny Carr.

The first woman expressed conventional sentiments. "Horrible," she said. "I'm scared to leave home after dark. I make Harold take out the trash. It's awful. You don't expect something like this to happen in Brookline. All I can think is, it could've been any of us."

In hushed tones, the second woman said, "I wouldn't be too sure about that."

I couldn't see the women, of course, but

the first woman probably gave the second a questioning look.

"Maybe she didn't deserve what she got," the second woman confided, "but she was no angel. I'll tell you something about her, but if anyone asks you, I didn't say it, and I'm not using names. I know about her because she had an affair with my best friend's husband. And he wasn't the only one. My friend was totally devastated. She lost fifteen pounds practically overnight. And besides everything else, she was terrified of AIDS. Her husband told her all about the affair, and she made him get tested, and he was negative. But it was strictly a matter of luck." She lowered her voice to a whisper. "And do you know what Bonny Carr did for a living? She worked with traumatized animals. What a joke! Here she was devoting her professional life to supposedly healing trauma, while all the while, she spent her personal life inflicting it. What she was, was a stinking little hypocrite. My poor friend is waltzing on her grave. And she isn't the only wife, either."

"Sounds like there'll be a chorus line."

"Oh, there will. There definitely will."

Chapter 21

From Monday through Thursday of that week, I was frantically busy. I finished my column for *Dog's Life*, worked on the proposal for *No More Fat Dogs*, double-checked the plane and hotel reservations for our honeymoon, and did my usual volunteer work for Alaskan Malamute Rescue of New England, meaning that I answered E-mail and returned phone calls about malamutes in need of new homes. I also sketched a seating plan for what Gabrielle called "the wedding breakfast," and Steve and I drew up a list of restaurants to consider for our rehearsal dinner. The "breakfast" would follow our afternoon wedding, and I saw no need to rehearse our simple service. Steve, however, having spoken with Gabrielle, explained that the point of the rehearsal was to provide an excuse for the mandatory dinner; therefore, we had to rehearse.

On Tuesday, Rowdy and I went to a cable television studio in Woburn to tape a show about pet care. Liver authority that I was, I was supposed to be the featured guest and was so nervous that my hands got drenched in sweat. Rowdy regarded the studio as yet one more splendid showring erected for the sole purpose of allowing him to strut his gorgeous stuff. To my relief, he stole the show by kissing the interviewer and howling for the camera. On Thursday, Steve and I took Sammy and Rowdy to dog training.

On Friday morning, I finally had time to get Rowdy to add his autograph to fresh copies of *101 Ways to Cook Liver.* Working in our usual cooperative fashion, Rowdy and I had developed a paw-printing system that limited the amount of ink tracked throughout the house and minimized the number of books spoiled by smears or dirt. Our "usual cooperative fashion" consisted of my making sure that the entire undertaking was saturated with dog treats and was therefore to the big boy's liking. At about ten-thirty, Rowdy was hitched to a kitchen cabinet with an old, stained leash. Stacked on the table were thirty copies of my book, each with a sheet of scrap paper inserted at the title page. Also on the table, on a thick pad of newspaper, was an ink pad that I'd moistened with a little water and repeatedly inked from a bottle. Near it, within my reach and out of Rowdy's, was a pile of my homemade liver brownies. On the counter next to the sink rested the ink bottle, a dog dish full of warm, soapy water for washing Rowdy's right paw, and a second dish of clear water for rinsing off the soap. A mop and a bottle of spray cleanser stood ready, as did a roll of paper towels and a dog crate lined with threadbare bath towels.

Our eccentric book signing went smoothly. I popped a treat into Rowdy's mouth, grasped his right leg with my left hand, raised his paw, and, using my right hand, pressed the ink pad against the bottom of his foot. I repeated the process until his paw was leaving dark marks on the tile floor. Then I re-inked his paw, held his leg in my left hand, wiped off my right hand, and used that clean hand to grab a book, open it to the title page, and shake the book lightly to allow the scrap paper to fall to the table. Chatting happily to Rowdy about what a good dog he was, I then held the title page just beneath his paw, pressed hard for about three seconds, removed the book, and re-inserted the scrap paper, which absorbed excess ink that would otherwise have smeared the facing page.

"Good job! That's a beauty!" I shoved food into his mouth, and off we went again. The trick, by the way, is to work fast. By the time we'd done all thirty books, Rowdy stood in a shallow pool of watery ink, and my worn-out, once-white running shoes were wet with ink, as were my holes-in-the-knees jeans, my knees themselves, and the cuffs of my ancient sweatshirt. That was when the front doorbell rang. Having sworn softly, I bellowed, "JUST A MINUTE!" My friends never use the front door. Delivery people do because my address is 256 Concord Avenue, and the front of the house is on Concord. Rowdy assumes, not unreasonably, that the front bell means a package from a kennel-supply company, a box that will contain toys and goodies for him. He bounced in the inky pool. I, in contrast, assumed that UPS or FedEx was delivering a wedding present, and I tiptoed around the ink and kicked off my shoes. Two gifts had already arrived, both sent by friends of my family even before they'd received invitations. One was a food processor that sat in its carton on the kitchen counter, and the other was a beautiful set of five thin but strong white leather leashes for the dogs to wear at the wedding. They, too, were on the counter.

The person at my front door, however, was Elspeth Jantzen, whose existence I had managed to forget. She was delivering the manuscript of her book for me to read and blurb. As soon as I opened the door, took in her usual violent redness of hair, face, and clothing, and invited her in, I warned her about the mess in the kitchen. Incredibly, she waited until she actually saw it to ask, "Is this a bad time for you?"

Without actually answering the question, I said, "Everything's hectic these days. Why don't you drag a chair away from the ink, and I'll clean up and make some coffee." Indeed, my mother raised me right. In other words, she taught me to be a fool.

Had Elspeth's mother raised her right, she'd have dropped off the damned manuscript and departed. As it was, she accepted my invitation and sat patiently as I scrubbed, rinsed, and dried Rowdy's foot, crated him, mopped the floor, and made coffee. As I did so, Elspeth took an inventory of my kitchen and narrated her observations. "Wedding presents! Well, I suppose a food processor is the last thing you need. I hope it's returnable. The leashes must be for the wedding. Aren't you going to get special collars?"

"Yes," I said. "Flowered collars. Or we're going to try. Rowdy and Sammy may eat theirs."

"I love the pictures!" She'd noticed the ones on the refrigerator, large photos taken with Steve's digital camera that I'd printed out on my computer. They showed Rita, Leah, and me having the hems of our dresses taken up. I'd seen no need to tinker with my perfect dress, but Mrs. Dennehy, Kevin's mother, had offered to do alterations, and Rita had insisted that my dress was an inch too long. "Are you going to wear a veil?"

"Flowers," I said. "Some sort of small headpiece."

"To match your dogs. That's beautiful. If I ever get married, my dogs are going to be part of the wedding, too. An essential part." Elspeth had two Irish terriers. Very nice dogs. Not pests. "And look at all your lists! You're so organized!"

"Steve is. He put up that bulletin board. He's much neater than I am." Tacked on the bulletin boards were drafts of the menu and various checklists, including one for presents received and thank-you notes written. Also displayed was a favorable review of my book that had just appeared in a major dog magazine. My kitchen could've been set up to announce that I was a published author who was about to be married.

"Is Mac coming to your wedding?" Elspeth asked.

"Yes." I resisted both her implicit plea for an invitation and my impulse to extend one.

"And his wife?"

"We wouldn't ask Mac and not Judith."

I served the coffee. Loading hers with four teaspoonfuls of sugar and a big slug of milk, Elspeth said, "Well, Mac does a lot of things without his wife. A lot of *interesting* things."

I said nothing.

"Don't pay any attention to me. I'm just . . . what I am, actually, is pissed off at him. Not that Mac and I made any promises to each other or anything like that, except that honest to God, would it be too much to expect him to remember my name? To show the slightest little bitty sign that he remembered me at all?"

If I'd wanted to give a truthful yes-or-no answer, I wouldn't have known what to say. As it was, I didn't want to participate in the conversation at all.

Continuing it without my help, Elspeth fortified herself with a sip of coffee before saying, "Misspelling my name would be one thing. That I could understand. Or getting it wrong. *Elsbeth* with a *b*. I get that all the time. And no one ever spells *Jantzen* right. Or hardly anyone does. But he totally forgot *me!*" Although Elspeth's face was redder than ever, she looked far more sad than angry. "Like we'd never been close! And Mac and I *were* close. We were about as close as two people can be. And not all that long ago. I mean, eight years ago? It's not like it was in some other lifetime."

I reminded myself that I hadn't invited this unwelcome . . . admission? No. And it certainly wasn't a confession. On the contrary, Elspeth was bragging about her affair with Mac.

"It was at a conference," she went on. "We hung out together. And then we met in the bar that night. Admittedly, he'd had a fair amount to drink. I mean, so had I, for that fact. But Jesus Christ! Is that any excuse?"

An *affair?* A drunken one-night stand. "Mac did say he'd blurb your book."

"He does that for anyone who asks." She drained her coffee mug as if she were tossing down scotch. With an ugly smile, she said, "Let me tell you something I haven't mentioned to anyone else."

Don't! I wanted to beg. But I remained silent.

"Mac knew Victoria Trotter." Elspeth's voice was low. She chuckled softly. "She donated one of her mother's paintings to his vet school. He had something to do with accepting it. And you know, I've been wondering who else he knew." The smile and the chuckle made me wonder whether Elspeth was making a malicious joke, as I thought she was. Then she suddenly became serious. With no sense of absurdity, she said, "Mac's wife really doesn't understand him." As if voicing a fresh, original thought, she added, "Or appreciate him. He's a very unusual man."

I felt almost sorry for Elspeth. But I felt far more sorry for Judith. Elspeth eventually left. I did not, of course, invite her to the wedding.

Chapter 22

From: Gabrielle@beamonres.org
To: HollyWinter@amrone.org
Subj: No time at all!

Dearest Holly,

Here it is, the fourteenth of September, with the twenty-ninth no time away! I find myself becoming more excited as each hour passes. Your father and I thank you profusely for the beautiful photographs of your gown and Leah's and Rita's dresses. Your gown is as perfect to my eye as it is to yours. Your father regarded your photograph solemnly and then asked whether the dress had pockets for dog treats! Doesn't Buck have a wonderfully dry sense of humor? The shade of pale apricot you have chosen for the dresses of your attendants is lovely, and I thoroughly approve of your plan for collars adorned with roses in the same hue, especially because your favorite flower, the delphinium, is so very toxic to dogs, more's the pity. Besides, there are no apricot delphiniums, are there? And pale pink or baby blue wouldn't suit Leah and Rita, somehow.

Buck asks me to convey his opinion that the task of carrying a floral basket be assigned exclusively to India. He understands your desire to have your very own dogs take an active role in the ceremony and heartily applauds the loyalty that this desire reflects, but he nonetheless maintains that absolute reliability is of the utmost importance for the occasion and that the German Shepherd Dog is far more trustworthy than is the Alaskan Malamute when it comes to toting floral arrangements in the vicinity of preparations for catered dinners.

Speaking of Malamutes, the acceptances are coming in, including one with a delightful letter from your friend Twila Baker from Washington, who will be in New Hampshire with her dog, North, for a mushing boot camp the following weekend and will arrange to arrive in New England a week early in order to attend the wedding. What a dreadful drive for her! Three thousand miles, isn't it? We did include North in the invitation, didn't we? Not that it matters. One more will add to the merriment. Buck, I must warn you, got his hands on Twila's letter and, once having read of the boot camp, is facetiously promoting the notion that you and Steve should cancel your plans for Paris in favor of the mushing event, which he proposes that he and I attend with you, Steve, and all the dogs. When Buck first made this proposal, he had me entirely fooled! I assumed that he was serious. He takes pleasure in putting forth the notion in extraordinary detail and with a remarkably straight face. Whatever my little Molly and I would do with all those sled dogs is more than I can begin to imagine, the sport of mushing not being one of the traditional pursuits of the Bichon Frise or, indeed, one of the traditional pursuits of yours truly! My pretend horror provokes your father to yet greater teasing. We have been having such fun!

I am ever so much looking forward to your bridal shower, which is practically here! How lovely of Ceci to host this event as well as your wedding. Rita is a dear to join Ceci in feting you, as the local paper always phrases it. Rita is such a devoted friend, as well as a person of excellent taste who will see that everything is just so.

With great love,
Gabrielle

From: HollyWinter@amrone.org
To: Gabrielle@beamonres.org
Subj: Re: No time at all!

Hi Gabrielle,
Ceci and Rita are planning what they promise will be a simple and small shower, but I am delighted that you will be here for it. I am also delighted that Twila and North have accepted the wedding invitation. He is a remarkable dog — a successful show dog and a great working dog. Buck will enjoy meeting both North and Twila — in that order! But Twila is crazy about North and won't mind.

We are spending our honeymoon in Paris, and that's that.

The atmosphere generated by the murders is in jarring contrast to what seems, by comparison, our frivolous preoccupation with the festivities. Ordinary shops, including my local pharmacy and the neighborhood convenience stores, are suddenly stocking personal alarm devices, flashlights, noxious sprays, outside floodlights, and even baseball bats. After dusk, it's rare to see a woman outdoors alone. I wish I could report that Kevin Dennehy offered the hope of a rapid end to this grim period of fearfulness, but he does not, in part, I suspect, because the investigation is in the manicured hands of the District Attorney, the state police, and so forth instead of in his capable, beefy paws. Please remember not to tell Buck that I knew Bonny Carr.

I can hardly wait to see you!

Love,
Holly
P.S. Tell Buck that my wedding gown does have pockets.

From: JudithOEsterhazy@post.harvard.edu
To: HollyWinter@amrone.org
Subj: Dinner?

Hi Holly,
Mac and I wonder whether you and Steve would care to join us for dinner a week from today, on Saturday, the twenty-first. Olivia and her husband, John, will be with us, as will Ian and perhaps a few others. Ian will probably be persuaded to treat us to some live music. How fearfully Jane Austen we are! But we will be quite informal. If you are free,

would seven suit you?

Best,
Judith

To: JudithOEsterhazy@post.harvard.edu
From: HollyWinter@amrone.org
Subj: Re: Dinner?

Hi Judith,
Steve and I would be delighted to have dinner on the twenty-first. Many thanks for thinking of us. We'll be there at seven. What would you like us to contribute? Salad? Dessert? Wine?

Olivia gave us some of Ian's CDs. We are thrilled that he has agreed to do the music for our wedding. The more Jane Austen, the better!

Best,
Holly

To: BuckWinter@Mainely-dogs.com
From: HollyWinter@amrone.org
Subj: Repeat!

Buck,

I do not believe in interfering in other people's marriages, especially yours, but I feel compelled to repeat what I just said to you on the phone, namely, that if you want to go to mushing boot camp, fine! And I am happy to have Rowdy and Kimi accompany you. They will have lots of fun. The same cannot be said of Gabrielle. I wish that you had not signed her up without letting her know what to expect. It is your responsibility, and not mine, to inform her of the realities of camp! She needs to understand that mushing is mushing and that boot camp is boot camp! Please have her call Twila Baker!

Love,
Holly

Chapter 23

On Saturday night, Steve and I had an early dinner at a new restaurant in Newton called Nuages, which means, as I translated for Steve, Clouds. His French still hadn't progressed beyond the statement that his wife didn't like the heat.

"Actually," I reminded him as we drove to Nuages, "when you're its source, your wife-to-be likes the heat just fine."

We were trying out Nuages in the hope that it would be a suitable place for our rehearsal dinner. Because Althea tired easily, we wanted a restaurant close to Ceci's house on Norwood Hill. Nuages was a five-minute drive from there. Our investigation was a great success. The food proved to be not only delicious but more substantial than the restaurant's name suggested; because I'm half malamute, I object to light fare, and I absolutely hate small portions. The decor, atmosphere, and menu at Nuages, while unpretentious, were trendy enough to make us feel that we were getting married in style. By the end of the meal, we'd agreed that this was the right place, and before leaving, we talked with the manager and reserved tables for Saturday, September 28.

If all had gone according to plan, we'd then have returned home to spend an hour or two poring over our guides to Paris and making notes on romantic walks we just had to take and museums we just had to visit. Unfortunately, thirty seconds after we walked into the house, the vet tech who was living in Steve's old apartment above his clinic called to say that a hospitalized cat had taken a bad turn. Instead of relaying the message to one of the vets who worked for him, Steve apologized to me and took off. His parting words were, "Don't go outside alone!"

Steve's dedication to the welfare of his patients was one of the reasons I loved him. Still, I resented the interruption and even felt a little jealous of the ailing cat. I was left with the task of giving all five dogs some time outdoors in the yard, and, in Steve's absence, not simultaneous time, either. Steve's three dogs were in the third-floor apartment. The simplest way to get them to the yard would've been to take them down the back stairs, out the back door, along the driveway, and through the gate to the fenced area. It seemed ridiculous to suppose that the serial killer would attack me while I was outside for a few seconds in the company of three big dogs. Even so, I crated Rowdy and Kimi, went to the third floor, and then, with Lady and India following me and Sammy bounding in circles around us, passed through my place and into the yard. In the short time since Steve and I had arrived home, a heavy rain had started. Consequently, his dogs got wet and, on the way back up to the third floor, tracked mud over my kitchen tiles and the stairs. I didn't bother to clean up yet, but put on a rain parka and gave Rowdy and Kimi their turn outside. Rowdy, with his hatred of water, relieved himself in about five seconds and demanded to return to the dry indoors. After letting him in, I stood under the eaves and waited for Kimi, who was cooperatively quick.

When I opened the door and let her in, I should've known that trouble awaited. Instead of shaking herself off, Kimi zoomed forward, and the next thing I knew, she'd tackled Rowdy, and the two big dogs were in the middle of the kitchen floor fighting over a horrible mess of coffee grounds, empty ice cream containers, dirty plastic bags, and other refuse that Rowdy had liberated from the trash can that belonged in the cabinet under the sink. Alaskan malamutes display what is known as "genetic hunger," a legacy of the breed's Arctic origins evident in the malamute's determination to devour everything that could possibly be edible — and anything else that happens to be in the vicinity as well, including rival dogs vying for the same spoils. Consequently, the cabinet under the sink was always supposed to be fastened shut with a tight stretch cord. Steve wouldn't have forgotten to fasten the cabinet. Either I'd been careless, or Rowdy had somehow defeated my dog-proofing. Bending my knees to put myself in a secure stance and bellowing at the dogs to remind them of exactly who was spoiling their fun, I grabbed Kimi's collar, yanked her off Rowdy, dragged her to a crate in the guest room, and locked her up. Then I returned to the kitchen, swabbed out Rowdy's mouth with my fingers to remove a greasy hunk of aluminum foil, and incarcerated him in the guest room in the crate next to Kimi's.

Without even removing my rain parka, I got a broom and dustpan. Only when I'd transferred most of the debris to a trash bag did I notice that under the rain parka, I still had on the new pale gray dress I'd worn to dinner. Its skirt was about four inches longer than the parka, and in sweeping up the coffee grounds and grease, I'd managed to soil the fabric with what I suspected were permanent stains. I began swearing, mainly at that damned Jack London, and let me warn you, as he didn't, that *The Call of the Wild* doesn't begin to prepare a person for the reality of life with the noble and legendary dogs of the Far North.

So, I changed out of my new dress and into ratty jeans and a T-shirt, finished sweeping the kitchen floor, vacuumed and mopped it, put a fresh plastic bag in the trash can, stowed it under the sink, and defiantly slammed the cabinet door shut and secured it with stretch cord. The big green garbage bag was still in the kitchen.

All this is to explain, although not to justify, why I went outside alone at night. With the dogs in their crates, I could've left the trash bag in the kitchen. Or I could've put it in a closet, in the back hall, or in the cellar. I succumbed, however, to an urgent desire to rid my house of the evidence of the dogs' misdeed. Reality aside, I liked seeing Rowdy and Kimi through Jack London eyes; the green garbage bag reflected an image of trash hounds that jarred with my treasured picture of Arctic nobility. Also, with the green trash bag in one of the barrels under the back steps to the house, Steve would never have to know what bad dogs Rowdy and Kimi had been and what a careless idiot I'd been to let them get in trouble.

"This is going to take two seconds," I called to the dogs. "I'm practically not going out at all. I'll be right back."

As if to demonstrate just that, I didn't put my rain parka back on, but picked up the trash bag, passed through the little back hall, opened the outer door, and considered dropping the bag over the railing so that it would land next to the barrels. But I didn't. For one thing, Steve might've seen it when he came home. For another, although we have very few loose dogs around here, we do have a few raccoons and occasional possums and other wild animals that raid trash; I had no desire to clean the same mess off the driveway that I'd just finished removing from the kitchen floor. And the rain had now changed to mist; I wouldn't even get wet. Besides, the original outside lights in combination with the new ones that Steve had installed meant that it was anything but dark outside. Clutching the bag, I ran down the back steps, yanked the lid off a barrel, deposited the trash, and put the lid back on.

That's when I heard the noise. It came from alarmingly nearby. Worse, it originated in a place where almost no one ever went and where no one belonged: the narrow strip of earth between my house and the low fence that separated my property from my Concord Avenue neighbor's. In contrast to the fenced yard on the opposite side of my house, this little passageway was about the width of a footpath. I kept it clear of weeds, but otherwise took no care of it and used it only as a place to rest a ladder when I painted or washed windows. Running as it did from

Concord Avenue to the end of my driveway, it wasn't a shortcut; no one but me used it at all.

When I say "noise," I don't mean a loud one. On the contrary, the sound was soft and muffled, as if someone lurking just around the corner of my house had taken a single step on the wet ground or had perhaps shifted his weight from one foot to the other. Ordinarily, I'd have ignored the sound; I wouldn't have investigated its origin or called out to ask who was there. In this extraordinary time of fear, I heard the sound as furtive and threatening. Feeling guilty and stupid for ignoring the warnings, I made a panicked run up the back steps and went hurtling indoors. Once inside my cozy kitchen, I caught my breath, double-checked the locks on all the doors and windows, and freed Rowdy and Kimi from their crates. If Kevin Dennehy had been at home, I'd probably have asked him to take a look around, but I knew that he'd had a date with his girlfriend, Jennifer, and I knew that his car wasn't in his driveway. As to dialing 911, Kevin had told me all about people who pestered the police by summoning officers to chase down and arrest what turned out to be tree limbs rubbing against roofs or paper bags blowing in the wind; I had no intention of becoming such a person.

"But," I told Rowdy and Kimi, "I did not

imagine that sound. I really did hear something. And you know as well as I do that no one ever goes on that side of the house. Something was there. Or someone. I would really like to know who. Or what. And I would like to know whether it's still there."

With that, I turned off the lights in the rooms with windows facing the passageway: the living room and kitchen. Feeling ridiculous, I then moved from window to window, stopping at each to peer out at what was, as far as I could see, the usual vacant strip of property.

"You know, it wouldn't hurt you two to bark when there's someone outside," I said. "I don't actually like barking, and I hate pointless yapping, but I wouldn't mind an occasional woof when the situation calls for one." The dogs, being malamutes, wagged their tails. "And this situation does, or at least did, warrant a woof because . . . hey, let me tell you something. You know how people are always saying, 'I'm not the imaginative type'? Well, I *am* the imaginative type, and that's the reason I've had to get good at distinguishing between my imaginings and what's really out there. And tonight, someone really was out there. Is out there. Maybe." I paused. "And here's something I'm not proud of. And I'm not telling this to anyone but you guys. But I'm different from Victoria Trotter. And I'm different from Bonny Carr.

I don't pass off other people's work as my own, and I'm not some self-aggrandizing phony. I try to be kind, honest, and all the rest! And that difference made me feel safe. Now it doesn't. And I don't like feeling threatened. So, what do I do? Call the police and report that I heard, quote, a noise, unquote? Do I take the two of you out there and poke around? Do I take India? Victoria's dogs were in her house. Bonny Carr's dog was crated in her car. Yes, exactly. What if the dogs had been right there?"

Rowdy and Kimi gave my monologue their full attention; they did so in the happy expectation that I was about to feed them treats. I ended up doing just that, but only because they tagged along when I went to the bedroom, opened the closet door, stood on tiptoe, and retrieved the ultrafeminine Smith & Wesson case that contained the world's weirdest hostess gift, a Ladysmith revolver once presented to me by my father as a token of his thanks for my hospitality. Rowdy's and Kimi's interest in the weapon made me uneasy, not because the dogs were capable of firing it, of course — even malamute brilliance has its limits — but because the innocence of the dogs' curiosity jarred with the reality of its object. Still, instead of leaving the Ladysmith in its case, I crated the dogs, fed them treats, and dug ammo out of a locked file drawer in my office. Then I loaded the revolver. I grew up in Maine. Therefore, I grew up with guns. I'm not the sort of person who accidentally discharges a firearm, nor am I the sort who cowers helplessly in her house because she suspects that an evildoer lurks outside.

After slipping on a jacket, pocketing my keys, and grabbing a flashlight, I quietly entered the back hall and eased open the outer door. The floods, both old and new, showed my car and Rita's BMW; everything looked normal. Moving slowly, I descended the stairs. With the flashlight in my left hand and the revolver in my right, I made a sudden sprint past the barrels and around the corner of the house. Almost to my disappointment, the narrow strip of land was empty. As if to justify my presence there, I aimed the flashlight at the wet ground and walked the length of the passageway. The beam showed wet leaves that I hadn't bothered to rake. If it also showed footprints, I didn't see them. Feeling foolish, I made my way back along the length of the house and had just stepped onto the brightly illuminated driveway when a human figure appeared on the sidewalk. The figure was female. Taking a look at me, she opened her mouth in a giant O that could have come right out of Munch's famous painting titled "The Scream." And scream Rita sure did.

Chapter 24

"Don't give me this line of yours about Maine and guns," Rita said. "The world is full of people who grew up in Maine and don't go around brandishing deadly weapons."

"Name one," I challenged.

We were seated at my kitchen table. I'd explained about Steve's feline emergency, invited Rita in, unloaded the Ladysmith, and returned it to its case, which I'd stowed safely in the bedroom closet. After locking the ammunition in the file drawer, I'd let Rowdy and Kimi loose. Then I'd opened a bottle of a red wine that Steve was considering for our reception. It was called Mad Fish. The name suited the present occasion. Rita was furious at me, and we were on a subject intimately related to fish and fishing, namely, the State of Maine. Then, too, there was the unmentionable matter of fishy Artie Spicer.

"The late Senator Margaret Chase Smith,"

Rita said. "Stephen King. Your own mother."

"As it happens, my mother was an excellent shot, and for all we know, so was Margaret Chase Smith, and I have no idea whether Stephen King owns a firearm of any kind, but since he lives in Bangor, it's perfectly possible that he does, although he obviously doesn't need one to scare people, does he? And I was not 'brandishing a deadly weapon.' You make it sound as if I'd been standing in the middle of Harvard Square taking potshots, and speaking of stupid behavior, exactly what were *you* doing wandering around outdoors alone at night with, I might add, no protection at all?"

"Spike heels are a very effective weapon." Rita cracked a little smile. I refilled her wineglass. "And I wasn't 'wandering around.' Artie and I went to dinner, and he has an early flight to catch tomorrow, so he dropped me off, and the only reason he didn't walk me to the door is that thanks to my dutiful landlady, the driveway is brighter than the Sahara at noon, so I could hardly be said to have been outdoors after dark, could I?"

"You certainly could. In fact, you were. And the garage of The Charles, where Laura Skipcliff was killed, is anything but dark, and it's indoors. And Bonny Carr was killed in the parking lot behind her building, which must've had lights. You should've made Artie walk you to the door."

"I'm not in the habit of *making* Artie or anyone else do things. I'm a therapist. Remember? I don't *make* people do things."

"We're not talking about your patients' mental health. We're talking about your physical safety."

"I'm safe," Rita said. "So, are you going to tell me what you were doing outdoors alone at night? With a gun?"

"I heard a noise." My statement undoubtedly sounded as childish in Rita's ears as it did in mine. "Really. And you've heard Kevin on the subject of people who call nine-one-one about a *noise*. And Kevin's out with Jennifer, so I couldn't just to have him come over. And I knew what I heard, Rita. I heard a footstep around the corner of the house."

"You heard a footstep from indoors?"

"I was taking out the trash. Rowdy raided the trash under the sink, and he and Kimi got into a fight over it. They made a real mess. And I didn't want the garbage bag sitting on the counter or in the hall."

"You couldn't wait for Steve to get home?"

"I didn't know when he'd get here. I still don't know. You know what Steve's like. It's perfectly possible that he'll sleep on the floor next to the cat's cage. Or with the cat in his arms. So I ran out."

"Maybe stupidity is the true basis of our friendship." Rita raised her glass.

I raised mine. "Friends," I said.

"Forever."

The clinking alerted Rowdy and Kimi, who'd been dozing on the floor. They loved Rita, but considered her to be a rather uninteresting guest, mainly because she never gave them human food or drink, and certainly never wrestled with them.

Instead of discussing our friendship, I said, "We found a restaurant for the rehearsal dinner." I went on to tell her about Nuages, a far easier topic than my strong suspicion that the man I'd seen in Artie Spicer's car had, in fact, been Artie. Rita insisted on seeing the wedding presents that had been arriving daily. The latest was an electric quesadilla maker.

"Returnable?" Rita asked.

"No. It's from my horrible cousin Janice. She probably got it at a yard sale."

"Is she coming to the shower?"

"No. We didn't invite her. Remember? Because if we had, she'd've turned up here two days early with all of her dogs and expect Steve to update all their shots for free and expect us to keep our dogs crated the entire time she was here. Inviting her to the wedding was a concession to Buck. Her dogs are very definitely not invited." Janice had fox terriers, both smooth-coated and wirehaired, and more of both varieties than she could manage properly. The dogs weren't the problem; they'd have been fine if they'd belonged to someone else. "Speaking of the shower, it's a week from tomorrow, and you and Ceci still haven't assigned me a task."

"Ceci and I are giving it. Period. Leah is helping. And there won't be all that much to do. Afternoon tea. Coffee, tea, pastries, little sandwiches with the crusts cut off."

After we'd talked yet more about my wedding, I realized that I'd asked Rita nothing about herself. Ordinarily, I'd have asked about Artie, but I just couldn't bring myself to do it. Instead, I raised the subject of her psychotherapy practice. "Whatever happened to your truth woman?" I asked.

"Who?"

"The patient you told me about at the mall. At dinner. She dropped out of therapy, and you were wondering whether she'd come back. She thought her husband was cheating on her, and you thought she was telling you *her* truth." As soon as the words left my mouth, I felt a ghastly conviction that Rita would correctly interpret my underlying meaning, and I wished to doG Almighty that I'd censored myself. I had the vivid fantasy, as Rita would say, that she'd suddenly rise to her feet and start singing a Patsy Cline classic: "Have You Got Cheating on Your Mind?"

Rita did not break into song. Oddly enough, she didn't even read my thoughts. "I

215

haven't seen her," Rita said. "She terminated." When therapists talk about the end of therapy, they always make it sound as if the patient has died. Rita went on. "She should've stayed in therapy, and I told her so. But there was nothing I could do except make sure she knew that I'm available."

I was only half listening. If I'd been willing to share my sudden insight with Rita, she'd have appreciated it. The Patsy Cline song? Its real title was "If You've Got *Leaving* on Your Mind." I am a Patsy fan. I hadn't just forgotten the correct name of the song; rather, I'd made what Rita would have called a "motivated slip."

"Are you all right?" Rita asked.

"Yes. Just . . . sorry. I was drifting." I almost added that I had something on my mind. The something was Artie Spicer. The something was cheating.

Chapter 25

The dossier on Elspeth Rosemary Jantzen began in the now-familiar fashion with page after repetitive page of results from AnyWho, InfoSpace, Yahoo! People Search, WhitePages.com, Switchboard.com, WhoWhere, SuperPages.com, 411.com, the MSN White Pages, and other people finders that I didn't even recognize. All agreed that she'd had a phone number with a Belmont prefix and that she'd lived where I knew she'd lived, on Payson Road in Belmont. Three maps showed that her address was near the intersection with Belmont Street. The people finders asked the usual questions about whether the searcher had gone to high school with Elspeth Jantzen or wanted to send flowers to her. They offered to find the names of her neighbors, friends, and colleagues, and to identify restaurants and hotels in her neighborhood. I'd driven along Belmont Street dozens of times. It had restaurants, no doubt. But hotels? My recollection was of tidy two-family houses. There was a golf course nearby and, I thought, a reservoir. At a guess, the closest hotel was in Cambridge.

According to a page printed from MissingMoney.com, Elspeth R. Jantzen, with a last known address in Allston, had unclaimed property at the National Bank of Jacksonville. Florida? The page didn't say.

The next section was devoted to information from the web about Elspeth's family. I skimmed an obituary of her mother, Eve, who had died two years earlier and been buried in a Roman Catholic cemetery in Watertown. Eve was survived by her husband, Edward Jantzen; two sons, Ron and Gregory; and a daughter, Elspeth. The bulk of the information in this section was about Elspeth's father, Edward, and specifically about his financial dealings. *Dealings* seemed to be the right word — as in wheeling and dealing. A great many pages from the corporate search site of the Commonwealth of Massachusetts showed that Edward Jantzen of Milford, Massachusetts, had been the president, treasurer, and clerk of eight corporations, all of which were now in dissolution, two voluntarily, six involuntarily. The companies had had names like Jantzen Just Enterprises and Jan-Go Corporation; I couldn't begin to guess what kinds of businesses they'd been. Next came UCC Public Search results, also provided by the web site of the Secretary of State. What I knew about UCC filings was that the letters stood for Uniform Commercial Code and that the filings had something to do with loans secured by borrowers' property. In any case, Jantzen, Edward, of Milford MA, appeared four times as a debtor. Two of the "secured parties," presumably the issuers of loans, were local banks. For the other two filings, the secured party was a loan company in Oklahoma. For all I knew, billionaires were always organizing and dissolving one-person corporations and practically lived to be listed as debtors to Oklahoma loan companies. Still, the impression I had was of small-time transactions and petty failure.

The final section consisted of copies of articles that Elspeth had published. Like me, she was a dog writer, and she'd published in some of the same magazines I had, including *Dog's Life*. Disgusting though it may sound, fleas are the bread and butter of dog writing. Consequently, like the rest of us, Elspeth had written on that pestiferous topic. She'd also done the inevitable breed profiles ("Meet the Nova Scotia Duck Tolling Retriever!"), the articles about protecting dogs from summer heat, and the comparisons of popular brands of dog food. I'd seen her pieces before, but having written on the same topics, I'd never read her presentations of what was bound to be the same material.

I leafed through the copies in the dossier until I came upon a copy of an article that had appeared in a newsletter about dog health published by an obscure veterinary school about four years earlier. There are zillions of dog publications; no one reads all of them. I'd never heard of this one. Anyway, I began actually to read the article because the subject surprised me. Elspeth's dogs were well-mannered pets, but she'd never shown them in obedience. Furthermore, I'd never heard her express any interest in obedience trials, formal obedience training, or, indeed, dog training in any form. Yet this article was about the dos and don'ts of using food in dog training. The topic was not one on which I held any sort of monopoly; it was a popular subject. Still, it was my subject and not Elspeth's. So was the article, which had originally appeared in *Dog's Life* magazine. With *my* byline. Elspeth had changed the first sentence. Every reference to malamutes had become a reference to Irish terriers. But I know my own writing, and this work was mine. Elspeth had stolen it from me.

Chapter 26

On the evening of Tuesday, September 17, Steve went out to dinner with two fishing buddies of his, fellow veterinarians who were on the staff of Angell Memorial Animal Hospital and who kept trying to persuade him to sell his practice and join them there. After feeding dinner to the dogs and then to myself, I decided to quit putting off the task of reading Elspeth's manuscript, which had been sitting in my office for four days. By now, Mac had probably mailed his blurb to Elspeth's editor. Of course, he had the advantage of not intending to read the book at all before generating a couple of quotable sentences of persuasive praise. *Highly recommended! Essential for everyone who wants to raise kind children!* His blurb would be followed by its truly essential components, namely, Mac's full name and the titles of his books.

As an antidote to my cynicism, I went to the third floor and got Sammy the puppy, and turned him loose in my kitchen. To the general public and to many pet owners, *puppy* means a very young pup, a ball of fluff, but in the parlance of the Dog Fancy, puppies are puppies until they're eighteen months old, long after they've grown to adult size. Sammy, who'd turn one year old this coming winter, wasn't yet as big as Rowdy, but was nonetheless a big dog, albeit a big dog with a ball-of-fluff brain. To encourage Sammy to play with actual dog toys rather than with objects that he'd happily redefine as such, I confined him to the kitchen by shutting all its doors and got out a couple of big black Kong toys, a fleece dinosaur, and, his favorite plaything, an eerily naturalistic stuffed squirrel that looked realistically dead. Ignoring the toys, Sammy plunged his head into Rowdy and Kimi's big water bowl, filled his mouth with water, and galloped across the floor while opening his jaws and shaking off the water that clung to his face. Having drenched the tile, he grabbed the squirrel, tossed it, and pounced. Cured of cynicism, I opened the manila envelope that Elspeth had left, extracted the two manuscripts it contained, and took a seat at the kitchen table.

What Elspeth had called her "book" was a children's book with a companion volume for parents and teachers. Until I examined the manuscripts, I knew nothing about the material except its theme: kindness. I began with

222

the children's book. Centered in the middle of the first page was the title: *The Story of Zazar.* With a sense of disbelief, I turned to the first page of text, where I discovered that the eponymous Zazar was, indeed, a juvenile elephant. The following pages explained that little Zazar lived in a city of animals, where he was friends with a monkey and with a little old lady. The city wasn't called Celesteville, and the monkey wasn't named Zephir.

"Even so!" I said aloud. "Outrageous! How could anyone be so stupid?"

What on earth kind of blurb did Elspeth expect me to write? *A must-read for fans of intellectual property theft!* I could go on to say that I eagerly awaited Elspeth's next work, *Zinnie the Boo.* But Elspeth had a publisher. What kind of publishing house had accepted stolen goods? In search of an answer, I shook the manila envelope, and out fell a note of thanks from Elspeth that contained the name of her editor and her publisher, together with an E-mail address and a mailing address in North Dakota. Neither the publisher nor the town in North Dakota was familiar to me. Still, the lowliest clerk at the smallest of small presses should have recognized one of the most famous characters in children's literature. Aha! Maybe the North Dakota outfit was a vanity press, a company that authors paid to get their books in print. Maybe the editor in North Dakota had cashed Elspeth's check without bothering to read about Zazar.

"But what about me?" I asked Sammy. "What about *me?* Did she think I was going to put *my* name on the cover of this ridiculous piece of damned larceny? I am insulted!"

Sammy sank his teeth into his squirrel and shook it vigorously.

On the off chance that Mac hadn't yet mailed or E-mailed his quotable injunction to buy Elspeth's book, I tried to call him, but got his and Judith's answering machine. Feeling uneasy about leaving a voice message about Elspeth's having stolen Babar, I went to my computer and E-mailed Mac a brief and remarkably tactful warning. I said that the elephant in her book bore what I at least found to be a disconcerting resemblance to Babar. I then E-mailed Elspeth a diplomatic and constructive message in which I pointed out that Zazar was likely to remind readers of Babar and suggested that she consider changing the character's name and species.

Elspeth Jantzen never received my E-mail. As I subsequently worked it out, she must have been killed at about the same time I sent the message, which is to say, at around nine-thirty on Tuesday night. The police were never able to discover exactly what Elspeth was doing out of doors when the assailant struck. Like every other woman in

Greater Boston, she'd certainly heard and read countless warnings not to go outside alone after dark. I suspect that she felt safe in her low-crime neighborhood, a section of Belmont just off one of the main drags, not a pricey locality like Belmont Hill, but a pleasant, middle-class area that I remembered from once having dropped off a book she'd let me borrow. Police speculated that she'd been dashing out to her car for a library book that she'd checked out earlier that day and left on the front seat. At any rate, when her landlord found Elspeth's body on Wednesday morning, her purse was still in her apartment, she wasn't wearing a jacket, and the library book was in her car. The cause of her death was blunt trauma to the head.

But I didn't even learn of Elspeth's murder until late on Wednesday afternoon. By the time her landlord found her body, the morning papers were being delivered, so there was nothing in the newspaper or on NPR's *Morning Edition*, and after Steve left for his clinic, I followed my daily routine of dog chores, housework, and writing. At about three in the afternoon, a terrific and totally unexpected wedding present was delivered: a beautiful picnic table from L.L.Bean sent to us by Steve's uncle Leon. Once I'd opened the package and seen its contents, I dragged the box out the side door and down the steps to the fenced yard, where the table would go, and like a kid with a new toy, unpacked and assembled the table. The weather was clear and warm. Feeling wifely, I planned a meal of pasta and salad to be eaten at the new table, ran out for ingredients, and thus didn't check my E-mail for a practically unprecedented length of time.

The news of Elspeth's murder reached me on Dogwriters-L. Elspeth had been planning to attend the annual conference of the Cat Writers Association, not only because she occasionally wrote about cats, but because the Dog Writers Association of America cosponsors the event with the CWA. This year's conference was to be held in Houston, Texas, in November, and one of the organizers had placed a call to Elspeth to ask her to fill in for a scheduled panelist who'd just cancelled. Anyway, the cat-writing conference organizer had spoken to a brother of Elspeth's, who'd answered her phone. After that, the news had spread to Dogwriters-L. The post announcing Elspeth's murder contained no details — it said only that she had been killed — and the responses to the original post were expressions of shock and horror, together with requests for the names and addresses of relatives who should receive condolences. Although I still thought that Elspeth had been wrong to do a book about an elephant named Zazar, I felt guilty about the E-mail

I'd sent to Mac and hastily sent him a message saying only that Elspeth had been murdered.

As I chopped tomatoes, fresh basil, and mozzarella, and washed salad greens, I kept switching the radio back and forth between WBZ, an AM news station, and WBUR, Boston's NPR news station. I first caught the story about Elspeth's murder on one of WBUR's news summaries. The announcer reported that the killer responsible for the deaths of two women in Cambridge and one woman in Brookline had struck for the fourth time. The victim, Elspeth Jantzen, had been killed outside her home in Belmont the previous evening. On WBZ, a reporter interviewed a gravel-voiced Belmont police spokesperson who gave brief answers. The police were cooperating fully with all authorities and agencies charged with investigating the serial homicides. Yes, the perpetrator had again used a blunt instrument to deliver a crushing blow to the head. Yes, the medical examiner had identified an injection site on the body, but the results of the autopsy were not yet available.

In between feeding my dogs and Steve's, and giving all five their turns in the yard, I finished dinner preparations and spent a little time searching the web. While the dogs were outdoors, I kept watch over the new picnic table, which I was determined that Steve and

I would get to enjoy this one time before it got marked by dogs and had to be washed. Far more than the previous murders and more than my own Saturday-night scare, Elspeth's murder frightened me in a personal way. I had known her; on Friday, she'd sat at my kitchen table. We'd been members of the same profession. We'd had acquaintances in common. Ordinarily, it would never have occurred to me to lock the wooden gate in the fence that led to the driveway. Now, while I scooped up after the dogs and carried out a tablecloth, plates, and silverware, I not only kept that gate locked but kept India at my side as I went in and out. Although the German shepherd dog is a popular choice for protection work, India's education had consisted of training for the American Kennel Club obedience ring, where anything even remotely like protective or aggressive behavior would have been highly unwelcome. Good girl that India was, she excelled in obedience. In daily life, she showed her breed's normal desire to watch out for her owner and his belongings, but she'd never been taught or even encouraged to protect Steve, never mind me. Still, I trusted India to inform me if a stranger approached the gate, and her strong, intelligent presence gave me the welcome sense of having a powerful ally. Also, unlike my own malamutes and Sammy the pup, India could be relied on to keep her jaws and her bodily fluids off the new table, and she wasn't a food thief. If anything, she did her job too well to suit me. Sensing my need, she glued herself to my side, gazed at my face, and cocked her head to listen for sounds of threat. I was used to Rowdy and Kimi, who never worried about anything because they assumed that if trouble arose, a fight would ensue, and they'd win. Period. They made the same flattering assumption about the inevitability of my own victory in all possible situations.

When Steve got home, I was putting candles in wedding-present candleholders. He'd never looked better, and I'd never been happier to see him. My love for him really had been of the at-first-sight variety and was as wholehearted as my love for my dogs. I'd often told him just that. How many men would have been pleased to hear such a sentiment? Damn few. A man like that was worth marrying. Anyway, I threw my arms around him, clung to him, and felt myself tremble.

"I heard about Elspeth Jantzen," he said softly. "You should've called me."

"I'm okay."

"Ms. Malamute." Steve understood the limitations of words and the power of touch; he was, after all, a vet. He held me as if he held a dog in pain, as if he had the rest of his life to keep me in his arms, as, in a sense, he did.

Finally, I said, "I've made dinner. Your uncle Leon sent us a picnic table from L.L.Bean. It's in the yard. I thought we'd eat out there. I need to keep doing normal things. We can eat whenever you want. No rush. I've fed all the dogs, and they've all been out."

"I'll open a bottle of wine," he said as he belatedly greeted the faithful India.

A half hour later we were where I'd envisioned us, seated across from each other at the new picnic table eating linguine with fresh tomatoes, basil, olive oil, and mozzarella, the pasta accompanied by a green salad and French bread. The wholesomeness of the food felt defiantly at odds with the murders of people I'd known. India had settled herself under the table. In her own dignified way, she was affectionate, but she wasn't cuddly. With some hesitation, I'd slipped my toes under her, and she was tolerating my need to draw on her warmth and strength. To avoid having the new floodlights transform the evening into an Alaskan summer, we'd turned off the lights in the side yard and were dining, as planned, by candlelight.

"You want to talk?" Steve's question was genuine. Still, I could hear Rita's influence in it. She'd been a good friend to Steve throughout his divorce and during the early stages of our reunion. "You don't have to," he added.

Mindful of talks I'd had with Rita, instead of pouring out everything on my mind the second he walked into the house, I'd given him a chance to make the transition from work to home. Now, we'd each had a glass of wine, and I did need to talk and to hear what Steve had to say. "When Elspeth was here on Friday," I began, "she told me she'd had an affair with Mac."

"You told me. A one-night stand."

"It really couldn't have been more than that. It was at some conference a long time ago. At that bookstore where Mac and I did our talks, he didn't remember her at all. I was right next to him, and I could tell. I'm sure that Elspeth didn't look even vaguely familiar to him."

"They kept the lights out. Or he was drunk, and they kept the lights out." His face a bit stiff, he added, "You sure Mac's never come on to you?"

"Never. With me, he's brotherly. Collegial."

"Any chance Elspeth was lying? Or imagining things?"

"She imagined that a one-night stand was something more than that. And she imagined that Mac would remember her. And naturally, she was insulted that he obviously had no idea that he'd ever seen her before. She was furious. Anyway, in a sort of half-joking way, or what I assumed was a joking way, she said that Mac knew Victoria Trotter and maybe the other victims, too. *Knew* in the Biblical sense. And that maybe he'd murdered them all."

"You're sure she wasn't serious?"

"I didn't take her seriously. And Mac? I know Mac. We both do. Steve, you've read those profiles of serial killers. Mac doesn't even begin to fit the picture. He's anything but some isolated, frustrated daydreamer. He's not depressed. He has a good opinion of himself, admittedly, but he's not grandiose in the psychiatric sense. His books are successful. *He's* successful. He has a very successful wife and two grown children. Even if he knew all the victims and slept with all of them, it's impossible to see Mac as some sort of deranged human male insect who devours his sex partners. And years afterward?" I turned my hands palms up and gave a little laugh. "Mac as a homicidal sex fiend? The whole idea is a bad joke." I paused. "But before you got home, I did check on the web for a minute, and this is freaking me out. Bonny Carr had a web site, and Mac is quoted on it. Some kind of endorsement of her methods. I forget exactly. That doesn't necessarily mean that he'd ever met Bonny. He's not discriminating about what he endorses. Maybe she E-mailed him, he visited her web site, and he E-mailed back what's there. Now *that* sounds like Mac."

Steve refilled our glasses. "Kevin said that

Victoria Trotter had a lot of men in her life. Mac could've been one of them."

"Victoria? With Judith at home?"

"It doesn't have to work that way." He didn't mention his ex-wife, Anita, one of whose lovers had looked like a toad, or so Steve had once confided to Rita. "There was Elspeth. And what we know is that this is a guy who knew a lot of women who've died."

"Who've been murdered."

"At The Wordsmythe. At your launch party. Mac was talking to Claire, and . . . you remember Claire? She's a veterinarian. Claire Langceil. Skinny blond."

"Actually, I ran into her in the Square the other day. She and her husband are going to be at dinner at Mac and Judith's this Saturday. They're friends of Mac and Judith's."

Steve said, "I wish we weren't going."

"We could get struck down by the flu. But you were starting to say —"

"Mac knew Victoria Trotter. Elspeth. And maybe Bonny Carr."

"So did I."

"You know him, too."

"Not the way they knew him! Or may have?"

"Good," Steve said. "Keep it that way."

Chapter 27

It's one thing for a man to have other women, but quite another for him to kill them off. By the time Steve and I were halfway to Mac and Judith's house in Lexington on Saturday evening, I wished that we'd excused ourselves by pleading illness. I almost wished that one of us would actually begin to throw up.

"We don't *have* to do this," said Steve, who was reluctantly at the wheel of what he considered to be my ill-gotten Blazer, which we'd chosen because it hadn't yet acquired the full doggy miasma and ineradicable coating of dog hair so notable in Steve's van. Dog vehicles are like pieces of meat: They take a while to ripen to gaminess.

"We do," I said. "It's too late to cancel, and each of us is a worse liar than the other."

Our knowledge and suspicions about Mac's infidelities might've made the occasion something of a minor social challenge. What made the prospect of the dinner almost intolerable wasn't just the speculation we'd engaged in immediately after Elspeth's murder, but new information yielded by the autopsy, which was that Elspeth had been injected with a drug familiar to all veterinarians and to many dog owners: acepromazine. An old-time and still popular veterinary sedative, ace was so widely used that dog breeders and show types shifted the word's grammatical gears from noun to verb, and routinely spoke of "acing" dogs. In effect, its presence in Elspeth's body proclaimed her death to be a dog murder.

I continued. "What do you want me to do? Call now and say, 'Sorry to cancel at the last second, Judith, but we think that your husband's been murdering his mistresses'? Steve, when I say it to *you*, it sounds preposterous. I'm not about to say it to *Judith*, and if I make up some excuse now, that one's going to hang in the air. I am not a good liar!"

"We could've sent E-mail. We should've cancelled before."

"But we didn't. We've been over this! We don't know anything! We just wonder. On the basis of freakish ideas we're going to shun someone who's been generous to me? Mac has done more to help me promote my book than everyone else combined, and Judith and Olivia have been perfectly nice to me. *And* Ian is doing the music for our wedding. *And*

Olivia and Ian are going to be at dinner. *And it's your next left!*"

Our spat was still going on two minutes later when Steve parked in a wide area at the end of Mac and Judith's long driveway. Their house, which I'd visited before, sat in the middle of a large wooded lot. Like my house, this one had three stories. Alas for Steve and me, there ended the resemblance. This place had lots of floor-to-ceiling windows, exposed beams, cozy balconies, and spacious decks.

"Shit," he said.

"We don't want to live in Lexington, anyway, and if this place were in Cambridge, it would go for four million plus."

"That's not what I meant."

"Steve, look. I wish we'd begged off, too. I'm sorry. We'll get through it and leave early."

As we were about to get out of the car, a silver Volvo station wagon pulled in next to us, and out of the passenger seat popped Claire Langceil, the skinny, wiry, wire-haired blond veterinarian who'd been at the launch party at The Wordsmythe. With relief, I said, "Claire's here. You like her. And she never shuts up, so we won't have to say anything at all."

Before Steve had opened his door, Claire was rapping on the glass, smiling brightly, and saying, obviously to him, "Hey, you're here!" Even after I was out of the car, Claire continued to address Steve. "Daniel and Gus are with me." She nodded at a man and a boy who'd also emerged from the Volvo. "Daniel loves Judith's cooking." Claire somehow sounded as if she were revealing a character fault.

"Hi," I said to the man and the boy. "I'm Holly Winter. And this is Steve Delaney."

"Daniel Langceil." The man shook hands with me and then with Steve. Daniel was short and round-faced, with curly brown hair, dark eyes, and an air of warmth and amiability.

"And Gus the Great!" Claire exclaimed.

Gus had curls, lighter than Daniel's and darker than Claire's. He had his father's dark eyes and a shy manner that he hadn't inherited from his mother.

"Gus the Great!" Claire repeated.

Although Claire's grand epithet for her son was neither witty nor funny, Steve and I compliantly responded to Claire's expectations by looking as if we found it clever and hilarious. Daniel's expression was unreadable. Gus looked miserable.

"Hi, Gus," Steve said quietly. "You want to go into the house now?" Accustomed to soothing nervous animals, Steve was wonderfully casual. The boy's face brightened. He silently moved to Steve's left and walked toward the entryway in such perfect heel position that Steve would have been justified in popping a treat into the child's mouth and saying, "Good Gus!" Steve did no such thing, of course; his kindness consisted of allowing Gus to meld with the group instead of finding himself singled out.

The rest of us tagged along. The house had a lovely front entrance. Glass panels framed a door made of teak and adorned with a brass knocker and a brass handle, both polished with Gilbertian care. Claire rang the bell, rapped the knocker, and then pressed her face against one of the glass panels and tapped eagerly. Dog person that I am, I assumed that she was in a desperate hurry to empty her bladder. When Mac opened the door, however, she didn't rush past him, but stayed with the rest of us. As we entered, Ian returned from walking Uli. The sweet old Bernese gave a soft woof and wagged his tail.

The foyer was a long, wide landing with a flight of stairs on the left that led down to the ground floor, where, as I knew from previous visits, Mac had his office. Four or five years earlier, he'd sold his prosperous veterinary clinic to a national corporation. By agreement, after the sale, Mac had continued to see a few old dogs and cats that he'd treated throughout their lives, but his one-man, home-based practice otherwise focused exclusively on behavioral consultations. Also, of course, he wrote articles and books.

Anyway, we didn't go down to Mac's office, but ascended the flight of stairs on the right, which led to the main floor of the house. Judith appeared and began to welcome everyone. As always, Mac radiated vigor. Judith was infinitely elegant and slimmer than ever in a loose black top over close-fitting black pants. Hearing Ian's voice behind me, I turned to see that he was murmuring to Uli as he gently supported the dog's hindquarters to help the old fellow climb the stairs. Claire, obviously watching, too, announced, "Time for a puppy, Judith!"

Judith's back was turned, not, I should add, in reaction to Claire's remark. Rather, our hostess was leading the way to the living room, which had more than enough square footage to accommodate a couple of showrings. There was a fireplace at one end. At the other, next to a wall of glass, was the dinner table. The furniture was all shiny wood and Scandinavian fabric. Oil paintings depicted bright, life-size poppies, peonies, and nasturtiums. Nothing in the room even began to hint at animals. There wasn't a cat or a birdcage or a fish tank anywhere. I couldn't even see a single strand of pet hair.

Seated on one of the two couches that flanked the fireplace was a man of thirty or thirty-five who looked so amazingly like Judith that I assumed he must be a close relative of hers. A nephew? Unless Mac was

Judith's second husband and this was a son from her first marriage? To my surprise, however, when Olivia appeared with a tray of appetizers, she introduced the man as her husband, John. To avoid mystification, let me state that John Berkowitz did not turn out to be some love child of Judith's whom Olivia had married without knowing that he was her half brother. Although John was entirely unrelated to Judith, he nonetheless had his mother-in-law's prominent cheekbones, blue eyes, and full lips. His individual features were Judith's, as was his overall look. He even had a manly version of Judith's lean elegance.

Seeing my startled expression, Olivia laughed and said, "It's okay! Everyone has the same reaction. It's how we met. We were at a party, and I saw John, and I said, 'Wow! You look so much like my mother!' But we checked it out. We're not even distant relatives."

I'd have felt comparatively relieved to learn that they were. In the world of purebred dogs, "line breeding," as it's called, is so common that breeders need a special term, *outcross,* for the mating of *unrelated* animals. By comparison with close line breedings — father to daughter, son to mother, brother to sister — a cousin-to-cousin mating of human beings would've struck me as unremarkable. But show dogs don't usually choose their own mates. And if they did, the females wouldn't knowingly, deliberately, and perversely go around picking studs who looked uncannily like their own mothers!

No one voiced any additional remarks about John's appearance, in part because we were busy taking seats, accepting Mac's offer of drinks, and devoting ourselves to the appetizers that Olivia had placed on the low table between the couches. The hors d'oeuvres weren't the usual raw vegetables and dips or selections of cheese and crackers, but slices of smoked salmon rolled around arugula and cream cheese, long strips of peeled cucumber wrapped around seafood, miniature crispy brown potato pancakes, and other such delicacies.

"Incredible!" I said to Judith.

"Thank you," said Judith, "but Olivia deserves half the credit. We've always cooked together."

"I'm just the prep cook," Olivia said. "Mom is the head chef."

Claire said, "I have yet to discover anything that Judith doesn't do perfectly."

Judith laughed. "It's so seldom that anyone asks me to sing." To Steve and me she said, "Ian did not inherit his talent from me. I'm tuneless."

So far, except for the small matter of Olivia's having more or less married her mother, the evening was far less awkward than I'd feared. Indeed, if viewed by a stranger, the scene could have been designed to illustrate hospitality and domesticity. A fire burned in the fireplace. Seated on the floor by the hearth, Ian tossed in a fresh log and then returned to stroking Uli, who dozed next to him. On one couch were Mac, Claire, Steve, and I, with little Gus between us; on the other couch were John, Olivia, Judith, and Claire's husband, Daniel. With the possible exception of Ian, we'd have seemed an attractive, appealing group. Mac had poured liberal drinks for everyone except Gus, of course, and me — I'd lost the coin toss for designated driver. Still, a stranger might have assumed that my mineral water was gin or vodka. An old-fashioned observer might have noted that the numbers were uneven: Ian was not part of a couple. What's more, in contrast to everyone else, Ian looked vaguely unhealthy. His skin was pale, and, as I'd noticed at the bookstore when Mac and I had given our talks, his pale blue eyes seemed somehow to make him look watery, even gelatinous. I had a ludicrous vision of him as a poached egg in aspic.

Chapter 28

I kept the unflattering image of Ian to myself. In fact, I remained unusually quiet over drinks. Judith and Olivia kept excusing themselves to check on dinner. At Judith's request, Ian brought in an armful of logs for the fire. John Berkowitz talked with Ian about a Bach concert they'd both attended. John shyly admitted that he played the piano a little. The three veterinarians, Steve, Mac, and Claire, discussed animals only as ordinary pet owners might have done. Mac asked Steve about Sammy, and Claire again advised Judith to get a puppy. "If Uli's mind starts to go," Claire said, "it's going to be impossible. You need to get one soon. It doesn't have to be another Bernese. You could get anything."

Neither Mac nor Judith responded. Miraculously, I didn't, either. Real dog person that I am, I tend to hand out unsolicited advice about all things dog on all possible occasions, but Judith didn't need my advice. The main reason that I kept silent, though, was my certainty that if a veterinarian husband and his dog-person wife had one old dog, no other animals, and no plans to acquire any, there was bound to be a reason, and that reason was bound to be none of my business.

An awkward lull followed Claire's remarks, but lasted for only a few seconds. Judith restored animation to the party by announcing that dinner was ready. As all of us rose, it became apparent that Claire, Daniel, and Gus were regular guests of Mac and Judith's and that the usual routine was for Gus to watch a video while the adults ate. Over Gus's objection that he wanted to stay with Steve and Judith's offer to set a place for him, Claire led him off. When she returned, the rest of us had taken our seats at the table near the big windows. Mac sat at the head of the table, with Judith at the other end. I was on Mac's right, and Ian was on my right, with John Berkowitz between Ian and Judith. To Mac's left was Olivia, then an empty seat for Claire, and then, to Judith's right, Steve. The table was set with bright place mats and napkins. Rita had educated me to recognize the good china and silver as such. The centerpiece combined flowers with candles. There were no place cards; rather, Judith had directed us to our places.

Mac, with typical warmth and conviviality, opened two bottles of wine and had just finished pouring it when Claire appeared, glanced around, and said playfully, "Olivia, you're in my seat!"

Olivia matched the teasing tone. "Next to Daddy is *my* seat. You're stuck with me, but you get to sit next to Steve."

To no one's evident surprise, Claire executed a nimble little dance and sang the chorus of that old song called "Daddy's Little Girl." Her voice was pretty good. Everyone laughed. When she'd finished the performance, she took the place that Judith had meant for her. If the table had been mine, I'd have been tempted to remove the chair and feed her a dinner of moldy leftovers in a dog bowl on the kitchen floor. Judith, however, displayed great sangfroid in serving Claire the same first course that she and Olivia had prepared for the group, namely, individual ramekins of truffle flan in Parmesan broth. A truffle custard in cheese soup might not sound like something to die for, but I spoke the truth when I said, "Judith, one reason I try to be good in this lifetime is that if I get to heaven, the food will taste exactly like this."

"I copied it from a restaurant," Judith said. "But thank you."

"Judith is amazing," her husband said. "She throws these things together in no time."

Olivia and Ian exchanged glances.

"Right," Olivia said. "No time at all. It also

took her no time to make Ian's special food."

Only then did I notice that Ian's ramekin contained something other than the flan.

"Fruit salad," Judith said. "That really did take no time."

"Ian is a vegan," Claire said. Although her voice carried no hint of ridicule, the bare statement somehow sounded like a taunt chanted in a schoolyard. "He lives on seeds and nuts."

"With the occasional tuber and root thrown in," Ian said mildly.

"Daniel," Claire said, "would you go check on Gus?"

Daniel excused himself and left the room.

"Now we can tell lawyer jokes," his wife said. "Only kidding." To me, she said, "He's a lawyer. Obviously."

I wondered whether she knew that Steve's vile ex-wife, Anita, was also a lawyer, albeit a disbarred one.

Soon after Daniel returned, Judith and Olivia cleared the table. Steve and I offered to help, but Judith and Olivia seemed to prefer to work as a team. They soon served the main course, which consisted of a leg of lamb, a fricassee of wild mushrooms, a fancy version of mashed potatoes, and, as I was disconcerted to learn, brussels sprouts. I hate the damned things. Rather, I'd always hated them until I tasted these, which were chopped into a sort of puree and were bright green, buttery, and in all other respects, entirely unlike the smelly little cabbages I'd avoided throughout my life. Mac made a show of playing the carving knife on a sharpening steel and did a capable job of carving the lamb. As probably goes without saying, Judith once again unobtrusively served Ian a special meal.

"The mushrooms are from the store," Olivia said. "They're wild, but you can relax. We didn't gather them ourselves and pick poisonous ones by accident."

It was, I think, Olivia's casual reference to unnatural death that triggered the subsequent discussion of the serial killings. The topic would have arisen anyway; everyone in Massachusetts was obsessed with the murders. With three veterinarians at the dinner table, the explicitly veterinary nature of the crimes made the subject inevitable. In any case, the mention of mushrooms somehow led to a conversation about the pharmaceuticals injected into the victims.

"Acepromazine was an odd choice," Claire said. "Injectable. Mac? Steve? Would you ever send a client home with it?"

Steve said, "Tablets."

There followed a technical exchange about the risks and benefits of a variety of veterinary tranquilizers, including ace, which emerged as safer for some breeds than for others. All three vets agreed that these days, the choice of anti-anxiety agents was so wide that they had the ability to prescribe on a case-by-case basis, selecting the best drug for each individual dog. Similarly, the three agreed on the importance of using behavioral interventions as well as medications.

"The same goes for amitriptyline," Mac said. "I'll tell you when I used to prescribe that — before Prozac became generic. If I had a client who couldn't afford Prozac or didn't want to pay for it, we'd give amitriptyline a try. It was cheap."

Everyone agreed, of course, that insulin was another matter; just as people with diabetes tested and injected themselves, so, too, did owners monitor and manage the disease in diabetic pets.

Ian listened eagerly and eventually asked, "So, where were they injected?"

"Ian, that's ghoulish!" Olivia said. "What does it matter? And these poor women were already dead. The point is that it was a creepy thing to do. Never mind anything else! Except the creepiest thing of all, which is that it's getting so veterinary."

"I'm curious," her brother told her. "In the arm?"

"Ian, enough," Mac said. "No one wants to dwell on gruesome details. And you're forgetting that these poor women, some of them, weren't strangers. Holly and I were blurbing a book that Elspeth What's-her-name had just written."

I didn't know what to make of the statement. Even Mac, I thought, wouldn't stoop to blurbing a plagiarized book. Maybe he'd missed the E-mail I'd sent him after I'd read about Zazar and before I'd learned of Elspeth's murder. Or maybe he was telling a pointless lie? I said nothing. With Elspeth dead, what did it matter whether I had or hadn't intended to have my name on the cover of her book?

"The scarlet lady," Ian said. "At the bookstore."

Olivia came down hard on her brother. "Ian, what a way to talk about someone who's just been murdered!"

"She was all red. Red hair, red clothes, red face. All I'm doing is saying what she looked like."

"No, you are not, and you know you're not. And it's not exactly as if you're in a position to criticize other people for the way they dress. You spend most of your life —" Olivia caught herself. To Steve and me, she said, "Sorry! I've scared you about your wedding. Ian does own a tux. He'll be perfectly presentable."

Whether deliberately or accidentally, Olivia thus shifted the conversation from murder to music, and the dinner party regained its normal atmosphere. As we finished the main course and ate the salad that was served after it, everyone joined in a discussion of Ian's music and the musical choices we needed to make for our wedding. Daniel was an especially helpful contributor. Claire excused herself twice to check on Gus, and when she was present, limited herself to humming snatches of songs that were mentioned. By the time we'd finished the salad, the idea had arisen that instead of having dessert at the dinner table, we'd move back to the opposite end of the room for live music.

The party dispersed. Daniel and Steve helped Ian to carry in his instruments. Mac added logs to the fire and set out liquors and glasses for after-dinner drinks. Claire took a seat on one of the couches near the fire. Meanwhile, I insisted on helping Olivia to clear the table and load the dishwasher, and Judith put together a chocolate soufflé. As the three of us did traditional women's work, we talked traditional women's talk about weddings, especially Olivia's and mine. Once the soufflé was in the oven, Olivia decided that I just had to see her wedding gown, which turned out to be stored at her parents' house. Consequently, Olivia, Judith, and I started upstairs to the top floor, where I'd never been before. With a look of happy expectation, Uli trailed after us.

"Oh, dear," Judith said, "Uli sometimes

forgets that stairs are a problem for him these days."

As Ian had done earlier, she supported the old dog's hindquarters and spoke encouragingly as she helped him up the stairs. "My best boy," she murmured. "You can do it! I know you can. Good boy!"

Impatient to show off her gown, Olivia raced up and said, "Mommy, Uli really isn't interested. Let him stay downstairs."

"He wants to be with me," Judith said gently. "All he wants is to be with me. It's not too much for him to ask." To me, she said, "He's on every old-dog drug there is. He's not in any pain."

"I'm sure he's not." Indeed, Uli wore a contented expression and softly wagged his white-tipped tail.

The flight of stairs ended at a spacious landing. Two doors were closed, and three stood open. Pointing toward one of the open doors, Olivia said, "Mommy's study. People always want to see where she writes."

Before I had a chance to get more than a glimpse of a computer sitting on a paper-laden desk, Olivia rushed into another room and announced, "Mommy's bedroom. My gown is here because she has tons of closet space."

It seemed to me that the whole bedroom had tons of space. It was furnished with a king-size bed, two night stands, two dressers, a small easy chair, and a large dog bed that looked unused. Olivia opened a door to reveal a walk-in closet. "Wouldn't you die for all this room?" Olivia exclaimed. "Mommy is so lucky."

Looking embarrassed, Judith said, "Uli and I both snore, and I have insomnia. And Uli gets restless at five in the morning. Mac can't sleep through the noise."

The awkward topic of the separate sleeping arrangements ended there. Olivia emerged from the closet with what she told me was a Vera Wang gown. It was elaborate and lovely. I took care to exclaim admiringly about it. Then the three of us and Uli made our way downstairs. Judith and I helped Uli, whose progress was slow. As I held him, I noticed how extraordinarily clean he was. His coat felt as if he'd just been bathed and groomed, and he had not a trace of the old-dog odor that's sometimes impossible to eradicate.

When we reached the main floor, Judith and Olivia went to the kitchen, and I joined everyone else by the fireplace. Arrayed near it were a guitar, a violin, and a keyboard connected to a big speaker. In my absence, the others had been talking about our wedding music. Specifically, although neither Steve nor I was a particular fan of classical music, we'd felt obliged to have a solemn, highbrow accompaniment for the service. Ian had a better idea. "Why get married to music you don't love? How'd you feel about jazz guitar?"

Steve and I looked blank.

Instead of regaling us with words, Ian picked up his guitar and began to play a medley of 1930s jazz songs. The sound was anything but solemn, and far more hot than highbrow. I was crazy about it. Steve squeezed my hand. Watching our faces, Ian smiled and began what it took me a second to recognize as the Wedding March.

By then, Judith and Olivia were serving the chocolate soufflé and pouring coffee. Daniel moved to the keyboard, and he and Ian switched to music we might want at the reception, mainly country and old Motown. Daniel had been modest about his own talent, but he seemed to have no difficulty in following Ian, and they both played requests. Although Ian assured us that he'd have a great female vocalist with him, I'd liked his singing on his CDs, and when he and Daniel sang, they sounded good to me. Steve asked for and got "My Girl." The chocolate soufflé, the upbeat music, and Steve's flattery took me out of myself, and I almost lost my discomfort and suspicion until Steve, as seduced as I was, made the faux pas of requesting "Your Cheatin' Heart." I could feel my cheeks turn the color of the flames in the fireplace. Fortunately, Ian and Daniel immediately began to play the song, and I practically buried my face in my plate as I scraped up the last of the chocolate.

When the song finally ended, I said, "We wondered about dog songs, but they're probably too corny for you."

Ian's response was sweet. "Nothing's too corny for me. And I love dogs." With that, he began a series of amazing guitar improvisations on "Hound Dog," "Hot Diggity Dog," and a few other sappy songs rendered unsappy by his good-humored brilliance.

When he finished, Mac said, "Play your mother's song."

" 'Uli's Tune,' " Judith said. "It's not mine. It's Uli's."

The instrumental was strong and melodic, with a theme that began simply and developed richly. It ended with soft, sad notes. Judith watched her old dog throughout it. At the end, she said, "My two good boys. Ian, thank you."

If Claire had yet again nagged Judith about getting a puppy, I'd have wanted to throttle her. As it was, she said nothing. Instead of sitting in respectful silence, however, she got up and walked over to Uli, who was lying at Judith's feet. Bending down, Claire stroked the dog's head.

"Claire, take your hands off Uli," Judith told her. "I need you to get your hands off my dog."

Chapter 29

"Mac and Judith have separate bedrooms," I said to Steve as I drove us home. "She sleeps in the master bedroom."

"And you found out where Mac sleeps, why he sleeps there, whether John and Olivia have separate rooms, what kind of birth control, if any, they use, and a whole lot of other intimate details of everyone else's life?"

"Olivia stores her wedding gown in a walk-in closet in what she calls 'Mommy's room.' After Olivia said that, Judith looked embarrassed, and she said that she and Uli snore, and she has insomnia, and Uli gets restless in the morning and wakes Mac up. I didn't pry. Besides, lots of couples have separate rooms. It doesn't have to mean anything."

"Don't let it give you any ideas."

"I won't. And if all five dogs and I snored all night in your ears, it wouldn't bother you. Speaking of which, Mac is the least animal-oriented veterinarian I've ever known. I've known a few who didn't have animals because they didn't have time to take care of them, but that's always been temporary, and it's pretty rare. Time isn't an issue with Mac or Judith. With Mac, it's got to be a lack of interest. I find that pathological."

Steve laughed. "The Holly Winter One-Item Mental Health Assessment Instrument. If you don't have dogs, you're crazy."

"Exactly. Other than that, Steve, I have to admit that as I watched Mac, I was the one who felt crazy. Yes, he cheats on his wife. But Mac as a serial killer? He isn't isolated. He isn't depressed. He's warm, connected, sociable . . . and he's very successful. Also, he knows he's successful. He doesn't feel rejected or unrecognized or resentful. He's self-confident. He doesn't fit the profiles. But you know who does?"

"Ian. In some ways."

"Ian. I hate the thought."

"He's a genius. He's the real thing."

"Largely unrecognized as such. Somewhat withdrawn. Odd. Shy. No relationships with women, at least that I've heard of. Or with men, although I don't think he's gay."

"He gets along okay with his sister and his mother. He helps with Uli. No one else in the family did, that I saw."

"Not that I saw, either. Actually, both children seem very devoted to Judith. After all, Olivia practically married her mother! John looks so much like Judith! It is really weird.

But it's a compliment to Judith, I guess."

"Logically, that gives them a motive. Ian and Olivia."

"But wouldn't the logical target be Mac? He's the one who cheats on Judith."

"He's their father."

"That didn't stop Oedipus. But it might stop Olivia. And speaking of Olivia, she really cannot stand Claire. At the table, when Claire told her to move and started singing 'Daddy's Little Girl,' I'll bet that Olivia *felt* like killing her."

"What is it about Claire that you don't like?" Steve sounded genuinely puzzled.

"Her hostility. Her meanness to her perfectly nice husband. Her high-handedness. I could go on."

"I love you when you're catty."

"Veterinarians have special dispensation to be catty, and you practically never are," I said. "I love you anyway."

We were rescued from greater excesses by our arrival at home. As we walked to the door, Steve, who'd enjoyed Mac's generosity with wine and spirits, wrapped his arms around me and began kissing my neck. I was midway between giggles and rapture when the back door flew open to reveal Rita, who called hoarsely out, "Thank God you're home! Do you have any Valium?"

The floodlights gave us a clear view of her. Her eyes were swollen, and her nose was running. For a second, I stupidly wondered why she wanted Valium for the common cold. Then I heard her sob. In no time, Steve and I were holding her, leading her to the kitchen, asking her what was wrong, and offering everything from Ovaltine to tea to brandy. Just as canine instinct compels dogs to lick the wounds of their own valued pack members, so human instinct apparently drives us to force beverages on our injured loved ones.

Seated at the table, Rita blew her nose loudly and said, "Could one of you get Willie for me?"

Rita was normally the sort of genteel person who avoided blowing her nose in the presence of other people. If she had no choice, she performed the operation silently and unobtrusively. Furthermore, although she loved Willie and took great care of him, she typically sought comfort from human friends.

"I'll get him," Steve offered.

Rita handed him her key.

As he left, I said, "Rita, talk to me! You never take Valium or anything else. You believe in talking. I'm here!" Only then did I notice that Rita was trembling. "I'm getting you a blanket, and I'm going to make you some tea." I put the kettle on.

With a hint of her old spirit, Rita said, "I don't want tea. You and your English novels."

Dashing to my bedroom, I grabbed a soft fleece blanket. When I returned to the kitchen, Rita had her head on the table. I wrapped the blanket around her and gave her a hug. Her shoulders felt thin and brittle.

"I read *good* English novels," I said. "Would you rather have Ovaltine?"

She shook her head. Her hair was a mess. "I look awful," she said.

"You look upset."

Steve returned with Willie, who, for once, didn't bark at me or eye my ankles. Instead, he ran to Rita. She always kept him as perfectly groomed as she kept herself. As usual, his coat was freshly clipped. His eyes glowed, and he radiated energy. For style, you just can't beat the Scottish terrier. It is not, however, a mushy breed, and Willie was not a cuddly dog. Even now, he didn't lean against Rita or jump in her lap. Instead, he stood boldly before her with his little tail flying back and forth. Then he uttered a single bark. At Willie's display of bravery and good cheer, Rita again started to sob.

The kettle was boiling. I made sugary tea and put a cup of it in front of Rita. Then I took a seat next to her. Steve sat opposite us. He reached across the table and took her hand. "I'm not real talkative myself," he said. "You want me to leave?"

"Of course not!"

"Rita," I said, "please tell us what it is."

"Holly, I can't even say his name. All I want is Valium. Ativan. Xanax. Sonata. Anything! I just want to go to sleep. What I cannot endure right now is consciousness."

"You and Artie split up," I said.

"I have not even spoken to him, and God knows he never said anything to me that would ever have . . . oh, Holly, I just can't believe it. It's so grotesque! I just can't believe it. I am such a fool!"

Steve covered her hand with his. "Welcome to the human race."

Rita managed a hint of a smile. "You *married* Anita. At least I . . . except that I would've married him. I wanted to! I am too stupid to live." She finally took a sip of tea. "This is awful. Do you have any gin?"

"Wine," Steve suggested.

"Wine it is."

While Steve opened a bottle, Rita went to the bathroom and then returned with her face clean and damp. "I can't begin to tell you how glad I am to see both of you. I couldn't stand to have anyone else see me like this."

Steve had poured wine for all three of us. He handed Rita her glass. "Hey, we love you."

Rita raised her glass, and the three of us clinked. "In dogs we trust," she said, "as Holly's always saying. I should've known. He and Willie never liked each other." She

260

sighed. "So, I had dinner with Ceci and Althea. I was supposedly there to help set up for your shower tomorrow, but Ceci's maid had done everything, really. The reason I was free — and by myself — is that *he* was at a bird conference at Cornell. Or so he said. And gullible moron that I am, I believed him."

Steve said, "Stop. Whatever happened, it wasn't your fault, Rita."

"Thank you. You are a love, Steve. So, I left early. Early for me. Late for Althea. At nine or so. I took that shortcut you told me about, Holly, the one that goes down Norwood Hill to Oak Square in Brighton. I'd gone a few blocks. I was still in Newton, still in the part with the gaslights. They're charming, but they don't give much light, and the street signs are hard to see. I took a wrong turn. Did I ever! In more ways than one. And then what did I see but —" She broke off without saying Artie's name. "What did I see parked on some little dark street but a distinctive Citroën. It was unmistakable. So . . . I am so stupid!"

"You are not stupid," Steve said.

"I want to get this out and over. That shithead knew that I was having dinner with Ceci and Althea, so I assumed that for some reason, he was in town after all and that he'd decided to look for me. Hah! And that he'd gotten lost. There was a little light coming

261

from his car. And I pulled up and got out and went over to it. I did not suspect one single thing. And there he was in the back with that piece of hypocritical pornography in lard, Francie Julong." Rita squeezed her eyes shut.

I said, "Rita, I am so sorry."

"On a public street! There he was with that gushy, smarmy little pig! That lump of lying filth! Turning tricks in cars! What did I ever do to either of them to deserve this?"

Steve said, "Nothing. Not a thing. Rita, you're beautiful. You're intelligent. Any man who cheats on you has something seriously wrong with him."

"I could kill him," Rita said. "I could kill her, too."

Chapter 30

"My objection to bridal showers," I told Rita and Leah, "is that marriage is not about *things*."

"In your case," said Leah, "it's about dogs."

At two o'clock on Sunday afternoon, the three of us were crammed into Rita's bathroom, where my friend and my cousin were trying to do something about my hair and my face in time for my shower.

"Not exclusively, although I would like it if Rowdy and Kimi would shape up so India doesn't steal the show. That hurts!"

Rita refastened a clip in my hair. "As everyone's mother used to say, you have to suffer to be beautiful. Leah, she needs more blush."

Rita had asked Steve and me to say nothing to anyone about Artie Spicer and the scene she'd witnessed. Before Leah's arrival, she'd showered, soaked her face in ice water, and performed various cosmetic miracles.

Her eyes weren't swollen, her face wasn't puffy, her makeup was careful, and her lightly highlighted hair was sleek and snazzy. I could see tension in her jaw and shoulders, but she looked good enough to fool everyone else.

"Also," I said, "I hate the idea of extorting presents."

"Your implication," said Leah, "is that whereas other brides are gross materialists, you are a saint."

Rita did something to my eyebrows. "Rites of passage are inherently social transitions. Your loved ones want to participate."

"Loved ones! You make them sound like the dearly departed. And I'm sure you've done enough to me. I need to get dressed. I can groom a malamute for the showring in less time than you're wasting on me."

Leah ordered me to close my eyes. "If Rowdy and Kimi hollered like this on the grooming table, you'd muzzle them. Hold still and behave yourself, or you won't get any treats."

"You're not giving me any now."

"Ceci and Althea will, but only if I tell them that you were a good, good girl."

Leah evidently gave the elderly sisters a positive report. When we arrived at their house just before four o'clock, the dining room table and sideboard were laden with what I'll refrain from describing as liver goodies for people. Ceci's china, silver, and crystal displayed cakes, pastries, strawberries, raspberries, and dainty sandwiches with the crusts cut off. A fire burned in the living-room fireplace, and flowers were everywhere. Ceci, dressed in champagne, flitted nervously about.

Althea, looking a thousand years old and none the worse for it, was resplendent in lavender. "Do you know the poem about old women and purple? I've faded beyond it." She sat in her wheelchair amid the potted palms in the conservatory area at the far end of the living room. "Holly, move close to me so I can see you properly. There! You look marvelous."

"Thank you. Leah made me wear black. Rita tried to veto it, but Leah has a gift for getting her own way."

"Skill in getting one's own way is not to be disparaged. Ceci enjoys the same gift."

"They both put it to good use with dogs. I don't look funereal?"

"Not in the least. You are all sophistication."

"I bought the suit for Paris. The dogs won't be with us, so I didn't have to worry about camouflaging undercoat."

At my insistence, we'd kept the guest list for the shower to about twenty-five. Although Rita was one of the hostesses, Ceci had insisted on having the shower at her house. The wedding, which was only a week away, had swollen beyond our original vision of a small, intimate gathering, and I'd been determined not to stick Ceci and Althea with two great big parties one right after the other. The doorbell rang for the first of what nonetheless seemed like many times, and Rita greeted my dear stepmother, Gabrielle, who had driven all the way from Midcoast Maine. As I watched Rita, I admired her strength in putting up a brave front.

Before long, new guests arrived, and I was busy making introductions and replying to questions about the wedding and honeymoon. The collective sound of women's voices reminded me of the twittering of a flock of birds. I kept the perception to myself. The People's Republic of Cambridge had made me paranoid about expressing gender bias. In the vicinity of Harvard Square, I'd have been afraid to observe aloud that women were shorter than men. Or that men were taller than women? The safe course was to limit myself to reporting that in Alaskan malamutes, the American Kennel Club standard called for a height of twenty-five inches at the withers for males and twenty-three inches for females, the withers being the part of the back that's above the shoulders and below the neck. In assessing the height of dogs, we don't measure heads. If we figured human height at the shoulders instead of at the top of the cranium, women would eventually turn out to be shorter than men, but it would take ages to remeasure everyone, and we'd all enjoy a politically peaceful interlude during which we'd have no idea how tall or short anyone was and would thus be temporarily liberated from the hideous possibility of causing height-related political offense. Just to prove how weird Cambridge is, let me add that it was perfectly acceptable in Cantabrigian circles to say that women possessed greater emotional intelligence than did men. I thought that the assertion was a sneaky way to suggest that women were stupid. But maybe I'd better be quiet about that topic, too, and confine myself to stating that although the American Kennel Club standard for the Alaskan malamute said nothing about preferred IQ differences between males and females, the girls were, in general, smarter than the boys.

Birds. We did sound like them. Our striking plumage was, however, more characteristic of avian males than of females. Steve's vet techs and assistants weren't wearing scrubs, and my friends from dog training weren't in kennel clothes. Still, I'd have bet that almost every outfit had pockets and that a lot of those pockets contained dog treats. Faith Barlow, Rowdy's handler, wore a dress I'd seen in the showring. Its color was a pale rose, chosen, no doubt, to hide dog hair, as Faith's dress almost did. Rowdy's breeder, Janet, wore a rather severe gray suit, but large sterling silver malamutes dangled from her ears, and her hair bore a startling resemblance to the stand-off coat so desirable in our breed.

Birds. I wouldn't mention them to Rita, who had, of course, met Artie when she'd taken up birding. Didn't some feathered species mate for life? Not Artie. As I chatted with friends, I kept darting glances at Rita. She'd discovered Artie with the gushy, perfidious Francie in this same neighborhood only the night before. To preserve our friendship with Rita, Steve and I would have to tell her about the scene I'd witnessed at the Wayside Wildlife Refuge. But not yet, not until she regained some strength. At the moment, she was in animated conversation with Gabrielle, who was due to spend the night in Rita's guest room. Rita held a cup and saucer in her left hand, but she wasn't drinking anything, and she wasn't eating, either. She'd told me that she'd been unable to swallow more than a bite of the scrambled eggs she'd fixed herself for breakfast. My concern for Rita made me realize that many of my best friends were absent. One of the few disadvantages of forming friendships through dogs is that you end up with close friends who live thousands of miles away. Some of mine would be there for the wedding, but they couldn't make separate, expensive trips just for a shower.

The one guest who wasn't exactly a friend of mine was Carla Guarini, who was doing the flowers for our wedding. Carla also had the distinction of being the only guest invited because her husband was a Mob boss and I'd consequently been scared to exclude her. For once, Carla's dog wasn't with her, and for once, I was glad that someone had left a dog at home. Under my tutelage, her tiny dog, Anthony, had progressed beyond disobedient insufferability, but I hadn't cured Carla of tucking him into her bosom, as if he were a silk scarf that prevented her from showing a lot of cleavage, a function that Anthony did not, in any case, serve. As usual, Carla's dress plunged. A turquoise satin cocktail dress with dyed-to-match pumps, it looked like an especially hideous bridesmaid's gown. Soon after Judith Esterhazy arrived, I was surprised to find that Carla, having learned that Judith was a famous novelist, had engaged her in what Carla clearly intended as literary conversation.

"You write books!" Carla exclaimed. "I just love to read! I've always got my nose stuck in a book. My favorite is Cecilia Ann Vesper. Don't you just adore her?"

Slim and refined, Judith Esterhazy was possibly the last woman on earth who'd accessorize by sticking a dog between her breasts. "Vesper?" she inquired.

"Well, some people think she's old-fashioned. She doesn't go in for these modern settings and career women and all that, but, hey, I live modern, and I'm a career woman myself, and when I settle down with a book, I want barons and baronesses and castles and ruins, because *that's* romance, and if romance is what you pay for, romance is what you should get, right?"

Judith's sangfroid remained intact. "Cecilia Ann Vesper. I don't think I've read her."

"Well, my favorite was *Moated Passion*, but *Towering Love* was pretty good, too. The new one is *Highborn Rapture*. I just got it, but I haven't started it yet. So what do you write?"

I abandoned eavesdropping. "Judith's new book is about a woman warrior," I told Carla. "A queen. It's set in England during the Roman occupation."

"I love queens! And we're Italian ourselves, my husband and me. What's it called?"

"Boudicca." I didn't offer to lend Carla my copy. She could afford to buy the book, and Judith needed every hardcover sale she could get.

"Presents!" Ceci announced. "Let's all get together by the fireplace!"

As we gathered for the ritual, I spotted Rita at the periphery of the group. She was no longer talking with anyone, but lurking silently and looking as if she wanted to disappear altogether. When Leah joined me and nearly shoved me to a seat in the middle of

270

the couch, I murmured, "Let's get Rita to sit with us."

For once, instead of speaking so that everyone could hear every word she enunciated, Leah whispered. "One of her patients is here. She wants to keep a low profile."

Rita ran into her patients all the time at restaurants, at movies, in shops, and at parties. She saw them in the pool at her health club and, worse, in the sauna, where, of course, they saw her, too. When I was with Rita during these encounters, I could always identify her psychotherapy patients as such because Rita would suddenly make what I recognized as an effort to behave as if she weren't privy to all sorts of secrets that these people hid from everyone but her. I was always itching to know the details of the hidden lives of these apparently ordinary people, but Rita never violated her patients' privacy. On the contrary, unless she was desperate, she wouldn't even admit that a particular person whose appearance had suddenly caused her to assume an expression of ultranormality was, in fact, one of her patients.

The first present I opened was from Carla Guarini: a black lace teddy and a matching thong. The gift drew laughs and exclamations that delighted Carla, who, I felt sure, was not Rita's patient. As I unwrapped the next package, it occurred to me that Rita had been outgoing and talkative, albeit in a rather brittle fashion, until the arrival of the last guest.

Who had been the last to arrive? Judith Esterhazy.

Chapter 31

More than any other human being I'd ever known, my stepmother, Gabrielle, established a special connection with everyone she met. When people described her as charming, they really meant that she made them feel uniquely understood and appreciated. They didn't just feel that way, either; Gabrielle was genuinely fascinated by everyone. Consequently, the world worked better for Gabrielle than it does for the rest of us. Repair persons returned her calls and efficiently fixed her appliances. Auto mechanics took pains to make sure that her car was safe. Doctors and dentists squeezed her in ahead of other patients. Even my impossible father was in her thrall. For example, had it not been for Gabrielle, Buck would not only have managed to attend my bridal shower, but would have done so dressed for a hunting expedition and accompanied by a large pack of dogs. As it was, she'd contrived to leave him in Maine, the state slogan of which is, of course, "Maine: The Way Life Should Be." When it comes to my father, that's my slogan, too, more or less: "Buck Far Away: The Way Life Should Be."

All this is to say that one reason I adored Gabrielle was that she possessed what I'd previously believed to be the exclusive power of Alaskan malamutes: the enchanting ability to make everyone feel special. Like Rowdy, Kimi, and Sammy the pup, she was observant, intelligent, and responsive. Her energy was theirs. At eleven o'clock on Sunday night, for instance, Gabrielle was still talking away, examining every wedding present Steve and I had received, asking about Paris, and deepening her relationship with Sammy the puppy, who was no more eager to let me go to sleep than she was. We were in my guest room, which served as Wedding Central. My gown hung in the closet, and presents were everywhere.

"Now, I know that you need to get to bed," said Gabrielle, sipping from a glass of wine I'd just refilled for her. "This is going to be the busiest week of your life. But I want to reassure you that even though your father and I will get here on Friday, we aren't going to be underfoot. Are you sure you want Buck and me to stay here? We could easily find a hotel. Or maybe Rita would put us up. She seems happy to have me use her guest room tonight, although there does seem to be something a little off with her. She seems fragile. Trouble with a man?"

"Of course you're not going to a hotel! The beds on the third floor aren't too bad. Steve had them in storage, but they're all set up. You and Buck are going to be in one room, and Twila Baker is going to have the other. Buck is going to be so crazy about one of her dogs, North, that we'll be lucky if he remembers the wedding. Steve's dogs will be in that apartment, too, at least some of the time, but Buck obviously won't mind, and Twila won't, either. She's used to teams of malamutes. She'll have her whole team with her, but except for North, they'll be outside in her dog trailer. Steve's three dogs and the two you're bringing won't bother her at all. She'll probably harness them up and put them to work. Actually, she'll be staying here all week, until she goes to mushing boot camp. Are you and Buck still . . . ?"

"Your father promises me that the accommodations are nothing short of luxurious," Gabrielle said. "He may be exaggerating a tiny bit. He and I do, after all, have rather divergent opinions of what constitutes luxury. But I simply didn't have the heart to crush his enthusiasm, especially after he'd reconciled himself to having you and Steve go to Paris instead, not to mention the matter of Althea's performing the service."

If I'd tried to enlighten Gabrielle about the true nature of mushing boot camps, we'd have been up for another few hours. By the time I crawled into bed, it was midnight. Steve was asleep, and eager though I was to talk to him about Judith Esterhazy, I couldn't bear to awaken him. We had no chance to talk in the morning, either. Gabrielle ate breakfast with us, and then Steve left for work. For the rest of the day, I was frantically busy. Gabrielle left for Maine at nine. After that, I stowed all five dogs in crates and supplied them with giant black rubber Kong toys that I'd stuffed with goodies and placed in the freezer. Having bought silence, I did two radio interviews that Mac had set up for me, one with a local station, the other with a station in California. Both so-called interviews consisted mainly of my listening to weather reports, station identification information, and news updates. The local station's news made no mention of the serial killings. The California weather sounded enviable. Our Cambridge weather was sunny and warm, too, so I was able to wash and groom Rowdy and Kimi outdoors. Mac had arranged to have a reporter from a small local paper do an article about my book. The reporter was going to get here at three, and I wanted the dogs looking their best because she was going to be accompanied by a photographer. The newspaper wasn't the *Globe* or the *Herald*, but promotion was promotion, and I wanted the dogs to create a good impression. Once they looked terrific, I cleaned the house, took a shower, and fixed myself up. The reporter arrived late and stayed for two hours. We talked mainly about the problems she was having with her Gordon setter, problems attributable to her failure to give the dog any exercise, as I tried to tell her in a tactful manner. After she left, I worried that her article would portray me as a nasty, critical person whose book no one should buy.

After I'd fed all the dogs and given them time outdoors, I tried to ease my worries about the interview by checking the web sites of the big online booksellers. Browsing by category, I got to Home and Garden, then to Pets, then to Dogs, and finally to Care and Feeding. Ridiculous! If I did the categorization, Dogs would be a subcategory of Religion. Anyway, having slightly narrowed the field of comparison, I found that *101 Ways to Cook Liver* was doing just great; in fact, if there'd only been a subcategory of liver cookbooks for dogs, I'd have had a bestseller. I also checked on *Ask Dr. Mac*, which was selling even better than *101 Ways to Cook Liver*, and, alas for literature, about 1001 times better than Judith Esterhazy's *Boudicca*.

At about the time I finished "ego surfing," as it's called, searching the web for oneself,

Steve arrived home with the takeout food he'd promised to pick up because he'd known how busy I was going to be. Sammy, who was loose in the kitchen, sniffed the bag.

"I feel guilty," I said. "You'd rather have real food than sushi."

"Your greatest fear about getting married isn't that we'll end up miserable or that I'll cheat on you. It's that you'll get stuck cooking every night. And I don't mind sushi. I like horseradish and ginger. And this isn't just sushi. I got shrimp."

"My greatest fear is economic dependence," I said. "But speaking of cheating, I have been dying to talk to you since yesterday afternoon. I love Gabrielle, but we haven't had a second together when we've both been awake, and this is about one of Rita's patients. It's confidential."

"Stop worrying about money. We're in this together."

"In a million years, I'm never going to earn half what you do."

"So what? It doesn't bother me. We do different things. We do things we love. We love each other. We share. Let it go, Holly."

"It's not that I want the kind of marriage where each of us pays exactly half of the electric bill and the gas bill and so on, and where we have to figure out who made which phone calls, and how much of the dog food got eaten by whose dogs."

"Yours steal more food than mine. We'd have to factor that in."

"Sammy does his share. Don't you, Sammy? And he's the only one who chews books."

"We'd have to hire a bookkeeper. Forget it. It's a socialist marriage. To each according to need. That's all. It's easy."

"Yes, but what's really a need? As opposed to a want? Or a whim?"

He laughed. "Dogs are a need. All the rest is extravagance. Let's eat."

As we set the kitchen table and spread out the food, we both kept an eye on Sammy, who had never been fed at the table, except possibly by Kevin, but who hadn't given up hope, either. When Steve and I sat down opposite each other, Sammy eased his nose onto the table and rested his chin.

"Leave it," Steve told him and then finally said to me, "So, what's up?"

"Judith Esterhazy," I said. "She was a patient of Rita's. Yes, no big deal, except that I think I know more about her than I'm supposed to. The day that Rita and I went shopping and had dinner at the mall, Rita had two margaritas and some wine. I was driving. Anyway, she started telling me about a patient of hers. No names, of course. And Rita wasn't gossiping. She was talking about a dilemma she was in. She couldn't tell what reality was. The patient was a woman who thought her husband was cheating on her. The husband said that the wife was paranoid. The woman had stopped treatment. That's the gist of it. And later, when I asked Rita, she said that she should never have said anything. What I think is that the woman was Judith."

"Rita didn't make any connections?"

"Why would she? I knew something was up yesterday, at the shower, because Rita was being her social self. She wants to keep up a brave front. She was valiant. She was talking to everyone. And then all of a sudden, she stopped. She had that look that she gets when one of her patients shows up. You've seen it."

He dipped a piece of sushi in soy sauce. "Yeah, it's unmistakable."

"And Judith was the last person to arrive at Ceci's. Judith arrived. Rita got quiet. And she got that look. And what I've realized is that Rita has heard all about Mac, and she's seen his book here, but I never call him anything but Mac, and his last name is McCloud. Judith is the only person who calls him Bruce, and it's all she ever calls him. Everyone else calls him Mac. And Judith's last name is Esterhazy. I've probably mentioned Judith to her, but it's a common first name. Rita had no reason to see a connection."

"I want you to try to remember exactly what Rita said."

"She said that the husband had sent the wife to therapy because the wife thought he was repeatedly unfaithful to her. He claimed she was imagining things. Rita said his infidelity was the wife's truth. From the patient's point of view, she was telling the truth. Something like that. And that her patient's reality was the only reality that she, Rita, had available. The husband wouldn't see Rita. Oh, one other thing. The wife had a dog, and Rita said that one issue was that the woman loved the dog more than she loved her husband."

"We could ask Rita to listen to us. And not say anything."

"Not now! Cheating and lying are the last things she needs to think about. I saw her for a second today. Steve, she looks as if she's lost five pounds since Saturday. We just cannot put any pressure on her about anything. She trusted Artie. The only one of us who didn't was you."

"Veterinary reflex. Nice guy. But if he'd been a dog, I'd've known to muzzle him before I got close."

"Well, I wish Rita had had the same intuition. And I wish we'd warned her."

"We went over that. It could've been some other guy."

"We were fooling ourselves. We wanted to be wrong." One piece of seaweed-wrapped rice remained. "Do you want that?"

"It's yours. I got ice cream."

As he dished out Ben & Jerry's, I asked, "So what does it mean? Mac sent Judith to therapy because she thought he was unfaithful. He told her she was imagining things. She told Rita she wasn't. And then she stopped therapy."

"She knew. And then something convinced her she was wrong? Or she just didn't like therapy. But, look, Holly, what we're doing here is leaping to conclusions. One conclusion. Mac. That's illogical."

"We've been over the murders. So has everyone else."

"One more time. All women. All killed in the evening. Not in the middle of the night. Killed at times when people go places or are on their way home. All killed right near where they lived. Or were staying. All except the first one owned dogs, and the dog or dogs were nearby. All except the first did some kind of work that had to do with dogs. All except the first were people you'd met. And Mac knew. Who else knew them?"

"You met Elspeth. So did Judith and Ian, at the talk at the bookstore. If Mac and I knew all of them, except Laura Skipcliff, there are probably other people who did, too. Other dog writers. Vets. Dog trainers. Vet techs. Veterinary assistants. And so on."

"You see? The value of taking a fresh look. Techs. Assistants. Think about it. Laura

Skipcliff doesn't fit the pattern. Or doesn't appear to. But someone else does. At your launch party. The woman who'd died?"

"Nina Kerkel. But she died a natural death."

"She worked with Mac. Veterinary receptionist?"

"Yes. I remember because Judith said that she was all too receptive. Yes! Judith was muttering about her. Venomously, too. And according to Ceci, who knows Greta Kerkel, her ex-husband's mother, Nina Kerkel, was, quote, no better than she should've been, unquote. But Nina Kerkel wasn't murdered."

"She died," Steve said. "If you look at it systematically, Laura Skipcliff was the first victim, but Nina Kerkel was the first in the series."

Chapter 32

The dog lover's hymn: "You'll Never Walk Alone." The melody ran through my head as I sat at a card table at the front of the mall bookstore on Tuesday evening. I obviously wasn't walking, and I certainly wasn't alone. With me were the two most fanatical fans any author could desire. One pressed his body against my left thigh, the other pressed hers against my right. The behavior was intimate, but when a signing draws only two attendees, the author welcomes almost any demonstration of high regard, even if, as in this case, the demonstrative individuals don't buy her book. Gazing into the adoring eyes of my worshipful public, I realized that I should have brought Sammy the pup along, too. Sammy, having eaten several copies of *101 Ways to Cook Liver*, knew it inside out, and if he'd disliked it to begin with, he'd hardly have gone back for second helpings. The dog writer's hymn: "You'll Never Sign Alone."

Mac had warned me about the signing and had himself declined the invitation on the grounds that no one would come. He had, however, advised me to accept. According to Mac, chain bookstores in downscale strip malls were always devoid of shoppers during a signing, but the autographed books did, in fact, sell once the downcast author had gone home. He'd said that such signings could be depressing, but that he knew the events coordinator at this place and that she'd probably keep me company. He'd ended by saying that I should do as I pleased about the invitation. *Pleased* wasn't exactly how I felt at the moment, but it consoled me to observe that no one else's books were selling, either. Indeed, the warm-blooded mammals in the store consisted of a clerk, the events coordinator, Rowdy, Kimi, and me. So much for never taking both dogs!

I felt sorrier for the events coordinator, Irene, than I did for myself. I'd written the book and had it published. The reviews had been good. In other bookstores, people were buying it. But how was Irene supposed to coordinate a nonevent that, as such, required no coordination?

As it turned out, Irene evidently had considerable experience in meeting this challenge. She did so by getting out a second folding chair and sitting with us. She was a little, fine-boned woman in her mid or late fifties. Her short white hair flowed backward and upward from her delicate face. The pitch of her voice, too, headed upward as she spoke, and she had a habit of lifting her gaze to the ceiling.

"It's always like this," she said, "and these days, women are afraid to leave home after dark. Or in daylight, for that matter, some women, anyway. A lot of our customers are women. They'll buy the signed books later."

"It's fine." It was, too. As a dog writer living in Cambridge, I was chronically plagued by the awareness that my neighbors were writing academic articles about verb forms in Aramaic, recent economic shifts in Argentina, the existence of thermonuclear something-or-others, and the role of women in the American colonies, whereas I was yet again discoursing on the methodology of the reliable recall. The publication of *101 Ways to Cook Liver* had made me feel slightly less marginal than I had before. But now, all of a sudden, I was doing a book signing to which no one had come. At last, I was undeniably a *real* author! Hurrah!

"It's too bad Mac wasn't free to come, too. You weren't nervous about driving alone?"

I smiled. "I'm not alone."

"Some of those women had dogs. That woman in Brookline had her dog in her car."

"Bonny Carr. Her dog was in a crate. She apparently got out of the car first. That's what I'd normally do. But now I've arranged the crates so I can open Kimi's from inside the car. She and I get out, and then we get Rowdy."

In a startling demonstration of his fearsome nature, Rowdy responded to the sound of his name by dropping to the floor, rolling onto his back, and imitating a giant bunny rabbit.

Irene laughed and then bent down to stroke his tummy. "He is so cute! It's funny that such a big dog can be so adorable."

Kimi, who misses nothing, decided that Rowdy was getting more than his fair share of the attention. Worse, she'd evidently taken a liking to Irene, into whose lap she suddenly tried to leap. Kimi weighed exactly seventy-five pounds. At a guess, Irene weighed a hundred and five. My first — and horrifying — thought was that the tiny Irene was at high risk for osteoporosis: a thin, fine-boned Caucasian woman in late middle age. If Kimi had to hurl herself into people's laps, couldn't she pick hefty, heavy-boned African-American men of twenty? I gave Kimi a full body shove. "Sit! Irene, are you all right?"

Luckily, she was. What saved her from being crushed was, I think, her small lap; Kimi simply hadn't had room for a solid landing. Still, I was mortified. I offered a heartfelt apology. I also put Kimi on a down-stay and put my foot on the section of her leash right near her collar in case she decided to break. Irene was lovely about Kimi's misbehavior. She laughed it off and said, "It's always the minister's children, isn't it! Please don't worry about it."

The incident, which could've broken Irene's pelvis, broke the ice between us. Its absurdity somehow made one of us mention Barbara Pym, who turned out to be one of Irene's favorite novelists as well as one of mine. We drifted into an enthusiastic discussion about Jane Austen and Penelope Lively. Kimi remained in a solid down-stay. Eventually, Irene asked me to sign the copies of my book that were stacked on the card table. I considered the signing a success. As I got ready to leave, Irene again raised the question of my safety.

"I'll be fine. I'll crate Rowdy. Then Kimi and I will get into the car together. Besides, I'm parked right outside. There's plenty of light."

"These women were murdered right near where they lived. Or were staying."

"I've made an arrangement at home. When I get there, I'll use the horn, and my fiancé will come out. I live in Cambridge. I'm used to being careful."

"I'm sorry if I'm being pushy. It's just that I knew the first victim. Victim! I can't think of her that way. Laura Skipcliff. I hadn't seen her for ages. Decades. But she and Mac and

I went to college together. I always liked the two of them. Mac was crazy about her, but she left him for someone else. And then she went off to medical school. I haven't seen Laura since we graduated. But I always liked her. What a terrible way for her life to end."

I was too surprised to do anything except echo Irene. "Terrible," I said inadequately. "Terrible."

Chapter 33

"The rest was speculation," Steve said. "What you're doing now is withholding information."

"What *I'm* doing? What *we're* doing. But it's got to stop."

The second I'd arrived home from the bookstore, I'd told Steve about Mac McCloud and Laura Skipcliff. We were now in the yard sitting at our wedding-present picnic table sipping wine from wedding-present glasses. The wine bottle was on the table. Next to it, a fat candle burned in a glass-sided lantern cleverly designed to prevent breezes from blowing out the flame. Wedding present. Good one. It's easy to see why some couples get married for the gifts.

"We're victims of dog osmosis." Steve gestured toward our five dogs, who were in the yard with us. "We've absorbed an attitude of unconditional loyalty. It's like that thing you've got framed in your office. Senator Vest's Eulogy on the Dog. 'Faithful and true even to death.' Only here, what's at issue is the death of other people, these women. Mac has been helpful to you, and in some ways, he seems like a nice guy, but he doesn't own you." Having left a crucial point for last, he said, "Besides, we're not dogs."

"You're right. When you've spent as much time with dogs as we have, it's easy to get the idea that the only kind of loyalty worth having is unconditional loyalty. Perfect fidelity."

"This is a friendship," Steve said. "And not even all that close a friendship. Okay, you don't want to be a lousy friend. Who does? And that's not what's required. All you have to do is tell Kevin one thing, and that's that Mac knew all the victims."

"I'm the one who has to?"

"We have to. Faithful and true, Holly. I'm on your side."

"I know you are."

"All the rest of what we talked about is guesswork. We're not getting involved in spreading rumors. Or gossip."

"Certainly not. Sammy, stop that! Steve, he's chewing the leg of our new table. Make him stop!"

More than with any other dog I'd ever owned . . . let me start over. The problem I encountered in disciplining Sammy was the difficulty of avoiding the most common pitfall in dog training, which was, is, and ever shall be the tendency to give unintended positive reinforcement for undesirable behaviors. Sammy was so damned cute that it was almost impossible to tell him to quit doing something without simultaneously letting him know how damned cute I thought he was. With his adult-size jaws wrapped around the leg of the table, he wore an expression of winsome innocence.

"Sammy," Steve said, "has taken a cost survey of available wedding presents, and he's picked the table because it's the most expensive one in reach. Sammy, leave it."

In part to avoid catching Sammy's eye, I stood up. "I'll go call Kevin."

"To arrest Sammy?"

I laughed. "Steve, you're starting to sound like me! We'll end up being one of those identical-twin couples. I'll get taller. You'll get shorter. My hair will turn darker. Yours will turn lighter. I'll suddenly discover that I know how to remove foreign objects from dogs' intestines, and —"

"Call Kevin."

To our shared relief, Kevin wasn't home. I left messages for him here and there asking him to call me. In fact, instead of calling me, Kevin showed up at my door at nine o'clock the next morning, that is, the morning of Wednesday, September 25, four days before the wedding.

The house was in chaos. I'd started the day

by preparing the third-floor apartment for the guests who'd be staying there, my friend Twila Baker, with her malamute, North, and my father and Gabrielle, with Buck's golden retriever, Mandy, and Gabrielle's bichon, Molly. I put fresh sheets on the beds, set up crates for the dogs, and carried up a supply of towels. I also dealt with calls from two people who'd lost the directions to Ceci's house and needed me to explain how to get there. While I was on the phone with the second caller, Sammy somehow managed to get into my own first-floor guest room, where he amused himself by opening four packages that had been delivered the previous day. When I came upon him, he'd raided all four shipping cartons. Sodden strips of cardboard were everywhere, and the floor was thick with wrapping paper and Styrofoam peanuts. What's more, he'd apparently eaten the gift receipt for a fondue set that we'd intended to return. Sammy lay happily in the midst of the wreckage with a miraculously unbroken bottle of special French brandy grasped between his beautiful big white paws. The brandy, together with a set of glasses, was a present from one of Steve's vet school friends. The glasses and the bottle had been on a table. Evidently intending to swig the stuff down, Sammy hadn't touched the glasses, but he'd used his paws or his mouth to steal the bottle and at the moment, with astonishing delicacy, was applying his teeth to the task of removing the cork. Considering the destruction he'd caused cold sober, I hated to imagine what he'd have done drunk.

When Kevin Dennehy rapped on the back door, I staggered to it with one hand grasping the collar of the unrepentant Sammy and the other hand wrapped around the neck of the rescued brandy bottle. Sammy was delighted with himself, with me, and with the sight of Kevin, who eyed the smiling dog, the bottle, and me, and said, "The thought of marriage is driving you to drink, huh?"

Sammy wagged his tail faster than ever. His eyes glittered.

One slow word at a time, I said, "I just found Sammy uncorking this bottle. He somehow moved it from a table to the floor. Without breaking it."

"Hey, Sammy, gotta watch out for drinking alone. Or did you know I was coming over? Well, I'll tell you, kid, it's early in the day for me. But I could use a cup of coffee."

"Of course. Kevin, come in. I'm sorry. He made an incredible mess. It was my fault. I should've kept an eye on him. Or crated him. At least he gave me the bottle with no argument. He isn't possessive with his treasures. But come in. I'll make coffee."

Kevin and I had radically different taste in coffee. When I was writing against a deadline, I self-medicated with Café Bustelo. Otherwise, I drank French, Italian, or Vienna roast. Kevin's cop loyalty to all food and drink purveyed by Dunkin' Donuts was so marked that I kept a bag of Dunkin' Donuts ground coffee in the freezer for him. As I made his coffee for him and mine for me, he fooled around with Sammy, but when we settled at the table, I managed to get his attention and said, "Kevin, thank you for coming over. I really need to talk to you. This is serious."

"Hey, marriage is."

"This isn't about marriage. It's about murder."

"Same difference."

"Kevin, please! I really am serious. It's possible that what I'm going to tell you means nothing. That's for you to judge. But I need you to quit fooling around and listen."

He did.

"You remember Mac McCloud. You met him at The Wordsmythe at my launch party. Which was also his. He was signing his new book."

Kevin nodded.

"He's a vet. He mostly does behavioral consultations these days. Counseling. Psychopharmacology. Dispenses advice about problem behavior. I've known him off and on for ages, but I got to know him better when my book was coming out. He's been great to me. Really, he's been my unpaid publicist.

And I know his family. His wife is a famous literary novelist. Judith Esterhazy. She was at The Wordsmythe, too. You might've met their daughter, too. Olivia. Their son, Ian, is a musician. He's doing the music for our wedding. We had dinner with them on Saturday."

Kevin waited for me to continue.

"Mac knew all of the murder victims. Every one. And the reason I'm telling you is that a lot of people knew the women who lived around here. Victoria Trotter. Bonny Carr. Elspeth. I knew them. Other people must've known all of them, too. But Mac went to college with Laura Skipcliff. She was his college girlfriend. I heard this last night from a classmate of theirs. She didn't make anything of it. Why would she? She had no way to know that Mac knew the other victims, too. But he did. He knew all of them."

"And?"

"Laura Skipcliff dumped him."

"Thirty years ago?"

"She was what? In her mid fifties? Mac's age, obviously. So it would've been more than thirty years ago. I have no idea whether they stayed in touch. For all I know, they didn't. Or maybe they did." Reluctantly, I added, "Elspeth told me that she'd had a one-night stand with Mac. She called it an affair, but I'm pretty sure that it wasn't, really."

"There money there?"

"What?"

"Mac. Does he have money? Or his wife?"

"They have a house in Lexington. A lovely house. They're not hard up. Mac had a successful veterinary practice that he sold to a big corporation. I don't know what he made on the deal, but it must've been lucrative. He probably still earns a lot."

"The wife?"

"Oh, she can't earn much of anything. Her books get great reviews, but they're very literary. They don't sell well. She probably makes even less than I do. A lot less."

"Family money?"

I shrugged. "I have no idea. Kevin, I have to say that I hate telling you this. These are not creepy people." I paused. Ian? He was odd. But not creepy. Was he? "They're friends of mine. Mac has been a good friend to me. In case you wondered, he's never even hinted that he wanted to be more than that, not that I'd have been interested. He's a nice guy. Friendly, sociable, all the rest. I've read all those profiles in the papers, and he's nothing like that at all. There is no one more different from those profiles than Mac McCloud."

The phone rang. "I'm sorry," I told Kevin, "but I have to get this. It'll be about the wedding."

It was. Our photographer's husband announced that his wife's brother had died. She was leaving immediately for Memphis, wouldn't return until Tuesday, and was terribly sorry to let us down. As I was struggling to utter expressions of sympathy, Kevin rose, mouthed good-bye, and left. For the rest of the day and, indeed, the rest of the week, I concentrated almost exclusively on our wedding and honeymoon. The new photographer I hired specialized in splendid portraits of show dogs. Since dogs were far more difficult to photograph than were mere human beings, and since there'd be five dogs in the bridal party, her qualifications were obviously superb. I confirmed our plane reservations, our wedding-night reservation at an airport hotel, our reservation at the hotel in Paris, the reservation for the tents, and the reservation for the rehearsal dinner. By the end of the week, I'd confirmed so many arrangements that I felt as if the forthcoming ceremony shouldn't properly be called a wedding at all, but a confirmation. In between sending and receiving E-mail, and making and answering phone calls, I kept checking weather forecasts on the web. We had rain on Wednesday and Thursday, but Friday was clear, and the outlook for Saturday and Sunday was splendid.

I devoted most of Friday to bathing and grooming all five dogs, a task I'd have hated to perform indoors. It would've been sensible to take the dogs to a groomer, but it felt important to me to do the work with my own hands. I wanted to perform a purification ritual with the two dogs who were already mine, Rowdy and Kimi, and with the three who were about to become mine. India, the ultimate one-man dog, would always be more Steve's than mine, but her acute intelligence would enable her to understand that Steve had a wife — and this time, a wife worthy of him and of India's allegiance. Lady the pointer was so touchingly dependent on Steve that she'd never be fully mine, either. Sammy, however, had a malamute's exquisite sensitivity to even the slightest shift in any relationship. Of Steve's three dogs, Sammy was the one who'd somehow know that Steve and I were married. When Althea pronounced us man and wife, Sammy the pup, my Rowdy's beautiful son, would understand that he had become my dog, too.

Chapter 34

The dossier on Claire Langceil, D.V.M., opened with the usual pages from the major online directories: AnyWho, InfoSpace, and so forth. All agreed that Claire G. and Daniel T. Langceil lived at 37 Windcrest Drive in Newton. MapQuest showed that Windcrest Drive was south of Route 9. I couldn't remember ever having been in the immediate neighborhood, which was somewhere near the Chestnut Hill Mall and a few miles from Norwood Hill, where Ceci and Althea lived. I didn't need to have seen the Langceils' house to get a detailed view of it: The results of a property search of the City of Newton's web site included an aerial photograph of the lot. Additional pages from the Newton Assessor's site provided copious, if tedious, information about the property. The lot size was 12,390 square feet, the frontage was 80 feet, and the house style was Victorian. The house had gas heat, central air conditioning, three fireplaces, two above-average baths, one half-bath, four bedrooms, a deck, a porch, and an in-ground swimming pool. Some of the codes and numbers on the assessment pages meant nothing to me: The land use was 101, and the zoning was SR1. A page devoted to the property's assessment history was, however, easy to interpret: In the past ten years, the assessed value had risen dramatically. In that respect, the Langceils' property was like everyone else's.

I had to wonder whether Ceci knew that the equivalent information about her Newton property was available online to anyone who cared to search for it. At a guess, Ceci had no idea. Had she known, she'd have felt outraged at what she'd have seen as an infuriating invasion of her privacy. She'd have babbled on and on about the matter, especially, I thought, because her old-fashioned kitchen and baths would've been rated as below average. She'd have taken the rating as a personal insult. Knowing Ceci as I did, I suspected that she'd immediately have renovated the offending rooms, not because she actually wanted to update them, but because she couldn't bear the humiliation of poor ratings.

To return to Claire Langceil, the next item in the dossier showed that her birthday was August 9. Next came the result of a search of the Commonwealth's Division of Professional Licensure site. Claire Gail Langceil,

Newton, MA, was, indeed, a licensed veterinarian. The status of her license was given as "Fee Paid." The page also gave her license number, the issue date, and the expiration date. At the bottom was the statement that the site displayed disciplinary actions dating back to ten years earlier and that this license had had no such actions taken during that time.

Next were copies of two articles from a local newspaper. One was about a rabid fox that had bitten a child. Claire Langceil, D.V.M., was quoted as saying that pet owners should remember to keep cats as well as dogs up to date on rabies vaccinations. She was described as an adjunct faculty member in the veterinary technology program at Saint Mary's Junior College in Boston. The second article had nothing to do with veterinary medicine. It was about a fall harvest festival in Newton. Local residents who'd attended the festival had included Daniel and Claire Langceil, and their son, Gus. Daniel had said that the event was "a lot of fun for our whole family."

The dossier then focused on a second person. According to Martindale.com's Lawyer Locator, Daniel T. Langceil was a member of the Boston law firm of Seed and Trout, which was so famous and prestigious that even I had heard of it. Daniel had gone to Harvard College and Harvard Law School.

His practice area was listed as "General Civil." FindLaw.com presented a listing from the West Legal Directory. This one simply gave Daniel's name, his firm, its address and phone number, and his area of practice, general civil law.

There ended the dossier. I found the ending anticlimactic. In fact, this dossier had a vaguely perfunctory quality, as if the compiler had surfed the web without bothering to rise to its heights or plunge to its depths. Missing was the sense of compulsive completeness that I'd perceived in the previous dossiers, the driven determination to discover everything. But perhaps I was reading in to this dossier and, in reading the others, had merely projected my own sense of compulsion and drive. After all, each of the dossiers was incomplete. In each case, the true last page was murder.

Chapter 35

At three-thirty on Friday afternoon, when all five freshly shampooed dogs had had their turns on the grooming table, I banished all creatures to the house and began to ready the yard for human use, namely, a lobster dinner. I can't help wondering whether Steve and I could have saved Claire's life by inviting Daniel, Claire, and Gus to our party. The invitation would've been strange. For one thing, I didn't particularly like Claire. For another, the Langceils hadn't been invited to our wedding; they were acquaintances rather than friends of ours. The party was for family members, close friends, and a few out-of-town guests. My father and Gabrielle expected to reach Cambridge at about five o'clock and were bringing real Maine lobsters and steamer clams. Twila Baker had called from New York State to say that she, too, should get there at about five. Two of Steve's uncles from Minnesota, Uncle Dave and Uncle Don, were flying into Logan.

They were renting a car and staying at a motel. The uncles, as well as Leah, Rita, Kevin, Jennifer Pasquarelli, and Steve's best man would arrive at about seven. The Langceils would've been out of place at the gathering. They might have declined the invitation. As I later learned, Daniel and Gus spent the evening at the Museum of Science, where they visited the exhibit halls and had pizza at the Museum's Science Street Café. Meanwhile Claire had an early dinner with Mac McCloud. Anyway, it's simply impossible to draw up a guest list with the goal of preventing murder.

That afternoon, I was preoccupied with thoughts about my wedding and specifically with my strategy for preventing Buck from ruining the festivities that he was generously paying for. My father didn't choose to be more moose than human being, did he? Well, maybe he did. In any case, no matter where he was, he always took up more space than everyone else combined. Fact! I'd seen him do just that at Madison Square Garden during the Westminster Kennel Club Dog Show. My house was, of course, a lot smaller than Madison Square Garden, as was Ceci's, and the entry at our wedding was a lot smaller than the entry at Westminster. Besides crowding everyone else out of any area, no matter how large, Buck bellowed in mooselike fashion. Finally, although I can't prove it, it seemed to me that he always breathed in more air than everyone else combined and then exhaled some odorless chemical that made all dogs worship him, but had peculiar and unpredictable effects on people. He irked both Steve and Rita, whereas Gabrielle had fallen in love with him at first exposure. My hopes for moose control rested in part on Gabrielle, who was a civilizing influence, but were pinned mainly on Twila Baker's dog team and especially on her lead dog, North.

The plan got off to a splendid start. Buck, Gabrielle, their two dogs, and fifteen live lobsters pulled into my driveway at five. When Buck got out of the car and greeted me, as usual, by asking about Rowdy and Kimi, he was immediately distracted by the rather startling appearance on narrow little Appleton Street of a big SUV towing a sixteen-foot-long dog-box trailer that was somehow going to have to fit in my urban driveway. Buck was at his best. He wore casual L.L.Bean duds rather than the hunting outfit I'd feared. Twila brought her car and trailer to a stop in the street, and my father immediately took charge. He moved my car and his own, and capably directed Twila as she, in effect, moored an ocean liner at a dock meant for rowboats. Buck took to her and to North immediately. Twila had long, dark hair and, in contrast to some of my Cambridge friends, was healthy-looking and vigorous. Women who supposedly run with wolves have got nothing on women who run teams of sled dogs.

What really impressed Buck, however, was North, properly, BISS American International Ch. Quinault's Northern Exposure, CGC, WLDX, WTD, WPD, all of whose titles Buck immediately elicited and all of which he understood. *BISS* is Best in Specialty Show, a speciality being a show limited to one breed, in this case, the Alaskan malamute. *Ch.*: Champion is conformation competition, in which dogs are judged according to the ideal spelled out in official breed standard. *CGC*: Canine Good Citizen, a title conferred by the American Kennel Club for passing a test designed to evaluate the dog's training and deportment, and the owner's responsibility in taking care of the dog. The last three titles are given by the Alaskan Malamute Club of America: Working Lead Dog Excellent, Working Team Dog, and Working Pack Dog. As my father was irritatingly quick to point out, Rowdy's and Kimi's work in harness had been occasional and strictly recreational.

Gabrielle tried to insert a few brags about the titles my dogs did have, but Buck's bellowing drowned her out.

"Gabrielle, don't!" I whispered. "Let him. The more he stays focused on North, the less attention he'll pay to the wedding, and —"

"An excellent plan," said Gabrielle, who, I should mention, looked entirely unready to run sled dogs. Or to run, for that matter. Her fabulous bone structure and pretty gray-blond hair wouldn't be assets on the trail, and she was distinctly plump rather than muscular. "North really is beautiful," she went on. "It does seem a shame that he had to do all that work, though! Leading a team! How would you like it?" She patted the fluffy white head of Molly, her bichon, whom she held, as usual, in her arms.

Although Gabrielle probably addressed the question to Molly, I said, "I might love it. And North certainly does, and please don't say any such thing to Twila. Working breeds like to work, and Twila positively dotes on North. She'd never ask him to do anything he didn't love." I paused. "Besides, aren't you going to mushing boot camp next weekend?"

"Yes, of course," Gabrielle said, "but that won't really be work, will it? It'll just be fun. A grand adventure! Molly and I can hardly wait."

I followed the wise course of not interfering in my father's marriage. By this time, my father was enthusiastically greeting the kennel help Twila had brought with her, a sturdy young woman who, as far as I could tell, reserved her powers of speech almost exclusively for dogs. He insisted on helping with the entire team, which consisted of North and seven other malamutes. As he did so, he got to examine the incredible box trailer.

In response to Buck's questioning, Twila said, "It's six thousand pounds. That's because of all the stainless steel diamond plate."

Gabrielle whispered in my ear. "Do the dogs have to ride in it?"

"That's what it's for," I said, "and they're a lot more comfortable than my dogs and I were in my old Bronco."

Meanwhile, Twila was showing off the luxurious dog vehicle, which had drops, as they're known, for twelve dogs, an elaborate venting and cooling system, and a gigantic sealed storage compartment for gear.

As the kennel girl let out one of the dogs, Hussy, and spoke softly to her, Gabrielle suddenly took an interest in the trailer and went so far as to stick her head into the box that Hussy had just vacated. "It's really a little private room, isn't it? And the door has louvers. It's very cozy and comfy. And perfectly safe. With padlocks for each little room. There's not a chance that someone could get hurt in there."

"Of course not," I said. "Twila is not about to endanger her dogs. Now we'd better unload everything. Everyone's expected for drinks at seven."

"Let's just leave Buck where he is. He had some fanciful notion of doing a real lobster and clam bake, but there simply isn't time, and you don't want your yard dug up, do you? And nothing would be ready for hours and hours, and we'd end up eating raw lobster, so if you don't mind —"

"Mind? I don't mind at all."

For the next hour and a half, Buck had no opportunity to cause trouble. On the contrary, he made himself useful by carrying luggage to the third floor, toting in plastic boxes of lobsters and clams, feeding and walking all five of Steve's and my dogs, and lending a hand as Twila and her helper fed and watered the dog team. When Steve got home, Buck acted glad to see him and happily introduced him to Twila and her crew. Meanwhile, Rita, Leah, and Steve's best man, Pete, had shown up, and with their assistance and Gabrielle's, Steve and I got pots of water going in my kitchen and in the kitchen in the third-floor apartment. Pete was a sandy-haired guy about six inches shorter than Steve, a veterinary oncologist with a cheerful, gentle manner. Recently divorced, Pete struck me as a possible match for Rita, even if only as a date. Despite her efforts, Rita looked exhausted. Her face seemed pinched, and she'd lost more weight than I'd have thought possible in so short a time. I prayed that my tactless father would refrain from commenting on her appearance. So far, he'd done nothing to embarrass me; for him, he'd been practically normal. Only one thing about Buck's behavior struck me as odd — namely, that although he and Gabrielle were signed up for boot camp, he made no effort to enlist Twila in convincing Gabrielle that boot camp would be a fantastic learning experience and that fluffy little Molly would fit right in with the teams of malamutes, Siberians, and Alaskan huskies. On the contrary, whenever Gabrielle approached Twila, he seemed to insert himself between the two women. I was, however, too busy preparing for dinner to pay a great deal of attention to the matter.

At seven, on schedule, Uncle Don and Uncle Dave arrived in their rental car. They looked remarkably like each other and remarkably like aged versions of Steve: tall and lean, with wavy hair and blue-green eyes. The picnic table and a couple of folding tables we'd put in the yard were set with paper tablecloths, paper plates, and plastic flatware, but we'd rounded up enough real wineglasses for everyone. White wine, bottled water, and soft drinks nestled in ice in two coolers. I'd been a little concerned that when Kevin Dennehy and his police-officer girlfriend, Jennifer Pasquarelli, arrived, she'd respond to the obvious presence of a great many dogs by

311

making sure that we were abiding by the leash and pooper-scooper laws, as we, in fact, were. Not that Cambridge dog laws were any of Jennifer's business. As I hoped not to have to remind Jennifer, she was a Newton cop and thus out of her jurisdiction. As it turned out, Jennifer was on good behavior. To my relief, she wore neither her uniform nor a Spandex running outfit. She did, admittedly, have a cell phone and pager clipped to the belt of her stretch jeans, but her lavender cotton sweater suggested neither law enforcement nor road racing. On the contrary, given her voluptuous build, it just looked suggestive. Her shiny, dark hair was loose, and her amethyst earrings and necklace had clearly been chosen for a purely social occasion. Kevin seemed proud to be with her. The two of them chatted with Steve's uncles. Steve made drinks and poured wine. Everyone, even Buck, ate the appetizers we'd bought at the Armenian stores in nearby Watertown: hummus, baba ganoosh, stuffed grape leaves, and various kinds of cheese with fresh Syrian bread.

The lobsters and clams were eventually cooked and served, and the whole business of carrying them outside and providing everyone with clam broth and melted butter was wonderfully diverting. By seven-thirty or quarter of eight, our guests were seated and amply supplied with lobsters, clams, butter, broth, baked potatoes, and big helpings of salad. Leah charmed the uncles by giving a lesson on how to eat a lobster. Glancing around, I was happy to see Rita seated next to Pete. Her plate was full. I hoped she'd empty it. Indeed, everything went beautifully until Buck, at my request, went inside to get a new pot of steamers. He'd been sitting between Gabrielle and Twila, at the same table with Steve and me. Since Gabrielle and Twila were now, in effect, next to each other, they naturally began to talk of what they had in common, which was, of course, the upcoming mushing boot camp.

"I had my concerns at first," Gabrielle told Twila. "I'm not a roughing-it type. I was very relieved when Buck explained that our cabin is going to be perfectly luxurious. You have a cabin, too, don't you?"

"North and I will be sleeping out under the stars," Twila said. "I've brought a bivy, but I probably won't need it. North sleeps right next to me."

"A bivy?"

"A bivy," Twila repeated. She went on to extol the virtues of the particular brand she owned. Because it had three poles, it was almost like a tent.

Gabrielle looked baffled.

I translated. "A sort of portable shelter for people who don't want to bother with a tent. It has just enough room for you and your sleeping bag, and it covers your head in case of rain."

Gabrielle was aghast. "But why aren't you taking a cabin?"

"There's only one," Twila informed her. "There's the big cabin. I'd rather be outside, anyway."

"One cabin?"

Unaware of the effect her revelation was creating, Twila added, "There are enough bunks for everyone, and after a day of hard work, you won't have any trouble falling asleep. The day starts pretty early. You'll need to begin getting the dogs ready at five for the morning run, so you'll want to be up by four-thirty or so. It's beautiful out then, and the dogs are all excited. It's great. You'll love it."

"Four-thirty." Gabrielle sounded dazed.

Twila laughed. "You can get up earlier. It depends on whether you want a big breakfast before the run."

"Oh, that's all taken care of," Gabrielle said. "Buck tells me that the food is delicious."

Twila laughed again. "Some people always like to cook communally, but you don't have to. There'll be a refrigerator in the cabin, so you can keep your own food there if you want. But you might want to just grab breakfast before or right after you hook up the dogs."

A gleam of comprehension sparkled in Gabrielle's eyes. "And the bathrooms?" Her throaty voice was strong and curious.

"I haven't been to this site before," Twila said, "but apparently there *are* a few. And the outhouse is supposed to be close to the cabin."

"Outhouse," Gabrielle repeated.

The sled dog having been let out of the bivy sack, so to speak, I said, "Gabrielle, it's possible that camp won't be exactly the way Buck has described it." Feeling guilty, I added, "But Ginny Wilson is supposed to be a wonderful instructor. The very best. And you'll like all the people there." That part was absolutely accurate. Gabrielle always liked everyone everywhere.

"Ginny is the best," Twila said. "How many dogs are you taking?"

"One," Gabrielle replied. "Molly. My bichon."

Twila naturally assumed that she was kidding.

"And Holly's malamutes. Rowdy and Kimi. And my husband's golden, Mandy."

I said, "Mandy will do anything."

"Molly," Gabrielle said softly to me, "will not do just anything. She can be quite fussy. As can I, of course. As can I."

My father chose that moment to show up with the pot of clams. Gabrielle waited until Buck had served seconds or thirds to those who wanted more clams. Then, in a dangerously sweet voice, she said, "Buck, I need a quiet word with you."

"Any time!" he roared. "Any time except right now. More clams?"

"No. No, thank you."

"Now, Gabrielle, this is no time to go off your food."

"I am not off my food. But speaking of food, perhaps you might tell Twila about the sumptuous breakfasts served at mushing camp. Someone has apparently misrepresented the nature of the camp to her, and I am counting on you to enlighten her. At this very moment."

I sprang to my feet, grabbed my glass, raised it, and said, "A toast! To my father and my beloved stepmother! Thank you for the lobster and clams! Thank you for everything!"

In groups of dogs, behavior is contagious. If one dog leaps up and starts running around in figure eights, other dogs are likely to do the same.

The next dog was Pete, Steve's best man, who proposed a toast to Steve and me. Leah raised her glass to Rita. Steve and I drank to the joining of our canine families. Gabrielle had no opportunity to have a quiet word with my father, who saluted her. The uncles rose and wished health and happiness to the lucky couple. My father again stood up and had us drink to Sammy the pup for having brought Steve and me together. As Rita was lifting her glass and opening her mouth, Jennifer Pasquarelli's cell phone rang. Jennifer dashed from her table and headed to a far corner of the little yard. Rita, ignoring the interruption, made a long and touching speech about her friendship with Steve and me. When she finished, everyone drank in our honor, and Jennifer finally returned to the group. She did not propose a toast. Rather, she whispered quietly in Kevin's ear. His jovial expression vanished. I felt sorry for him. On his own, he'd never have ruined the happy mood. Jennifer, however, was making a silent fuss. Everyone, of course, responded by asking what was wrong. Unfortunately, Jennifer answered the question. There'd been another murder, she said. In Newton. This time, the victim was a veterinarian. Perhaps Steve had known her? Her name was Claire Langceil.

Chapter 36

Not all that long ago, Newton Police Officer
Jennifer Pasquarelli had almost lost her job
over a highly publicized dispute she'd had
with the presumed perpetrator of the heinous
crime of violating the leash law. Thereafter,
Jennifer had completed some sort of social
skills training course, whether graded or un-
graded I didn't know, although I suspected
that if the course was indeed graded, Jennifer
had squeaked by with D minus. Jennifer
clogged the cogs of social machinery as effec-
tively as Kevin made them spin. But she and
her law-enforcement partner apparently got
along well. The call she'd received hadn't
been a summons to rush to the murder scene
and solve the crime. Jennifer wasn't even a
detective. Her partner had just wanted to
keep her informed, or so she said.

If our behavior immediately following the
announcement of Claire's murder had been
analyzed to determine aptitude for detective
work, the person attaining the highest score

wouldn't have been Jennifer. Kevin himself would've scored lower than Steve, who heard the news and vanished into the house. When he came back a few minutes later, he drew me aside and said, "I tried to call Mac and Judith, but all I got was a message. I tried Mac's cell phone. Same thing."

I shrugged. "They're both out? Not answering? His cell phone is off? But it was a good idea."

"Not necessarily. Their house is right near Route 2 and 128. With no traffic, you could get back there from Newton in no time. Or from Cambridge. Brookline. Belmont. It's maybe twenty minutes from Newton. Convenient location. If someone had answered, it wouldn't necessarily mean anything."

"Still, it was worth a try. Dear God, how awful! And here we are with all these people and this mess to clean up. And four strawberry shortcakes in Rita's refrigerator. Steve, this is going to sound so horrible that I wouldn't say it to anyone except you, but I have no intention of ever marrying anyone else. This is it."

"That's not so horrible, is it?"

"This is my only wedding! I don't want it ruined. By anything. I wanted this whole weekend to be for us. I know it's selfish. I should be thinking of Daniel and Gus and Claire and the other women. But I don't have any other life to marry you in! I don't want this weekend wrecked. I don't even know what to do right now."

"Gabrielle seems to have it in hand," Steve said.

While browsing recently in a Harvard Square bookstore, I'd noticed a book called *How To Make People Like You in Sixty Seconds*. Or maybe it was . . . *Ninety Seconds*. Anyway, the title had made me think, as usual, of Alaskan malamutes, but also of Gabrielle. I hadn't bought the book; I assumed that I knew what it said. When a new visitor appeared, Rowdy made repeated trips to the toy basket and presented our guest with carefully selected fleece dinosaurs and chewmen. Kimi specialized in gazing intently at her subject's face. *You fascinate me,* she seemed to say. Sammy's strategy consisted of fulfilling his mission in life, which was to be infectiously happy and thus to spread his happiness to everyone he met; he carried a benign virus of joy to which no one was immune. I, of course, was sick with love for him. Like Rowdy and Kimi, Gabrielle made people feel special. Like Sammy, she passed along happiness. But the crucial reason that people immediately liked Gabrielle was the same reason they immediately liked the dogs: Gabrielle's contagiously happy fascination with people wasn't some pretense she'd learned from a book; it was utterly genuine.

I should also mention that Gabrielle was a superb organizer. As Steve had noticed, she now had everyone busy depositing refuse in trash bags and carrying glasses and serving dishes to the kitchen.

"When Gabrielle gives orders," Steve said, "people feel flattered."

"Holly," Gabrielle said, "we have more paper tablecloths somewhere. Could you find them? Pete is helping Rita with the short-cakes, and the cream will need to be whipped."

"Thank you for taking charge, Gabrielle. I love you. Is Buck being impossible?"

With a confiding smile, she said, "He does *do* things, doesn't he."

"He's planning something mortifying. Do you have any idea what it is?"

"It will sort itself out. We'll think of something. We always do! The tablecloths?"

After I'd found the tablecloths in a kitchen drawer, I kept running back and forth between the house and yard. I set the tables for dessert, answered questions about the locations of household items, and caught scraps of conversation.

"SHOUTING?" my father bellowed. "I'M NOT SHOUTING!"

In saying that she wanted a "quiet word" with Buck, Gabrielle had referred to her own part of the proposed conversation on the subject of mushing boot camp. She'd known him to be just about incapable of quiet words.

After she'd said something inaudible, he bellowed, "MISREPRESENTATION? Ask Twila! She's been to Ginny Wilson's boot camps, and she'll be the first person to tell you that she's had a wonderful time. You can hear the gusto in her voice."

Gabrielle's reply got lost in a lecture that my cousin Leah was delivering to Twila's kennel helper. "The term *kennel girl* is sexist. You aren't a girl, are you?" The silent kennel person must've whispered a reply. "Well, yes," Leah conceded, "*kennel woman* does admittedly sound ridiculous. But there's no reason you can't stand up for yourself and insist on *kennel help,* is there?"

"No," my father boomed, "I did not imagine that you were the bivy type. We're staying in our own private cabin." After evidently listening for an unprecedented ten seconds, he said, "Because everyone else there *will* be the bivy type, that's why. Everyone else will be in bivies or tents or out under the stars. Therefore, we'll have the cabin to ourselves. And that's about as private as you can get! And Twila didn't think that you were joking about taking a bichon. If she had thought you were joking, there'd have been only one thing for you and Molly to do, and that'd be to get right out there and show her! Gabrielle, when life issues you a challenge, there's only one way to respond, and that's to get yourself right out there and show what you're made of!"

At about that time, Pete and Rita came downstairs with shortcakes and strawberries. As I supplied Rita with cartons of heavy cream and a handheld electric mixer, Pete kept talking to her in a hushed, fervent tone. ". . . drunk," he said. "And then she came on to me. It was the last thing I expected. And then she sent me this E-mail about the moon."

"Embarrassing," Rita said.

"Yes. And I'll have to go to her funeral. I don't know what I'm going to say to Daniel."

"Anything," advised Rita, "except the full truth."

"Poor Claire," Pete said. "I won't mention the moon."

When all of us reassembled in the yard with strawberry shortcake and coffee, the gathering took on a superficial tone of returning to normal. Uncle Don and Uncle Dave acted in a way that Steve usually dismissed as "Minnesota nice." At Buck's request, Twila got North, who greeted everyone by flashing his eyes and wagging his tail, and displayed a rare quality in an Alaskan malamute: the ability to be in the presence of food without stealing it. Buck tried to persuade Gabrielle that in hearing a reference to an outhouse, she'd misheard an innocuous reference to an outbuilding. "At our age," he said with hideous sympathy, "it's easy to get confused." Jennifer kept plucking at Kevin's sleeve and muttering in his ear. He nobly resisted her efforts to break up the party. Now that a semblance of order had been restored, however, I wished that everyone would leave.

In fact, no one stayed late. The uncles left for their hotel. Kevin and Jennifer gave Leah an unofficial police escort back to Harvard. My father helped Twila and the kennel woman with North and the rest of the team. Pete insisted on accompanying Rita in walking Willie, who unaccountably displayed no desire to bite Pete's ankles. While Steve and I were giving our own dogs a chance to run in the yard, I kept thinking of Mac and Judith. Maybe they hadn't answered the phone because Mac had gone to the police to turn himself in. As I imagined the scenario, he'd made a full confession to Judith, who was bravely accompanying him. Or maybe it was Ian or Olivia who had confessed, and both parents were loyally accompanying the murderous child.

Chapter 37

When I walked into my kitchen at seven-thirty on the morning of September 28, which is to say, on the day before my first and only wedding, Buck was standing at the stove burning things. The entire stove was covered in grease. Six slices of blackened bacon rested on a paper towel set directly on a countertop, not on a plate. The air was thick with droplets of hot fat. Eight revolting-looking brown objects sizzled in a pan. They appeared to be lumps of rubber and certainly smelled that way.

"Sunny side up!" my father proclaimed.

He was not alone in the kitchen. Sammy the puppy lay at his feet. On the counter next to the burned bacon and the battery from the smoke detector rested my directory of the membership of the Alaskan Malamute Club of America. The thick booklet was held open by a grease-covered sugar bowl. Jabbing an elbow toward the directory, my father said, "You see that? The centerfold! That's how proud Twila is of North. Two full pages, thirteen photographs, smack in the center of the directory, everything from a puppy picture to show photos to shots of North working in harness. Now that's what I call pride!"

"Good morning," I said. "Yes, since you asked, I slept well."

Reading from the centerfold, Buck said, " 'North, as we travel the path together, you enrich every moment of the journey. Thank you.' And you know what that represents, Holly? It represents appropriate gratitude to a deserving dog."

"Yes, it does," I agreed.

Turning from the stove to look me in the eye, Buck said, "And where, I ask you, is *your* public expression of gratitude to *your* Alaskan malamutes?"

"May I remind you that I am getting married tomorrow afternoon? And that this is probably not the best time to criticize me?" With an expression of transparently fake abashment, Buck made a show of shifting his gaze to Sammy, who continued to hold his down-stay while whipping the floor with his happy tail. "I'm in the doghouse, kid," Buck said. "With my daughter and my wife."

I was tempted to go to the third floor to make my own breakfast. With the intention of keeping Buck two floors away from us, we'd stocked the refrigerator with milk, eggs, butter, yogurt, juice, and fruit, and the cupboards with coffee, sugar, cereal, and English muffins.

"With Gabrielle, you deserve to be," I said. "Has Sammy had his breakfast?"

"Steve fed all the dogs an hour ago."

"Where is he?"

"Taking a shower. And in his absence, let me tell you that you've got my approval for this marriage."

"I'm glad," I said.

Smiling at Sammy, he said, "Nothing to be ashamed of! Quality dog! Best reason on God's green earth!"

"If you ever so much as hint at any such idea, if you ever so much as *think* it —"

The phone rang. The first of many calls, this one was from Ceci, who apologized for the early hour, but needed a consultation about the tents. Would we really need them? The forecast sounded perfect, but New England was, after all, New England, and . . . I'd no sooner promised to check the National Weather Service web site and hung up than the phone rang again. Uncle Don needed a reminder about directions to my house. I supplied them, and then made coffee and toast. Buck leaped to the conclusion that my polite refusal of his bacon and eggs indicated morning sickness. This new explanation for my marriage delighted him. I didn't have the heart to disappoint him. Or the stomach to digest his cooking. Not long after Steve emerged from the bathroom, the uncles arrived, and Buck inflicted breakfast on them. I escaped into the shower. When I'd finished bathing and dressing, the uncles and Gabrielle were leaving to pick up Leah, who was accompanying Uncle Don, Uncle Dave, and my stepmother to Ceci's house to assist in preparing for the wedding. To my relief, Twila had consulted my father about the possibility of finding a place to run her dog team, and Buck had not only suggested a state forest south of Boston, but had inveigled an invitation to go along. Before our guests departed, I reminded Gabrielle that she, Leah, Rita, and I had a one o'clock appointment to get our hair and nails done, and I reminded everyone that the rehearsal was at five o'clock at Ceci's. We'd go directly from there to Nuages for the rehearsal dinner.

My father and I had a little tiff. He wanted to take Rowdy and Kimi with him. Having groomed them for the wedding, I refused. On September 28, there was obviously no snow, and Twila's team would be pulling a cart, not a sled, along trails and dirt roads. Buck and I were still arguing when Twila's car and her immense dog-box trailer were in the street and she was ready to leave. Buck was in the passenger seat.

"No, you will not have time to groom them when you get back," I insisted, "and I want them clean for the wedding. Twila is skipping the rehearsal, and she's going to groom North then, but you need to be at the rehearsal! Rowdy and Kimi are going to camp with you. They'll get plenty of time in harness there. It will not hurt them to miss today's run."

Twila ended the spat by smiling at me from the driver's seat, giving a conspiratorial wave, and driving off.

As I was standing on the sidewalk loudly thanking Twila and heaven, Kevin Dennehy's back door opened. He was on his way out, but stopped for a minute to give me a few pieces of information about Claire's murder. To my shame, I realized that I'd been so preoccupied with my own plans and with my impossible father that I'd almost forgotten about Claire.

"Sodium pentobarbital," Kevin said. "They rushed it through." He meant the autopsy, I assumed. "You know what that is."

"Of course." Sodium pentobarbital is the drug that veterinarians use for euthanasia. The brand names for it are a bit grotesque: Euthasol and, worse, Beauthanasia. "Was that the cause of death?"

"No. Same as the others. Head trauma. Blunt instrument."

"That talk we had. I know you must've passed along what I told you. Has anyone followed up on it?"

He rolled his eyes and shrugged his shoulders.

"The world would be a safer place if you ran it," I said.

"I gotta go."

"Claire Langceil was a friend of Mac McCloud's. She and her husband and son were at Mac and Judith's when we had dinner there last Saturday night. Mac and Judith's son and daughter were there, too. Ian and Olivia. And Olivia's husband, John Berkowitz. Someone needs —"

He interrupted me by pounding his right fist into his left hand.

"You're a Cambridge cop," I said. "I know."

"Hey, you got beautiful weather for your wedding."

We did, too. But Kevin's remark and the warm sunshine reminded me of my promise to Ceci to check the forecast and make a decision about tents. I scurried inside to my office, dislodged Tracker the cat from my mouse pad, and visited three weather sites, all of which predicted that Sunday and Monday would be clear and mild. Finding itself on the mouse, my right hand automatically performed the familiar act of checking for E-mail. As usual, I had dozens of new messages from my dog lists. Scanning for personal E-mail, I saw that I had a message from Mac McCloud. The subject read: Urgent.

Holly,
I need a great and unpleasant favor that I cannot ask of my family. Please meet me at my house as soon as possible.

Best,
Mac

The message had been sent only ten minutes earlier. The time was now nine forty-five. It struck me as more than odd that Mac had E-mailed instead of calling, but the phone had been busy off and on all morning, and he knew that I read my E-mail all the time. Still, I tried to call him, but got no answer. On the off chance that Kevin hadn't actually left, I checked his driveway, but his car was gone. I made no effort to track him down, mainly because I somehow had the sense that Mac's urgent message had to do with dogs rather than with murder. I found Steve in the yard with Sammy. After quoting Mac's E-mail and saying that I'd tried to call him, I said, "Steve, Mac knows that we're getting married tomorrow. I have a bad feeling that this is about Uli. I need to go there. I need to go there right now."

Chapter 38

Steve refused to let me go alone. I argued that when we exchanged wedding vows, I wasn't going to promise to obey him and that I had no intention of accepting orders from him now, either. He countered by saying that if he were setting out for some destination that I considered risky, I'd refuse to let him go alone. I reminded him that all the murders had taken place in the evening near the victims' houses or, in Laura Skipcliff's case, at her hotel. He said, "So what?"

I called Ceci, told her to cancel the tents, and managed to end the conversation. Then Steve and I left. We took separate cars. I had no idea how long the urgent favor would take. Steve and Pete were meeting at one o'clock to pick up the champagne and the rest of the wine, hard liquor, and mixers. I, of course, was getting my hair and nails done. It made sense for each of us to be mobile. Still, as Steve's van followed behind my

Blazer out Route 2, I missed his company and kept glancing in the rearview mirror to make sure he was with me.

As Steve had remarked, Mac and Judith's house was conveniently close to Cambridge as well as to Belmont, Brookline, and Newton. For once, there was no traffic by the Fresh Pond Mall or on Route 2. Only twenty minutes or so after we'd left home, I turned into the long wooded driveway that led to Mac and Judith's house. One car was parked in the rounded area at the end of the drive. I couldn't tell whether it was Mac's or Judith's, but Steve said it was Mac's. Almost everything about the house looked just as it had on Saturday when we'd arrived for dinner. In the morning light, I couldn't tell whether any lights were on. As Steve and I walked to the front entrance, I noticed that two big pots of blue asters now sat on either side of the door. The glass panels were clean, and the hardware still shone. No sound came from the house. Steve rang the bell. We waited silently.

Reaching past Steve, I rang the bell again. No one answered. Then I rapped impatiently, just as Claire Langceil had done. Feeling annoyed, I said, "Why would you summon a person on some urgent mission the day before her wedding, and then not answer the door?"

Steve replied to my question by trying the

handle and then by opening the unlocked door. "Mac?" he called. "Judith?" His deep, strong voice reverberated in the spacious entryway. It seemed to descend the stairs to Mac's office and to ascend to the first floor. "Mac? Judith? It's Steve and Holly." This time, he shouted. He must have been audible throughout the large house, even in the bedrooms and in Judith's study on the top floor.

I'm not a reader of gothic novels, but I didn't need to be one to have the vaguely unreal sense that we'd been cast as characters in some melodrama, or perhaps in a parody of one. Even so, I felt compelled to play my role. "Mac?" I called. "I'm here. Where are you? Judith, are you here?"

With no discussion, Steve and I simultaneously decided that enough time had elapsed to justify our actually entering the house. Also by unspoken agreement, we headed side by side up the stairs in search of Mac or Judith. The immense living room, with the fireplace at one end and the dining table at the other, was as tidy as it had been when we'd arrived for dinner. There was no fire. The ashes had been removed and the hearth cleaned. Except for a basket of yellow chrysanthemums, the table was bare. The kitchen, too, was neat and presentable, but it showed signs of use. The scent of coffee lingered, and a large skillet in the dish drainer was still damp. A few droplets of water were visible on the tile floor near a large blue pottery dish that had a blue floral motif and bore Uli's name. The dish was half full of water.

Noticing a collection of message pads and a pen on a counter beneath a wall phone, I said in an undertone, "Maybe there's a note."

"Why leave a note there?" Steve asked sensibly. "Why not on the front door?" He, too, spoke very softly, as if we'd become intruders who wanted to avoid detection.

Still, I checked. The message pads were blank. As if compelled to search for proof that I was expected, I ran my eyes over the cabinets, counters, and appliances. The kitchen was remarkably uncluttered. The cooking utensils must have been in drawers or cupboards. A wall calendar with a photograph of a Bernese mountain dog hung near the phone, but there was no corkboard or message board.

"Nothing," I said. Suddenly inspired, I called, "Uli! Uli, come! Here! Uli, here!"

We listened, but heard nothing.

"Probably with Judith," Steve said.

A quick look in the other rooms on that floor revealed no one. The bathroom was obviously meant only for guests: Small lilac towels hung on a rack, and there were no bottles of shampoo, no tubes of toothpaste, no cosmetics. What seemed to be a guest room held a double bed, a dresser, and little else. Another room served as a pantry and storage area. With a sense of increasing alarm, I headed upstairs. Steve followed. Absurdly, we called out Mac's and Judith's names. When I reached the landing, I looked through the open door of Judith's little study and then entered. In contrast to the rest of the house, the room was messy, but only in the manner of a writer's workspace. A computer and printer sat on the desk, the surface of which was thick with paper. Yellow legal pads were piled on the floor. Books leaned lopsidedly against one another on shelves. Paper spilled from a wastebasket. Hurriedly, I led the way to Judith's bedroom. The bed had been made. All the drawers were closed. I opened the door to the big closet. No one was in it. The other two bedrooms on the second floor had evidently once been the children's. In one, framed photographs of stringed instruments suggested Ian. The other room had a flowered comforter and matching pillowcases. Neither room looked used.

"No one," I said at normal volume. "Mac's office is on the ground floor. I guess his bedroom is there, too. We probably should've looked there first."

We both ran down the stairs to the first floor, then down to the entryway, where we paused to locate light switches and illuminate the stairs that led downward. Foolish though it was, we again called out for Mac and Judith.

This time, we heard a sound. It was difficult to identify. A soft groan? A sigh?

As I was about to go straight ahead toward Mac's office, Steve unhesitatingly opened a door on the left. We stepped into a large bedroom with off-white walls and a full bed with a handwoven rust-colored spread neatly tucked in. On the far side of the bed was a nightstand with a pottery lamp, a stack of paperback books, an empty glass, and a prescription vial, the kind of plastic bottle used to dispense tablets and capsules. Its cap lay next to it. Sprawled face up on the floor at the foot of the bed was Mac McCloud. He wore a navy turtleneck sweater over khaki pants, and he had shoes and socks on, expensive-looking white running shoes and thick ragg wool socks. His eyes were closed, and his face looked lifeless; despite the sound we'd heard, my first impression was of death. Steve, however, dropped to the floor next to Mac and felt for a pulse. I didn't need to see Steve's face to understand that he'd automatically shifted to his professional mode; the set of his shoulders alone conveyed absolute concentration and effortless efficiency. As he checked Mac's mouth and jaw to make sure that Mac had an airway open, he said, "Go see what's in that bottle on the nightstand.

Don't pick it up. Don't touch it."

"Steve, that's pointless. He's obviously tried —"

"Just read the label. Don't touch the bottle."

I had to walk around Mac and Steve to reach the nightstand, and when I got to it, I had to bend down to make out the print. "Ace." Needlessly, I added, "Acepromazine. The bottle is empty. The prescription is five years old. It was prescribed for Uli."

"Find a phone. Call nine-one-one. Do you know the address here?"

"Yes."

"Give them the address, the phone number, his age. Any medical history? Heart?"

"No. Nothing."

"Tell them that he's apparently ingested an unknown quantity of acepromazine. Stay calm. Speak slowly. Call right now."

As I made my way back around Mac and Steve, Mac began to groan, and as I left the room, I heard him retch. In dogs, vomiting could mean a serious risk of aspiration. If there was anything Steve could do to minimize that risk, he'd do it. Adopting Steve's calm manner, I suppressed the urge to dash frantically in search of a phone. Instead, I walked smoothly to Mac's office, picked up the phone on his desk, dialed 911, and tried my best to give the crucial information as clearly as Steve would've done. "An unknown quantity of acepromazine," I said. "The address is 89 Milford Street. The door will be open. There's a flight of stairs on the left, going down. That's where he is."

Still cool, I went up the stairs to the front door, opened it, and left it open. Then I returned to Mac's bedroom, which now reeked of vomit. Steve had moved Mac to the bed and was holding him so that he leaned over with his head between his knees. One sleeve of Mac's turtleneck was spattered, and on the floor where Mac had lain was a mess that I'll avoid describing.

"They're on their way," I said. "He waited until Judith left. He didn't want her to be the one to find him. That's what the message meant."

"This isn't suicide," Steve said.

"Obviously not. He's alive." Even so, we spoke as if Mac weren't there. Indeed, there was an absent quality about him. His eyes remained closed, and he hung heavy in Steve's arms.

Steve shook his head. "Ace can be lethal. Suicides use it. But Mac had lots of other options that would've been quick and sure. Mac didn't do this."

"Then someone set it up. Someone staged it." I thought for a moment. "To spare him a trial. And a jail sentence. Someone who loves him. Judith."

"Unless it's someone's idea of justice. Maybe both at once. Execute him. And spare him."

Another possibility came to me. Indeed, what came to me was the likely possibility, the one that would account for the presence of the empty bottle of acepromazine in a prominent place on the nightstand. I was about to say so when sirens interrupted me. The taxes in wealthy suburbs get spent, in part, on extraordinarily rapid emergency services. In what seemed like two seconds after the first scream of the first siren, I heard people in the entryway. Although I'd given directions about going down the stairs, I stepped out of the bedroom and pointed to its door. The first two EMTs descended and entered the room, and two others followed almost immediately with great quantities of medical paraphernalia. A uniformed police officer told me to get out of the way. At first, I lingered in the hallway outside the bedroom. I heard Steve say something about injection sites and about finding none. Then someone asked me to move. Still feeling weirdly like an intruder in the house, I went outdoors. In the driveway were an emergency medical van, a second emergency vehicle the size of a truck, and a police cruiser. The cops, Steve, and the EMTs, with Mac on a stretcher, all emerged from the house. Steve was walking right next to the stretcher, near

Mac's head, and speaking quietly to him, as he did with sick animals. Steve left Mac for only a moment to come to me and say, "I'm going along with Mac. He's conscious. Go ahead and go to the beauty shop."

"But what about Judith?"

"Let the police handle it. I've got to go." He wrapped his arms around me and squeezed for just a second. "I love you, Holly. I'll see you at Ceci and Althea's. At five." With that, he ran to his van and jumped in. Both medical vehicles drove off, the siren of the one transporting Mac already wailing. Steve followed.

I was left in the driveway with two cops, a young woman and a sad-looking man with salt-and-pepper hair and a lined face. "It's worse when they shoot themselves," he said to me.

"What?"

"It makes an awful mess. It's hard on the families. This way's ugly, but it's easier. More considerate. But this one's going to be all right. Lucky he lost his lunch, I guess." He paused. "He got a wife? Kids?"

"A wife. The children are grown. They don't live here."

"You got any idea where the wife is?"

"No. I'm sorry. I have no idea."

I expected the cops to return to the house. It was my understanding from Kevin Dennehy that the first officer on the scene had the obligation to decide whether a crime had occurred and to act accordingly. In this case, it seemed to me that the house should be declared a crime scene and appropriately sealed off. It also seemed to me that I should be questioned. Nothing of the kind occurred. All the officer asked me was whether he should close the front door or whether I'd do it. I said that I would. The cops got into the cruiser and drove off.

As promised, I went back to the entrance to Mac and Judith's house. As promised, I closed the front door. I pulled it shut. From the inside.

Chapter 39

In scanning the kitchen in search of a note from Mac, I had, as I've mentioned, seen a wall calendar with a photo of a Bernese mountain dog. My dog-loving eyes had centered on the handsome animal, who'd looked wonderfully like a young, healthy Uli. Only one other feature of the calendar had caught my eye, namely, a heart-shaped red sticker on the square for September 1; the little handwritten notes on other dates had barely registered on me. My own calendar had the same red hearts, reminders to give my dogs their monthly doses of Heartgard, a medication to prevent heartworm disease, the packages of which contained sheets of red hearts to affix to calendars.

Now, alone in the house, I returned to the kitchen to reexamine the calendar. This time, I read the handwritten notations, all in the same writing: *4:00 dentist, 10:30 cut & color,* and so forth. *Color* had to mean Judith; she used this calendar. In the square for the previous Saturday was *Dinner here*. Also noted in that square and in those for the other three Saturdays, including today, was *11:00 Sirius*. Sirius is, of course, the dog star. The cryptic notation evidently referred to a regular Saturday morning appointment that had something to do with Uli. Opening the cabinets near the calendar and the phone, I soon found a telephone directory. In the business listings was Sirius Dog Grooming. I dialed the number.

A woman answered. "Sirius!" In the background, dryers roared. A dog barked.

I said that I was trying to reach Judith Esterhazy.

"Hang on! She's around. Let me see . . . she's drying Uli. JUDITH? Can you take a phone call?"

Judith's voice was cool and unrevealing. "Hello? This is Judith."

"Judith, it's Holly Winter. I'm at your house. You need to come home."

"I'm almost finished. What's . . . ?"

"You need to get home now. This is something we can't talk about on the phone. Just come home."

She said that it would take her fifteen minutes. I hung up. If I'd wanted to snoop, I could've done so before I'd placed the phone call. Far from feeling even the slightest impulse to poke through Mac's and Judith's possessions, I felt an urgent desire to get out of the house. My most acute sense, however, was of missing my dogs. I desperately longed for Rowdy's strength, Kimi's intensity, and Sammy's contagious optimism. Cursing myself for having left them in Cambridge, I went outside, paced around, and eventually sat in my car, where I kept checking the time. Exactly eighteen minutes after I'd hung up the phone, Judith's car appeared. When I groom my dogs, I end up damp, disheveled, and furry. When Judith got out of her car, I could see that her short hair was as sleek as ever. To take Uli to what was evidently a do-it-yourself grooming shop, she'd had the sense to wear jeans and a T-shirt, but her jeans were unfaded and unripped, and the T-shirt was bright raspberry with decorative stitching at the neckline and on the sleeves.

She didn't smile at me, but gave a little nod and said, "Just let me get Uli out."

Judith opened the rear passenger door of her car and then the door of a metal crate. Remembering the help Uli had needed with stairs, I moved next to Judith and, without asking, joined her in taking most of the dog's weight as he climbed out. Once Uli was on the ground, he shook himself, wagged his tail, and eyed me happily. In the daylight, his old-age cataracts were plainly visible.

"I groom Uli every Saturday morning," Judith said. "It's a special arrangement I have with the shop. He's too big for me to lift onto my own grooming table, and he hasn't been able to jump up for a long time. We need the hydraulic table at the shop. And the people there are very kind about lifting him in and out of the tub."

"Every week. That's a lot."

"He's beginning to lose bladder control. These old-dog drugs do wonders, but they stop short of performing outright miracles."

We were walking toward the house. When we reached the door, she said, "This is about Bruce, isn't it? It is. Come in."

I'd closed the door, but left it unlocked. As if she knew exactly what I'd done, Judith didn't insert a key, but simply opened the door. The entryway showed no sign of foot traffic; it was just as it had been when Steve and I arrived.

Glancing to the left, Judith said, "Bruce isn't here?"

I shook my head. Then Judith and I supported Uli as he slowly climbed up the stairs. Judith's T-shirt exposed her arms. It would've been easy to believe that they belonged to a weightlifter who'd overdone liposuction and been left with nothing but skin, bone, and contrastingly massive muscle. "When there's no one here to help," said Judith, "I use a towel. But this is much easier. Uli likes the feel of hands. Coffee? Tea?"

"Tea would be good."

"Endless pots of sweet tea," she said. "The

British answer to any crisis. Soothes the nerves."

My own nerves were beyond the powers of tea. Judith, however, was composed. As she ran water into a kettle, set it on the stove, got out a heavy blue-and-white teapot, and put cups, saucers, spoons, sugar, and cream on the kitchen table, her thin face remained calm, and her hands were steady. The only sign of strain I saw in her was the absence of body fat, sad evidence of chronic stress rather than the acute distress I was struggling to conceal. The water seemed to take an hour to reach a boil. While she waited to make tea, Judith picked up Uli's big ceramic bowl of fresh-looking water, took the bowl to the sink, washed it, rinsed it thoroughly, re-filled it, and replaced it on the floor. Then she coaxed Uli toward it and rested a hand on his back as he took a small drink. As soon as he'd done so, he looked up at Judith as if to assure himself that he'd pleased her.

When the tea was finally ready, Judith and I sat at the kitchen table. I was on one of the long sides, and Judith was to my right, at the head of the table. Uli seated himself on her left, between us, not in the manner of a dog who intends to beg at the table, but in the companionable way of a dog who simply wants to be with the one he loves. When Judith had poured my tea, I stirred in two tea-spoonfuls of sugar and so much cream that the tea turned almost white.

I sipped, cleared my throat, and said, "I got an urgent E-mail message from Mac this morning. He asked me to come here immediately. His E-mail said that he needed a great and unpleasant favor that he couldn't ask of his family. When I got here, no one answered the bell. The door was unlocked. I found Mac on the floor of the downstairs bedroom. He'd taken an overdose of ace. The empty bottle was on the nightstand."

The hollows under Judith's cheekbones deepened. Her full lips thinned. Her face and body were rigid.

"I called nine-one-one," I continued. "Two ambulances came. When everyone left, I checked your calendar over there by the phone. And then I looked in the phone book for Sirius. I didn't want you to have to come home and . . ."

"Thank you." Judith brought her mug of tea to her mouth, but seemed to drink nothing. "Kindness always surprises me, somehow. I've had so much of the opposite. It's a blessing, really, a grace, if you will, that I still know kindness when I see it. And you are kind. In return, I think you're owed an explanation. I'm tempted to slip into triteness and say that I've been worried sick about Bruce, but it's not true. What I've been, really, is worried thin. I saw a therapist this

348

summer. For only a few sessions. But she gave me courage."

"It can't have been easy," I said with deliberate vagueness.

"In a way, it was. Oddly. Really, once I started, it was easier to confront Bruce directly than it had been to overlook things and, once in a while, to ask questions and get lies for answers. I didn't see the therapist after that. I always *knew*, in one sense, and at the same time, I didn't know. Both. Equally. It was a bizarre state. I knew about some of them. Bonny Carr. He talked about her. 'My friend Bonny Carr.' Endlessly. And Laura Skipcliff, the love of his life. That was strictly an emotional affair. A big deal is made of those these days, but let me assure you that it didn't even begin to cause me the gut-wrenching pain that the real affairs did. Strangely enough, Holly, Bruce didn't love those women. He loved Laura. But the others were nothing more than his whores. His real affairs had nothing to do with love." She paused. "Where was I? Yes. The most bizarre feature of the whole catastrophe was its effect on Bruce. I confronted him. And he went completely to pieces. He begged me to stay."

"And you did."

"With great ambivalence. Great conflict. He admitted everything. In some ways, one of the worst things he'd done was to send me to therapy. I didn't actually *go*. Bruce *sent* me. For help with my paranoia!"

"It sounds to me as if Mac was the one who —"

"He absolutely refused. We needed couples therapy. We needed to talk it all out. Bruce insisted that we had to let bygones be bygones. He wanted us to enjoy what we had now and what we were going to have. But he could not endure the guilt. The sight of me ate away at him. One night, I remember, he began to cry, and what he said was, 'You've never done a single thing to deserve the pain I've caused you.'"

"So he tried to undo what he'd done."

"He tried to eradicate its causes. He tried to atone." Judith sighed deeply. "He came to see those women for what they were. This morning, of course, he finally eradicated what he saw as the root cause. I have been dreading this all along." She bent down to seek solace as I'd often done myself, by burying her face in her beloved dog's thick, clean coat.

"Judith, did you know?"

"Bruce stalked those women. He cyberstalked them. Is that the word? On the World Wide Web. Strange, isn't it? In a way, of course, he knew them intimately, but some of them he hardly knew. It sounds melodramatic to say this, but Bruce led a double life. Once he was jolted out of his trance, once he really got it that he'd almost lost me, and almost lost his real life, this life, he saw those women for what they were. He kept . . . well, let me show you. I'll be right back." She rose. Uli got to his feet. "Uli, wait here, sweetheart," she said gently. "I have to go downstairs. I'll be right back. Holly, there's a bag of liver brownies in the freezer. Your recipe. Could you give him one? Distract him?"

I did as Judith asked. Uli nibbled at pieces of the liver brownie, and he listened as I babbled nonsense to him, but he'd obviously have preferred to be with Judith. When she came back, he moved toward her as if he hadn't seen her for weeks. Her face brightened and softened. She was carrying a stack of manila folders. Instead of showing them to me right away, she put them on the table, knelt next to Uli, and hugged him. Then she turned her attention back to me by sliding the folders toward me and saying, "You're welcome to look at these. In fact, take them! I want them out of this house."

I opened the first folder, which was, of course, devoted to Laura Skipcliff.

"There's quite a bit about their professional lives," Judith commented. "Laura Skipcliff. Anesthesiologist. She made a career of blotting out pain."

"Victoria Trotter lost her AKC privileges," I said. "A long time ago. For abusing a dog on show grounds."

Judith looked delighted. "I didn't know that! What I know about her was that she was a drunk. Bruce told me that much. Very little else, I might add. As you can imagine, I read books, a great many, about surviving infidelity, and Bruce read some of them, and every book, every single one, said that it was vital to get everything out in the open, to be able to ask and answer questions. But Bruce simply could not do it. He saw how much pain I was in, and he felt convinced that discussing things would cause me yet more pain. At first, he didn't even want me to know who these women were, but he came to see that I had to know. It was inevitable that I'd run into some of them. I was humiliated enough as it was without having to take the risk of seeing one of these women socially and not knowing. Of course, when I did see them, it was far from easy. But I wasn't made such a fool of all over again. And we simply had to keep seeing Daniel Langceil. And Gus. A child changes everything. Gus didn't choose to have a slut for a mother. It seemed best for me to endure seeing her. And I was so used to being hurt, you see! And then there were chance encounters. That signing and talk that you and Bruce did? Where that scummy little plagiarist had the nerve to show up?" Judith reached out and found the dossier on Elspeth Jantzen, and then pushed it in front of me. "Did you read

352

that manuscript of hers?"

"I thought it was outrageous. And stupid. Zazar! As if no one would see the similarity!"

"Yes."

"Judith, I had no intention of blurbing her book. I hadn't decided how I was going to get out of it, but I wasn't going to do it. You know, I thought that Mac . . ."

"That was just a reflex with Bruce. He was generous with his colleagues. Always. His first impulse was always to say yes." She evidently heard what she'd said. "In more ways than one."

"Judith, when did you begin to realize? When Laura Skipcliff . . . ?"

She winced at the name. "Bruce and I had separate rooms. So it wasn't as if I'd be aware if Bruce left. And we've always been quite independent. I do a fair number of readings and talks. We'd occasionally go to each other's events, but there was no obligation, and each of us had heard what the other had to say a million times. That night, I went to bed early, and for once, I slept. In the morning, when I listened to the radio, I had to wonder. I knew how terrible Bruce felt. Once he came to his senses, he couldn't come to terms with how he'd degraded himself. And me. So the thought crossed my mind. But I didn't take it seriously, I suppose. And an underground parking garage? So, it seemed like an ordinary urban crime.

But then when that horrible tarot woman died, I knew. And then, of course, he began to incriminate himself. The injections. I suppose that he found the police very slow to catch on. Eventually, he might as well have left notes saying that he was a veterinarian."

"You never asked him?"

"Never."

"Did you think about turning him in?"

"He was my husband! And he was trying to atone. Misguidedly. But he was trying to make amends. And my children! How could Olivia and Ian bear it if I turned their father over to the police?"

"And now?"

"Olivia is strong. She has my strength. But Ian! He is so sensitive. He always has been. A trial would have been dreadful for Ian. Worse for Ian than for Bruce. We talked about Ian just this morning, about the music he'd be playing at your wedding. Bruce was in an odd mood. He'd decided, I suppose. He cooked himself a big breakfast. Eggs with hot sauce. Sausages. He knew I'd be going out, of course. To groom Uli. I do that every Saturday morning. He waited until I left. And then he E-mailed you. To spare me. I'm sorry that you've had to go through this. The ugliness! And on the day before your wedding."

"Mac trusted me."

"It's strange, but I almost do, too. A

woman who's been betrayed as I've been trusts almost no one. But you and I are bonded. Through dogs. We know what love is. And I'm happy that you've found Steve. You won't have a life of lies and betrayal."

"The only perfect fidelity I ever expect isn't from human beings. It's from —"

"Your dogs. Of course." She leaned over to stroke Uli's head.

I quoted Senator Vest's eulogy, which is not, as Judith certainly knew, a eulogy on marriage: " 'Faithful and true, even to death.' "

Then, feeling close to Judith and ashamed to deceive her, I told her that Mac was still alive.

Chapter 40

"I've had a life of unconditional love," I said to Judith. "I know what it is to be loved by someone who'd never betray me and who cannot lie. Whenever I've thought that I'd never again know absolute trust and absolute fidelity, life has surprised me by sending that grace in some new and unexpected form."

"Sammy," she said. "Because Rowdy can't live forever."

Now and throughout the conversation that followed, Judith always kept at least one hand on Uli. Although it would have been easier for the old dog to sleep at her feet than it was for him to sit at her side, he made the effort to keep his head where she could touch it effortlessly. Sometimes he leaned his body against her for support. Sometimes he shifted position to rest the weight of his great head on her lap.

"And Kimi," I said. "Their love for me isn't identical. Their styles are different. Rowdy is lighthearted. He can turn serious if the need arises, but Kimi is a deeply serious soul. And I love them for who they are."

"No dog of mine has ever wanted other women," Judith said.

"No dog of mine, either." It somehow felt right to rest my hand, too, on Uli head's, near Judith's hand. "Judith, I cannot begin to imagine your pain. I don't know whether you know that Steve was married before. Recently. And briefly. But he was. I'd refused to marry him. So he married someone else. Precipitously. On the rebound. Stupidly. But he did it. And she was more horrible than I can begin to say. She cheated on him. Almost worse, for Steve, she was vicious to his dogs. He has a pitiful little pointer, Lady, who was brought to him for euthanasia. Steve rescued her. He kept her. And that monster kicked Lady. I saw her do it. To this day, I can barely make myself say that woman's name aloud. For all that she and Steve are divorced, for all that he is marrying me, I hate her with all my heart. I would truly like to strangle her."

"But you love Steve. Peculiar, isn't it? That that's humanly possible?"

"It is peculiar," I agreed. "But I do love Steve. I love him in spite of . . . I love him in spite of Anita."

"With dogs," said Judith, "there's never that *spite*, is there?"

"I didn't mean —"

"Are you sure? But I'm diverting you with word games. It's a bad habit of mine."

"Mine, too," I said. "Word games and dog talk."

"Distraction from agony. The fascination of true love. There's nothing wrong with either one, Holly."

I slid my hand slowly and tenderly across Uli's soft, clean coat until my palm rested on Judith's hand. "Judith," I said, almost whispering, "Mac wouldn't have taken that acepromazine. He might have injected it. He wouldn't have swallowed it. Steve and I have been together for years. We were together before . . . before Anita. We've been together since then. Judith, veterinarians know *everything* about euthanasia. They *know* how to end life. Mac wouldn't have had to bludgeon those women. He'd been all too close to all of them. He wouldn't have bludgeoned them first."

I pressed my hand firmly on Judith's. Her hand was so cold that it felt bloodless, but Uli's warmth seemed to radiate around it and up into my fingers. Her eyes were locked on Uli's; she didn't raise them even briefly to meet mine.

"Someone else gave Mac that ace this morning," I continued. "Someone else rid the world of his women."

I waited, but Judith said nothing.

"There are only three logical possibilities,"

I said gently. "Two of them are Ian and Olivia. Judith, I can see how much your children love you. When Steve and I were here for dinner, I watched when Ian helped you with Uli. And I heard the tune he wrote for Uli. He wrote that for you, too. It was about the love you share with this wonderful dog. Ian is an unusual person. He's almost miraculously gifted. And in other ways, he simply isn't like everyone else. And I've seen your relationship with Olivia. She even married a man who looks like you! You and Olivia are more than mother and daughter. You are almost sisters, too. Dear friends. I have a relationship like that with my cousin Leah. Leah is as close as I have to a daughter. I'd do anything for Leah. She'd do anything for me. So I have to ask myself, if your children knew how Mac has betrayed you, just what would they do for you?"

"Olivia adores her father," Judith said. "You had the opportunity to hear Claire on the subject. Loudly and intrusively. As usual. The others at least knew what they were. But Claire was deluded. She threw herself at Bruce. She actually imagined that Bruce was going to leave me for her and become a doting second father to her son! She made a fool of herself. Bruce always understood the distinction between his wife and his whores. It was a distinction that was lost upon Daniel's slut of a wife. Daniel is a sweet man. He deserved better. He put up with her endless jibes at him and her boundless narcissism. You know, Holly, she and her family were here many times. I cooked for them. I made them feel welcome. When I could have ridiculed her coarseness and her ignorance, I didn't do it. And in return . . . !"

"Someone exacted revenge."

Even now, Judith couldn't let go of her rage. "The hypocrisy! She knocked herself out to put on a show of friendship. Not that she was alone in her hypocrisy. Just look through these folders. They're a study in hypocrisy. Irony, if you will. Saint Bonny, who devoted her professional life to healing trauma and her personal life to causing it. Elspeth Jantzen, the red freak, with her stolen book about kindness to animals! And her personal devotion to cruelty. Every one of them!"

"Someone got even. Did Olivia do that for you, Judith? Did Ian? I admire Ian. I like him. But he is very devoted to you, and he is not like other people."

Suddenly brushing off my hand, Judith finally looked directly at me. "In this sham of a marriage, I have managed to hold to a few truths — my children, my writing, and dogs. Dogs! I have only one, and for someone like you or me, that's a dangerous state. And exactly what did Bruce do in response to the pitifully little that he knew was mine? My children were his children, too, so they were off limits. But just before your launch party, no time ago, it seems, he went after me yet again because my poor little books didn't sell, because I wasn't ambitious and didn't promote my work, because I was still not earning my keep, because I was nothing but a parasite! And do you know exactly what he threatened?"

"Uli," I said. "From the moment I read that E-mail this morning, I knew that this had something to do with Uli."

"It had *everything* to do with Uli. Bruce said that unless I started earning money, Uli would be my last dog. He said that when Uli died, that would be it. No more dogs. Ever." Judith's composure deserted her. Her thin face was contorted with grief. Her tears fell on Uli. "Uli is old! I'm all that's keeping him alive! How much longer can I keep him going? I cannot live without a dog! I cannot! Uli would love a puppy! Uli would teach a puppy his special ways, his little quirks! He would pass himself along through a puppy! When Bruce made that threat, my heart broke. Those vicious women had had my husband, and now I was going to lose the strength that kept me going!"

Softly, I said, "You must have thought about a divorce."

"And explain it to my children? Never! And what would I have done for a living?

Writing is all I know how to do. I could teach writing, but teaching would pay nothing, and it would leave me no time for my own work. In essence, Bruce threatened to kill me! He killed me over and over with his women and his lies, and then he threatened to take my life's blood away. I was on the verge of death."

"I can see that."

"And then a solution presented itself. You were there when it happened. At your launch party at The Wordsmythe, I learned that that filthy piece of trailer trash had died a natural death."

Reluctantly, I said, "Nina Kerkel."

Judith's eyes lit up. "Dead! I was overjoyed! The nonexistence of that conniving little slut was utter bliss. It was better than that! It was *repeatable* bliss."

"These files," I said. "These dossiers."

"Bruce can barely manage to send and receive E-mail. The World Wide Web is a truly marvelous resource, isn't it? Aerial photographs! Plot plans. And people continue to imagine that privacy still exists. It's an illusion. Like human fidelity. Human commitment. Human loyalty. Without dogs, there'd be no reality at all."

When Uli rose, I thought for a second that he was responding to the word *dog*. Then I heard the deep tones of Steve's voice. "Holly?" he called out.

"Here! In the kitchen." I felt frozen in place.

Steve entered and, with him, Mac, who looked pale and old.

"Mac refused to be admitted," Steve said.

Ignoring me, Mac said, "Judith, it's over. You and I need a few minutes alone together."

Judith merely nodded. Mac walked to her and held out his hand. She took it. He seemed to lift her to her feet. Then he rested an arm across her shoulders. Together, they made their way out of the kitchen. Uli, of course, followed them. It should, I suppose, have seemed strange to me that in their own house, they'd been the ones to leave when they could so easily have asked us to step outside. It simply didn't occur to me, mainly because I felt so relieved to be free of the intense contact with Judith and so comforted to be with Steve. Although I heard soft sounds from the staircase, I didn't wonder or even care where Mac, Judith, and Uli were going.

I stood up and melted into Steve, who said, "Holly, I love you so much. I can't begin to tell you how much I love you."

"I love you, too. I have never loved you more than I do right now."

"It was Judith," he said. "Maybe you know by now."

"When you left with Mac, I stayed here. I

363

figured out where Judith was. I called her and told her to come home. I wasn't frightened. I wasn't one of Mac's women, and I knew that she knew that. Steve, you were right about Nina Kerkel. All those articles in the papers? About serial murderers? We took those profiles much too literally. The resentful person, the isolated person, the person lost in daydreams, all of it — that was Judith. We knew that her books didn't sell. We knew all about Mac's attitude toward promoting sales. What we didn't know was that Mac had told her that unless she started to earn her keep, she couldn't get another dog after Uli died. Right after that, she heard about Nina Kerkel's death. And that was the trigger the papers talked about. Judith said that Nina Kerkel's death was bliss for her. She called it 'repeatable bliss.' What she didn't say outright was that she set Mac up. At first, she wanted me to think that he was the murderer. When that didn't work, I suggested that it might be Olivia or Ian. She couldn't see her children accused. She told me the truth. But she never got around to admitting outright that she'd set Mac up."

"He wants to go with her when she turns herself in. He feels responsible."

"He *is* responsible."

"They both are."

"So are those women, really. They did to

Judith what that horrible Francie did to Rita."

"Not by themselves."

"No, of course not. But —"

Mac interrupted me by suddenly and calmly walking into the kitchen. To my surprise, Uli was with him. Mac was breathing audibly and looked very ill.

"I carried Uli up the stairs," he explained. "He said his good-bye. Judith said hers. More times than I can remember, I've helped in just this way. A dog should leave this world peacefully, cradled in his owner's arms. It's always sad, but it's easier when the dog has bitten repeatedly, when everyone understands that the dog is a danger, a menace, and that all you can offer is that final act of caring. I always perform that act with love. As I did this time. A final act of caring."

Chapter 41

I returned home filled with overwhelming love for everyone in my life. As I drove back to Cambridge, I didn't even miss Steve, who was staying with Mac until the police arrived and Mac turned himself in. Steve's love and kindness traveled with me. When I got home, Leah, Rita, and Gabrielle were in the midst of a crisis; they barely noticed that I was late for our trip to the salon. My family being my family, the crisis was a dog crisis: Sammy the puppy had somehow managed to eat the rolled leather collar right off his own neck. He'd rejected the buckle and his tags, but he'd treated the leather as what it was, namely, a length of dead animal. My cousin, my best friend, and my stepmother had Sammy in the kitchen and were hovering around him so closely that he was in immediate danger of suffocation. Still, his tail was wagging, and he had a big, satisfied smile on his gorgeous face. I hugged Sammy, and then hugged Leah, Rita, and Gabrielle. I would, of course, tell them about the horror and sadness. But at the moment, I needed their fidelity, their commitment, their loyalty to me, which were not, as poor Judith had thought, illusory, but almost palpably real.

"The chances are good," I said, "that the collar will either come up or pass right through him, probably in the middle of our wedding. But don't worry about it. Steve won't let anything bad happen to Sammy."

Or to me, either, I thought.

By the freakish coincidence known in my family as "God spelled backward," Mac and Judith's wedding present had been delivered during my absence. Leah, ever herself, had high-handedly opened the package. I'd ordinarily have scolded her. Now, I felt nothing but gratitude to her for being her bossy self. The gift was a set of five large hand-painted ceramic dog bowls, duplicates of Uli's, but marked with the names of Steve's and my dogs: Rowdy, Kimi, Sammy, India, and Lady. I was running my hands over them and crying when Rita announced, "Holly, what's with the sentimentality? I know you! You're looking for an excuse to get out of having your hair and nails done. Remember? This is your show, and you're about to go Best of Breed. You're not walking into the ring of marriage ungroomed! We need to leave now!"

"But what about Sammy?" I protested. "Someone needs to keep an eye on him."

God spelled backward. Pete, Steve's best man and fellow vet, arrived, having already delivered the champagne and other drinks to Ceci and Althea's. Pete didn't really need to come to our house. I strongly suspected that he was just hoping to see Rita. As it was, he ended up keeping a watch over Sammy.

I don't have a clear memory of the salon. I know that on the drive there in Rita's BMW, I told Rita, Leah, and Gabrielle about Judith and Mac. It distressed me to tell the story. When I'd been with Judith, my emotions had been under tight control. Safe with my bridal party in Rita's posh car, I suffered from delayed shock. For some reason that I couldn't explain to myself, however, I omitted all mention of the dossiers. Before I'd left Mac and Judith's, Mac had said that Judith had wanted me to have the file folders on the kitchen table; she'd begged him to promise that I'd take them away. I'd complied. Last wishes and all that. Before leaving for the salon, I'd hustled them into my office, the abode of my cat, Tracker. Tracker had, as usual, hissed loudly and scratched me. Still, I felt such a surge of loyalty to her that I didn't even mind being scratched.

For the rest of the afternoon and evening, I was in a daze. I returned from the salon to discover that Steve, the last person to abandon a dog, had brought Uli home with him. I didn't mind. Far from it. In fact, rattled though I was, I made a quick phone call to Carla Guarini, our florist, to order yet one more floral collar. I know that the salon made us look beautiful, but only because I have the photos taken during the rehearsal and at the restaurant, Nuages. In entirely uncharacteristic fashion, I kept bursting into tears and didn't notice what I ate. I remember that Pete and Rita sat together. My father and Twila, after a successful day of running dogs, concocted a plan. Instead of spending the week in Cambridge, Twila and her team were driving to Gabrielle's house in Bar Harbor to enjoy the outdoors. Twila had never been to Maine before. She said that she wouldn't need a bedroom; she and North would sleep under the stars. At one point, Steve and I decided that it was too late to arrange recorded music for our wedding; we reconciled ourselves to having no music at all.

As I'd said to Judith, however, Ian wasn't like other people. I am, of course, a real dog person, which is to say that I'm an expert on human oddity, and even by my standards, Ian was very odd. It's more than a little peculiar, isn't it, to provide the music for a wedding the day after your father has euthanized your serial-killer mother? As Olivia had promised, Ian dressed formally, as did the other musicians. Olivia and John Berkowitz did not attend. Mac, of course, was also absent.

Everyone else we expected was there. As Rita, Leah, and I got dressed in Ceci's bedroom, I kept peering out the window to see who was arriving. Twila's dog-box trailer was parked on the street in front of the house; she intended to leave for Bar Harbor immediately after the reception. I saw Kevin escort his mother along the sidewalk. Behind them were Hugh and Robert, Althea's Sherlockian friends, and from the other direction I saw —

Ceci interrupted me and rattled my nerves by popping into the bedroom to free-associate. "Althea is being pigheaded!" Ceci exclaimed. "I have rehearsed my lovely poem about love and the moon for her, and I've offered over and over to help her with what she intends to say, but she refuses to let me so much as look at it, and I'm convinced that she's going to make a fool of herself and humiliate you by reading from the Canon of Sherlock Holmes instead of from *The Book of Common Prayer*, a foolish title if I've ever heard one, what on earth is common about it, for heaven's sake? My nerves are all on edge, I can't help thinking that it was a dreadful mistake for you to ask Althea to marry you, well, not marry you, you're marrying Steve, but it's too late now, Althea, of course, not Steve, and speaking of veterinarians, has Sammy produced his collar yet?"

"We think he's waiting for the service," Leah said. "And it's not Althea we're worried about, it's Buck. We think he's going to mortify Holly by saying that she's marrying Steve because —"

Ceci interrupted her. "What is that horrible noise? It sounds for all the world like a moose! Wild animals do wander into the suburbs these days, you know, deer, foxes, possums, not to mention rabbits and skunks, it couldn't be a skunk, could it?"

Returning to the window, I saw my dear stepmother, Gabrielle, standing next to Twila's dog-box trailer, which was all too obviously the source of the moose calls. Gabrielle looked beautiful, as did her bichon, Molly, who was, for once, on the ground instead of in Gabrielle's arms. Gabrielle's hair had new highlights, and she wore a tiny hat that would've looked outlandish on anyone else, but somehow became her perfectly. She faced one of the dog boxes and was evidently addressing its occupant. I opened the window, but even then, I caught only a little of what she was saying. Her hat was bobbing up and down, and her arms were folded across her ample bosom. My father, however, was clearly audible.

"NOT A WORD!" Buck hollered. "NOW LET ME OUT OF HERE! I SWEAR TO GOD, GABRIELLE, I WON'T SAY A WORD ABOUT SAMMY!"

When Gabrielle unfolded her arms, I saw that in one hand she held a key. She went on to insert it in the padlock of the paternal dog box. She turned the key and opened the door. My father climbed out feet first.

By then, Rita, Leah, and Ceci had joined me in watching the performance.

"How did Gabrielle get him in there?" I wondered aloud.

Leah answered. "She told him that part of Molly's training for mushing camp was being in a dog-box trailer. Then she said that one of Molly's tags was missing and that it had to be in that dog box. That was her plan, anyway. I guess it worked."

Fifteen minutes later, Buck took my arm and led me to the terrace at the back of the house, and down the steps to the lawn, where the people and dogs I loved most were assembled to bear witness to my marriage. The human guests sat in folding chairs to the left and right. Those with dogs had aisle seats. North looked especially handsome wearing his collar of white flowers. Twila had an arm resting on his head. Ahead of me, at the end of the grassy aisle, Althea sat in her wheelchair, which was festooned with white ribbons and pink rosebuds. To one side, Ian McCloud and three other musicians played a solemn version of the song Ian had suggested and that Steve and I had chosen: "I Only

Have Eyes for You."

For once, Buck spoke quietly. "You sure you don't want me to give you away?"

"You can't," I said. "I don't belong to anyone but my dogs."

India preceded us. She carried a basket of orange petals. Ahead of us, waiting, were Rita, Leah, Pete, and, of course, Steve, whose blue-green eyes radiated confidence and trust. There, too, were Lady, who quivered, and Kimi, Rowdy, Uli, and Rowdy's perfect son, Sammy, all wearing their elaborate collars of white flowers. When I reached Steve, Buck let go of my elbow, and Steve took my hand. Real dog person that he was, instead of whispering sweet nothings in my ear, he murmured, "Sammy's collar. Up and out. Restored to health."

Ah, romance.

The music stopped. Althea cleared her throat. She looked older than ancient and transcendently lovely. I prayed that she'd stick with the uncommon *Book of Common Prayer* instead of uniting us by performing the Sherlockian Musgrave Ritual.

"Holly and Steve," Althea said, "have done me the honor to ask me to solemnize their marriage, a match that is very welcome to all of us. From the first moment that Steve saw Holly, he appeared to be strongly attracted by her, and I am much mistaken if the feeling was not mutual. Indeed, their feelings for each other are most deep and honorable; they love each other devotedly. For other couples, marriage may mean a complete change in life and habits. Such is not the case for Holly and Steve, whose interests rise up around them and draw them together in the path toward complete happiness. Each would lead a lonely life without the other."

A grin spread across my face. I'm happy to report that Steve's and my interests, our dogs, did not actually rise up. Althea had chosen the phrase because it appeared in *The Hound of the Baskervilles*. I heard Hugh and Robert chuckle. They were undoubtedly able, as I wasn't, to identify the precise sources in the Holmes Canon of almost everything else Althea had said. I loved her dearly. She was solemnizing our marriage according to Sir Arthur Conan Doyle, and she was doing it without embarrassing us.

"Dearly beloved," she continued, "we are gathered here . . ."

Then Steve and I exchanged vows. In his deep, strong voice, he promised to have and to hold, from this day forward, for better for worse, for richer for poorer, in sickness and in health, to love and to cherish. As he spoke, he kept one hand wrapped around mine and reached out his other hand to rest it briefly on Kimi's head and then on Rowdy's. In turn, I made the same solemn promises. Just as Steve had done, I reached out to touch his dogs, first India, then Lady, and then Sammy.

Rowdy's son was finally mine.

Till death us do part.

About the Author

Susan Conant is a three-time recipient of the Maxwell Award for Fiction Writing given by the Dog Writers' Association of America. She lives in Newton, Massachusetts, with her husband, two cats, and two Alaskan malamutes.